DEAD MAN'S SHOES

Brian Labinsky, determined to drag the Everglide Shoe Company into the twentieth century, decides to sack half the workforce and transfer most of the production to sweatshops in India. Before long, a local supplier goes bankrupt and its manageress, Tina Grimston, suffers a heart attack but the series of undisguised death threats from Tina's husband has little effect on Labinsky. When Labinsky's body is discovered mown down by Grimston's Land Rover, DCI Sidney Walsh believes he is looking at an open and shut case. But Grimston has a cast iron alibi and Walsh is forced to rethink his methods.

DEAD MAN'S SHOES

DEAD MAN'S SHOES

by

Richard Hunt

Magna Large Print Books
Long Preston, North Yorkshire,
BD23 4ND, England.

British Library Cataloguing in Publication Data.

Hunt, Richard
    Dead man s shoes.

    A catalogue record of this book is
    available from the British Library

    ISBN   0-7505-1534-1

First published in Great Britain by Severn House Publishers
Ltd., 1999

Copyright ' 1999 by Richard Hunt

Cover photography ' Last Resort Picture Library

The moral right of the author has been asserted

Published in Large Print 2000 by arrangement with Severn
House Publishers Limited

Magna Large Print is an imprint of Library Magna Books Ltd.

Printed and bound in Great Britain by
T.J. (International) Ltd., Cornwall, PL28 8RW

One

Although the tapering mini spires of King's College's chapel, and the bold square tower of Cambridge's Great St Mary's could be seen in the distance, this area of the City, just off the Newmarket Road, boasted no buildings that would truly light up the architecturally appreciative eye, unless, that is, one was fanatically into industrial sites of a mere Victorian antiquity.

One such rectangular block of red brick and round-topped windows was very easy to date accurately, for high up on its facade, in faded blue letters nearly two feet tall, were the words, 'The Everglide Shoe Company – Limited est. 1895'.

It was not a derelict ruin, or even a museum of industrial heritage – on the contrary – this remnant of the days when the British Empire had flourished worldwide, was evidently still in business, for an area beside it, allocated to the parking of employees' cars, was nearly full, and a particularly expensive and prestigious model had just been added to their number.

Brian Labinski parked his metallic grey Jaguar on the prime spot in the broad car park which was reserved specifically for the use of the managing director. No one else dared use it – at least not since the time, six months or so ago, when he'd accepted the financial package offered to him by the headhunters who had sought him out, and almost begged him to undertake the task of dragging this once flourishing, but now sick and ailing company, out of its Victorian stupor and into the big, wide real world.

Before then, Labinski had been a globe-trotting troubleshooter for a huge international corporation. The power and influence that he had wielded then had been enormous, but he'd still been a back-room operator, and out of the limelight. Now, in this job, his name was becoming known in the right circles, and the eyes of a whole industry were watching him – success might even bring him a knighthood.

Those six months had not been wasted, and now, thanks to his efforts and tireless determination, there was an even chance that the factory might still be in business in another hundred years.

Not that Labinski would be there to see it.

He was nearly fifty years old, with already enough money invested to finance a comfortable life of leisure, but this job would bring more riches, and prestige as well, and maybe, in five or six years, he would go into semi-retirement, and share the occasional board meeting in England with a spacious villa in the élite part of Minorca that he'd set his heart on.

He was a very fit, dark-haired man, with the self-discipline necessary to keep to a strict diet that allowed no fat to appear on his lean body.

He straightened his back, bringing his height up to all of five feet nine, and strode proudly to the office door. That pride was an inner feeling though – no emotions at all showed on his well-schooled face. With the exception of his alert, all-seeing eyes, the rest of his facial features might have been chiselled from marble. Not a pale white marble, but one with a brownish tint – as if it had recently been smiled on by a foreign sun. It had to be a foreign sun, because the skies of Cambridgeshire had been damp and overcast for weeks, and even if the late March sun had deigned to show itself for the odd minute or two, it would still never have had the warmth to raise a blush, let alone a tan, on the local pallid goose-pimples.

'Good morning, Sir,' the young girl at the reception desk said respectfully. For which welcome she was rewarded with the slightest of curt head nods, as he went past and up the broad stairs to his office.

Brian Labinski's secretary was a soberly dressed woman with soft sad eyes. She was of average height, in her thirties, and rose solicitously from her chair to take the coat that he was shrugging off.

'Good morning,' she said briefly, in a husky but well-modulated voice.

'Are you well this morning, Emily?' Brian Labinski asked politely.

'Yes, thank you. The Chairman and the other managers are already in the Boardroom, and you are three minutes late,' Emily said, running the fingers of one hand through her short brown hair, and shrugging her slim shoulders in mild reproof.

'I'll go straight in then, but I'm parched, so bring me a coffee, will you?'

The long boardroom was spacious, but not very cheerful, for the tall windows let in too much of the gloom from the outside skies for that, and it was also rather chilly.

12

However there was one feature which should have brought a warm glow to the discerning viewer, a beautiful long table of highly figured English walnut, French-polished to a mirror gloss. The large hand-painted Chinese porcelain bowl, on a small, elegant sideboard at the far end, might also have set the palms of a few collectors' hands itching.

Brian Labinski shivered slightly as he looked round the faces of the people seated at that table, and his eyes glinted even more coldly than usual.

The Company Chairman was sitting at the head of the table. He was a short plump man with an ever-smiling red face, but cool shrewd eyes, and he was there to demonstrate the full support of the Main Board, which was only right and proper.

He nodded as Labinski came to sit by his right hand, then leaned back in his well-padded armchair, to watch the reactions of the others present.

'Well, Gentlemen, I arrived back at Heathrow from Bombay early this morning, and I am pleased to tell you that my trip to India was completely successful,' Labinski announced sombrely. It would not have been difficult to laugh, some of those faces staring at him already looked as miserable as sin. 'So, Everglide Shoes now owns a very efficient production unit in India. I left Carter out there to finish reorganising their quality control and planning functions. The computer systems are being made compatible with our own, and next week the link lines between us will be tested. I want to be controlling all their systems from here in England within three weeks. Is that clear?' Labinski paused to sip the coffee Emily had just brought him. 'We have set them a very high quality level, and if their workers don't achieve it, they won't get paid. It's as simple as that. They're getting the message pretty smartish. The first container left last week, and a second was nearly ready when I came away,' Labinski's mask-like face glowered round at the assembled company, but found no raised eyes to stare at. 'So plan 'A' goes into immediate effect. George!' He looked across the table at the harassed looking production director with the balding head and the bushy moustache. 'Have you done what I told you to do last week on the phone?'

George stopped studying the backs of his hands, and nodded reluctantly. 'Yes, I've arranged a meeting with the union representatives for this afternoon,' he announced blandly.

'And you've stopped all work going out to subcontractors?'

'Yes, but I want to have a word with you about that. We made some of them promises, if you remember. We must give them time to find other work, otherwise they'll go bust. Mrs Grimston's unit certainly will. She's in a right state,' George protested, his fingers drumming nervously on the polished table.

'Promises? What promises? Are they in writing?' Labinski demanded icily, frowning in annoyance at this digression from matters of real importance.

'Well no, but its only three months ago that we – that is – you, asked Mrs Grimston to give us all her unit's production until the end of the year, because at the time we needed it so desperately. It's not fair to leave her in the lurch now,' George responded defiantly. The glare from Labinski's eyes went into a deep-freeze mode that would have earned him a massive fortune in the frozen pea business.

'Do you really want to pay subcontractors to work while our own production people sit on their backsides doing nothing? Have you no sense? That could mean trouble with the union, and I won't take the risk. While the shop-floor operatives are working out their statutory periods of notice I want every single piece of surplus leather we have in this place made into shoes. I don't care if we've got orders for them or not. If we can't sell them to retailers, then we'll put them in our Factory Shop as seconds, and get our money back that way. Right! You all know what's happening and what you've got to do. Be back here at four o'clock this afternoon, and we'll run through the plans again, just to be on the safe side. That's excepting you, George. Your task is to get the union's co-operation. That's vital. I don't want any disruptive action from the workforce.'

'You're a hard bastard,' the Chairman said amicably, when the others had gone, leaving just himself and Labinski in the big boardroom.

Labinski shrugged his shoulders and sipped again at his coffee. 'That's why I'm here. No omelettes are ever made without the cracking of eggs. The important thing is, we're going to be getting top quality shoe uppers from India, for less than we could

16

buy the leather in this country, and you know what effect that will have on our gross margins. Now all we will have to do in this place is to put the soles on, and they'll still be classified as *Made in Britain*. Everglide Shoes is on its way back into profitability, and you can't complain. It'll make your shares worth millions again, so it's worth a bit of other people's blood and tears, isn't it?'

'Most definitely, and with your share options it'll put a few millions in your pocket too – but I'm not so optimistic as you. Other companies are also buying from countries with low labour costs, so we're not going to have that much of a price advantage.'

'True, but unlike us, they're in the cheap and nasty end of the market, and if they don't control their overseas suppliers properly, as I intend to do, they'll suffer from the Indian malaise of erratic quality standards and broken delivery promises.'

'I hope you're right. When are you planning to prune your management team?' the Chairman asked politely. Coffee was not his choice of refreshment, so he took a sip from a glass of sherry.

'When they've done all the dirty work

17

down-sizing this factory, of course,' was the curt reply.

'I'd like a schedule of all the management staff you'll be getting rid of eventually, and how much it is going to cost us. Is that all right with you?'

Brian Labinski's facial features relaxed into something that might possibly have been a grin. Months ago he'd ground down any opposition from this Chairman and his other shareholders, and now he had a slavish acceptance for any of the changes he'd wanted to make. 'No problem. I'll get Emily to run off a copy for you.'

The end came much sooner than anyone in the little factory unit had expected, but the possibility of closure had reared its ugly head so many times over the past few years that Shirley, for one, had come to believe that it would never actually happen. She was long and lanky, and unmarried, and one of the very best edge-folders of leather footwear in the shoe business, but then, she ought to be good at it – she'd been doing it ever since she'd left school. In those days all the big companies had had small factory units in any decent-sized village or small town – wherever they could find a supply of cheap female labour, in fact – but now most of them had gone out of business. Shirley had been lucky, because when the unit she had worked for had closed, her friend Tina had bought a half-dozen sewing machines cheaply, and had set up in a tiny leased factory unit, to do subcontract work for the bigger shoe manufacturers. It had done quite well really, in the early days, once they'd earned the reputation of turning out a good quality product. As many as fifteen people had once squeezed into that small unit. Lately though, things hadn't been quite so good, and only one of the big companies was still sending them work on a regular basis. Last week they'd all suddenly gone on to short-time, but that sort of thing often happened when factories were cutting new patterns, or changing from spring and summer styles to autumn and winter ones.

Shirley glanced towards the tiny office tucked away in the corner. Tina had been in there with the door shut all morning. No doubt she was phoning round to see if there was anyone else with work to give them. That husband of Tina's – Gordon Grimston – he was in the office too. No one liked him much, although they would never say so in front of Tina. He was a gamekeeper on a nearby rural estate, a tall paunchy fellow in his fifties, with a big weathered red face, thinning fair hair, and close-set piggy eyes, and he always gave off a smell that was something like a mixture of sweat and dog muck, and always looked in a bad mood. The only things she could find in his favour were that he was devoted to Tina, and his two dogs.

Another man had come in earlier. A short dapper man in a neat dark-grey suit, carrying a black briefcase. It was a good thing that he was only a little bloke, or he'd never have managed to get into the little office with the other two.

Shirley blotted the dull irrelevancies of the world out of her mind, and got back to the far more pleasant task of daydreaming what she would do when she'd won a million or two on the lottery.

It was something of a surprise then, when the dapper man came out of the office on his own, and in a voice that was strangely deep and earthy for a little bloke, called out. 'Ladies! Would you switch your machines off for a moment please. I have something to say to you.' He paused, while the startled faces of the workforce looked at each other in amazement, then fingers pressed at the

20

little red stop buttons. Gradually the whine, rattle and hum of electric motors and machinery stilled into silence. 'I am very sorry to have to tell you,' the dapper man went on in his soothingly confident voice, 'that, because your main customer will not be sending you any further work, and because it would appear that there is no prospect of any work coming from anyone else either, the directors, Mr and Mrs Grimston, have reluctantly decided that this company can no longer continue in business. So...'

'I thought we'd been promised work until the end of the year,' Jean, one of the flat-machinists interrupted suspiciously.

'And so we had,' snarled the angry voice of Gordon Grimston, who had also come out of the office with his arm protectively round the red-faced and sobbing Tina. 'It was only three months ago that the bloody managing director of Everglide Shoes himself begged Tina not to take work from anyone else, because he wanted all we could produce, but last Thursday, when Tina phoned up to ask what styles were coming this week, the girl in their planning department said they weren't giving us any more.' Gordon's piggy eyes glittered wildly. 'We know why too. The van driver told Tina on Friday. They've been stringing us along while they've been sorting out their bloody supplier in India. It's bloody slave labour out there – ten-year-olds – given a bowl of rice a day, if they're lucky. If I had their bloody managing director here now, I'd wring the bugger's neck.' His big gnarled hands twisted viciously, and none of those watching had any doubts that, had that managing director indeed been there, he would shortly have taken his last breath of fresh air.

The silence that followed was broken by the calm dapper man from the firm of liquidators, who had obviously seen such tense situations played out dozens of times before. 'It is most unfortunate. However, there is a formal procedure that has now to be followed for such instances of voluntary liquidation, and I am afraid I must tell you, ladies, that your employment with this company must cease as from this moment. I'd like you each to take one of these little booklets, and read it carefully. It explains your rights, and what money might be due to you, but I'll answer any questions you ask me now, as best I can.'

There was an appalled silence as the women there realised that they were now unemployed, and that this little group of old friends, with whom it had been so nice to work, was going to break up for ever. Several started to weep, and all looked horrified, shocked and very miserable.

'Are we entitled to redundancy money?' one girl asked sheepishly.

'Yes, if you've been employed for over two years.'

'What happens if the company hasn't got the money to pay it?'

'Then you'll be paid what you are due from a special government fund. They get their money back when the company's assets are realised. Now–'

It was at that moment that they all had something far more serious than a mere common factory closure to worry about. Tina Grimston, who until then had been standing quite still, and quietly sobbing to herself, suddenly had a heart attack. She gave a groan and an agonising gasp, and collapsed onto the floor, or she would have done if her husband's strong arm had not been round her. Then, while most of those there panicked and lost their heads, the long and lanky Shirley became the most important person in the room, because she was the only one with any first aid training, and it was up to her to keep her friend Tina alive, until the paramedics arrived in the ambulance and could take over.

Denise Labinski was more than twelve years younger than her husband Brian, but it would have been easier to have assumed that their relationship was rather one of father and daughter, because she was very slim, and her skin and figure still had the bloom and firmness of youth. That was all genuine enough, but her girlish mannerisms were mostly contrived. The almost continuous use of one hand to smooth her fair hair back from her face, and the widening of her eyelids to express innocence and surprise, were the now habitual results of much practice before the mirror. She was not quite a beautiful woman, but she wasn't far off from being so. She also had an extensive wardrobe of elegant clothes to go with her good looks, but one would expect that, with someone who owned and ran one of Cambridge's small but up-and-coming salons.

When Brian Labinski arrived at his spacious house on the outskirts of one of Cambridgeshire's more attractive villages, it was to an excited welcome from his two black Labradors, and the sight of his lovely wife, in a stunning and rather low-cut dress of silken green, waiting hopefully for some words of admiration or approval from him. She would undoubtedly have had them from most healthy males, particularly those who had been away from the marital home and had suffered the consequent agonies of deprivation for more than a week. Regardless of the damage to make-up or the creasing of an elegant gown, such normal men would have whisked her upstairs, demanding, insisting, or even begging and pleading on bended knee, that she perform her desperately needed wifely duties. In this case – for some reason – that did not happen. Brian Labinski stared at her coldly, and was totally unmoved.

'You're off out, are you? Well, I'm not going with you,' he said bluntly. 'I've got work to do, and I'm tired.'

That was received, not surprisingly, with a furious scowl, a flashing of eyes and a tossing of locks of fair hair.

'You're being selfish again, Brian. I always have to go out on my own these days. We never do anything together. You're so wrapped up in your damned shoes that you haven't got time for anyone else,' Denise retorted bitterly.

'Tough. You had the chance of coming to India with me,' Brian replied icily.

'You only asked me because you knew I wouldn't go. I don't like India. All those beggars and poor people, they upset me. Please come with me, Brian,' she said, opening her big beseeching eyes even wider.

'You heard me. No!'

'Well I'm not going to row with you, however unkind you are to me, but there is something important I must talk to you about. I've got problems at the salon again. Jenny's been off sick, and because of the weather things have been rather slow, and the bank won't increase the overdraft again. Would you let me have another cheque please, like the one you gave me last month? I'll pay you back, honestly. Things are bound to pick up soon,' she pleaded, turning on her very best girlishly innocent expression, which normally never failed – but did tonight.

Brian threw his briefcase onto the soft leather settee, and turned to stare at her with his cold ruthless eyes. 'Have you sacked two of your staff, as I told you to do last month? What have you done about turning your old stocks into cash?' He demanded bluntly.

Denise's bottom lip fluttered and her mouth fell open, but no words came out.

'You've done nothing, have you?' he went on inexorably. 'Well, your grotty little shop gets no more money from me, so try your tears on your bank manager.'

Denise was indeed about to resort to floods of tears, but the realisation that it would be a waste of time brought instead a tirade of angry words, of which *I hate you*, was probably the most frequently used phrase. Then she thought of something else that might just penetrate her husband's thick skin. 'There's been a man called Grimston on the phone all weekend, threatening you, and me too. Well, today he says he's had enough, and that you've nearly killed his wife – so he's going to kill you, and I hope he bloody does.'

That ought to have made him quake with fear, but Brian just stood there and smiled his cold confident smile, impervious alike to threat or tantrum.

Denise stamped her foot with frustrated rage, grabbed her coat from the back of a chair, snatched up her bag and stalked out of the house, shouting that he was a horrid man and that she hated him.

The cool evening air dampened her fury only a little. There were still blinding tears in her eyes as she drove too fast out of the shingled drive, and nearly knocked down a lone old man who just happened to be walking past.

The slamming of the front door and the tearing sounds of gravel being sprayed from beneath wildly spinning tyres, sufficed to confirm to Brian, if there was any need, that his wife had left in a mood.

It was not a matter that seemed to give him any concern at all.

He took his briefcase into his study and opened it preparatory to reading some papers, and then Denise's taunts about the Grimston phone messages finally had a reaction. There had been abusive and threatening phone calls made to the company at the end of last week, while he had been in India. They had already been referred for prompt legal action to the company's solicitors, who should by now have informed the police, and have prepared for an appeal to the courts for a restraining order to curb the activities of the abusive caller. The calls made here by Grimston were probably similar to those others, but if the word *kill* had really been used, it all became rather more serious. So he played the recording tape through, and listened carefully, not so much to the words, although he heard their meaning and intent, but more to the way they were expressed. This Grimston fellow, clearly the husband of the woman who ran the small local subcontracting unit that Everglides had been using for so long, sounded like someone verging on mental instability. The threats were uttered too casually for Brian to feel that they should be taken too seriously, but nevertheless, the sooner the weight of the law was pressing hard down on this Grimston's shoulders, the better. If the company's lawyers had failed to act promptly, then he would ask his own solicitor to deal with the matter when they met in the morning.

He went into the kitchen to pour himself the daily glass of red wine which the medical world had decreed was good for the maintenance of a healthy heart. The dogs nuzzled him expectantly, but failed to get the response from him that they were after. Instead, their master returned to the lounge, to recline in an armchair, sip his wine and peruse those reports and memos in his briefcase that he had not had time to read, or properly mentally digest, in the office.

Later Brian yawned. He felt tired, yet before he could go to bed he must comply with that essential requirement of good health – exercise. That was what his dogs were for. As well as being a useful deterrent against burglars, they made him get out in the fresh air and walk a mile or so each morning and evening, when he was at home.

He drained the glass of wine and got up to do this self-imposed duty. So too did the dogs, who had clearly been patiently waiting for this event from the moment they had got back to the house with their mistress after their early morning walk, if they'd had one, and they started leaping about with excitement.

Labinski closed his briefcase, and put it back on the desk in his study, then went to slip his feet into green Wellington boots. He donned an anorak, and pulled a black woollen fisherman's hat over his head to prevent the cool night air from giving him a cold, and went out of the side door, locking it carefully behind him. He strode down the shingled drive and sternly called the dogs to heel at the lane. They obeyed promptly enough, for once across this lane they knew they would be free of further interfering commands, and could dash off at full speed down the track opposite that led to the village green, on the far side of which was the main road, the pub and the shops. There was a pond there too, but the most numerous inhabitants of that were not ducks, but Chinese geese. The track which the dogs rushed down was the last reminder of the days when cattle had grazed the common and the land, which now contained several expensive executive houses, had once been a farm.

The track was rarely used. It was overgrown and darkened by the spreading branches of trees and bushes from the adjoining woods, but there was a worn, if rather muddy, path snaking down the middle, and enough light from the far street lamps to just about see where one was going. So, with the dogs already far ahead, Labinski strode cautiously along it alone, with his eyes looking down at the ground, watching for the muddy patch or rut which might send his feet slipping or sliding from under him. Once on the green he could stride out more briskly on the level grass, to get his heartbeat rate up and exercise those important coronary muscles, and prevent the hardening of his arteries. On these occasions he might allow his mind to wander into a daydream – of Minorca's warm sunshine, of the sailing and the diving in clear waters, and of the select and intellectual society that frequented its more elegant villas.

Daydreaming was a rather unfortunate thing to have been doing on that particular evening, for had he been more conscious of his surroundings he might have seen the looming bulk of a vehicle parked further up the track, under the trees. As it was, he was only aware of its presence when the noise of a fast-approaching high-revving engine broke into his reverie, and then it was too late for him to do more than utter a sharp cry of alarm and to make a despairing leap to one side, to try and avoid it. The driver of the now speeding vehicle had, however, presumably anticipated such a manoeuvre, for a quick twitch of the steering wheel ensured a near frontal impact with the leaping man, and a heavy thud as the body was flung into the nearby bushes.

Fortunately for Brian Labinski, that initial impact rendered him unconscious, so he felt nothing further when the vehicle braked and reversed over his sprawling arms and torso, before driving forward again, out of the track.

He might indeed have survived the injuries he had sustained, had help come quickly, but it was a long time before even the two bewildered dogs decided to go back and look for their errant master, and they were quite unable to do anything to help stem his internal bleeding, and so, eventually, Brian Labinski's heart stopped beating.

Two

If a member of the public uses the hallowed 999 call to report the finding of a dead body, the emergency services will generally act as though that member of the public doesn't know what he or she is talking about, and they will probably send an ambulance and a doctor to the scene as well as the police. Which is fair enough, for they work on the principle that no one can be considered properly dead until a qualified medical doctor says they are, and anyone who has collapsed in the street from a heart attack would surely agree that they too would want a doctor and an ambulance to turn up pretty smartish, to sort them out, regardless of the opinions of people whose medical knowledge might be limited to the use of aspirin or elastoplast.

However, as it so happened, the man who found and reported Labinski's dead body, had probably seen more corpses than many general practitioners see in a lifetime.

Jamie Hamilton was a silver-haired man in

his seventies. He was quite physically fit for his age, still straight-backed and perfectly sober, and he had been an infantry soldier in a Highland regiment in World War Two.

At El Alamein, like the New Zealanders and the Australians on his right, he too had charged through minefields in the darkest of dark nights, with only the thin lines of tracer bullets from anti-aircraft guns in the rear to give them any idea of the direction they had wanted to go. Wanted was hardly the correct word to use. None of them had wanted to advance towards those tenacious, well dug – in German troops, across ground that was swept by machine-gun and artillery fire. Even so, the night attack down the coast road area was made with an almost fanatical ferocity. Daylight had brought no rest or respite, as possession of their meagre territorial gains was re-contested with a vengeance by an enemy so proud and used to military success that it would not abandon a single inch of that worthless stony desert, until the dead of their own defenders lay thick upon the ground – and the dead of their attackers lay even thicker.

The Highlanders never reached their objectives that first night. As the sun came up, those still left alive dug frantically for cover as best they could in the hard ground. Jamie Hamilton had lain on his belly in a shallow scrape behind a low stone sangar all that first day, thirsty, tired, hungry and frightened, yet ruthlessly determined to thwart the enemy's counter-attacks, and as a sniper, he'd had a part to play in that. Circumstances had forced the Germans into making the very same mistake that Monty's predecessors had made. Now it was their tanks and their SPs, or self-propelled guns, that were out in the open, advancing into the trap of well dug-in anti-tank guns. It was Jamie's rifle that may have got one little battle off to a good start. At 500 yards his sights had lined up on the driver's vision slot of the first Panzer Mk III to breast the ridge. His shot must have been an extraordinarily lucky one, for that tank had suddenly lurched to the right, exposing its vulnerable flank to a 6-pounder armour-piercing shell. That tank had brewed up, as had six more before the rest backed off, but Jamie had by then picked off several of their grey-clad emerging crews. Two hours later the tanks came on again, and later, yet again.

There were eleven such relentless hellish days until the final breakthrough, and the young Jamie was red-eyed and near total physical and mental exhaustion, yet the infantry, the lowest of the low in the Army, were deemed to have no human feelings, for he and the remnants of his company were promptly packed on board a truck, to follow up the enemies' retreat for hundreds more dry and dusty North African miles. Then had come a different kind of vicious warfare, that was no less bloody, in the mud and mountains of Tunisia, Sicily and Italy, places where a now hardened young warrior, armed with a new rifle and telescopic sights, could really wreak a vengeance.

So, Jamie Hamilton had certainly been used to the sight of dead and mangled bodies – Italian ones, and German, Indian, American, British, and plenty of others from all parts of the Empire, and a fair few of the enemy's had fallen to his sniper's rifle. Callous it all may have been, but war had been war, and war had been callous, and the battle cry had been as it always had been: kill the enemy before he kills you.

So, even though more than fifty years had passed since the days when Jamie Hamilton had had a life risk that no insurance company in the world would ever have considered taking on, when he'd told the emergency call operator that Labinski was dead, he really had known what he was talking about.

After having made the 999 call from his little bungalow, just down the lane from the row of new executive houses, Jamie Hamilton took a torch from the cupboard that boxed in the electricity meter, and hurried back to await whoever from officialdom was the first to arrive. That turned out to be the calm and phlegmatic Sergeant Masters, in a police panda car.

'Are you this Mr Hamilton, who dialled 999 about a body?' He asked almost accusingly.

'That's right. I found him on me way back from the pub. He's up there – on the left,' Hamilton replied grimly, pointing up the overgrown track. 'Keep well right. There's tyre tracks up there. You'll want them.'

Masters looked thoughtfully at the older man's face, but he seemed reasonably sane, so it might be wise to do as he suggested. 'You'd best wait here then. I'll go on my own.'

Hamilton shrugged his shoulders and watched the bulky figure walk steadily up the lane, keeping well to the right, and sweeping the beam of his torch slowly from side to side, until the moment came when it illuminated Labinski's crumpled corpse.

Carefully placing his feet where they disturbed no tracks, Masters bent down and sought for a pulse at the body's neck, but found none. Then he observed the mud of the tyre tracks that crossed the body's clothes, and noticed particularly the depression that may have been caused by wheels momentarily pushing the body forward before rolling up and over it, then he stood up again to make his radio report back to headquarters. His final comment –to the effect that he, personally, thought there was no way that it could have been an accident – sent an already alerted 'scene of crime' team on its way.

An ambulance turned up, followed very shortly by a doctor, and soon the lane was seemingly full of vehicles with flashing lights, and no one had time for old Jamie Hamilton. Not that it bothered him much. He was tempted to go back home where it was warm, but he didn't – he just stayed on the fringes of the gathering crowd of neighbours and watched. However, when Sergeant Masters was free of other more important things, he came over with an open notebook in his hand.

'Do you know the dead man, Mr Hamilton?' he asked.

Jamie nodded, and pointed a finger at the house with the shingle drive. 'Lives there. Name's Labinski,' he replied briefly.

'Is he married – has he got a family?'

The old man shrugged his lean shoulders and became almost talkative. 'Only him, his wife and two dogs. Moved in six months back, they did. She's all right, but he's a stuck-up bastard. He was out walking his dogs, most likely. Does that, when he's home.'

'Dogs? Where are they? Have you seen his wife? Have you told her what's happened?' Masters asked.

Hamilton looked startled at the suggestion, and shook his head vigorously. 'No bloody fear. It ain't for the likes of me to tell her her husband's dead. As for the dogs, I dunno. Maybe they went home.'

Masters grimaced. Telling a wife that her husband was dead wasn't a thing he wanted to do either. Fortunately, unless circumstances forced the issue as they sometimes did, in the Cambridgeshire Constabulary it was standard practise for that task to be undertaken by someone with training in bereavement counselling. Masters' duty, as a patrol car officer, was really confined to holding the official fort in such incidents as this, until such time as the scene of crime team or the CID people turned up to take over, but if this death was not accidental, then ascertaining the whereabouts and safety of the man's wife ought to be given a high priority.

'We'd better go and see if there's anyone there, then,' Masters suggested. Hamilton looked reluctant when that word *we* came out, but nevertheless he followed the police sergeant across the road to the Labinski residence.

There were lights in the house itself, and others illuminating the sweeping shingle drive, and Labinski's metallic grey Jaguar.

'That's his car. Hers ain't here,' Hamilton grunted in relief. 'Hers is a red one. There's their dogs too,' he went on, pointing towards the side door where the two animals lay sprawled out, waiting for someone to come and let them into the house.

As guard dogs, they left a lot to be desired. They neither barked, nor came rushing over to defend their territory. One of them did raise his head to look in their direction, but otherwise the two intruders were totally ignored.

'So much for *Man's best friend*. They ought to still be whining and pining by their master's body,' Masters muttered scornfully.

'Maybe he didn't treat them right. Dogs have feelings too, you know,' Hamilton uttered defensively, and when Masters went to ring the front-door bell, he walked round to the side door.

'You'll have to wait longer yet,' he muttered dryly as the two dogs got to their feet, gave a half-hearted wag of their tails and moved to the door, clearly expecting him to open it for them. Hamilton pressed gingerly down on the shiny brass door handle and pushed, but the door was locked. He passed that piece of information on to Sergeant Masters, who had got fed up with ringing the bell and was peering through the front windows.

'There's obviously no one at home. You've no idea where she might have gone?' Masters asked as they walked back to the lane.

Hamilton shook his head irritably. 'How the hell would I know?'

More people had turned up while they had been away. Plastic-clad forensic officers were carrying a metal-framed tent structure

43

down the lane to where bright lights now glowed. Masters spent the next few minutes telling the man in charge what he had learned about the dead man, then he was free to get back in his panda car and drive off to resume his interrupted tour of duty.

Denise Labinski had slipped into what passed for a social set in Cambridge, with great ease. It had been only six months since she had taken over the salon, but right from that moment she had played her cards well. The first charity event invitation that had come her way had not in fact been meant for her, but for the previous owner. Still, she had accepted it anyway, and had made a smallish but adequate contribution to the Rumanian orphans or Rwandan refugees, whichever it was, and had set about meeting the so-called rich and influential of Cambridge with a relaxed vivacity that was not all that much different from her normal everyday personality.

Attractive and tastefully dressed, she caught the eye of men and women alike. Even if her conversational topics tended to be rather childish, she was nevertheless a good listener, and further invitations to such events, although they did not exactly come flooding in, arrived with a satisfying frequency. It was good for business too, and a number of those wealthy women had actually come to visit her salon, but not enough yet to swing a small loss into a profit.

So, she had done very well, in such a short period, but to turn up too early at one of those events, red-eyed from weeping and still full of anger at Brian's beastliness, would have been to court social gossip and disaster.

So Denise drove instead into the City, to her side-street salon, where she could calm herself down in private, and repair damaged make-up. The fact that she had failed to get a cheque from Brian was not the end of the world. She did have a small nest egg of her own in the building society, but it wasn't a very large sum, and she'd far rather have used Brian's money than hers. What was of great concern was the realisation that lately her judicious use of charm and femininity on her husband was failing to achieve the happy-family result that she expected, and that was bewildering, and rather frightening. He did not even seem to want her body nowadays either, and that was even more upsetting, because since her teens she'd always thought of that as her greatest asset. Now she was filled with self-doubt.

She felt tired and bewildered as she sat before a mirror in the inner room of the salon, staring with dread at the tiny crow's feet lines below her eyes. Making the effort to appear relaxed and lively tonight was going to be a great strain, and getting so worked up sometimes had the effect of making her mind go a bit scatty, so she would need to be extra careful. A couple of early drinks might help quell her anger with Brian, and stop her thinking all the time of how she could pay him back for his continued horrid behaviour towards her. However, the time was now getting on, and if she was going to this event, she must soon make a move. She leaned forward before the mirrors to study an eyelash, and suddenly realised just how revealing this low neckline really was. She had worn it to try and stir Brian's cold emotions, and it had utterly failed. She looked around, but to change it would take too long. No, she would just have to remember not to bend forward, or all the men would be trying to peer down there. Damn all men, she thought, and Brian Labinski in particular.

'Working late?' asked the uniformed

46

policewoman, who was out walking the beat with a male companion as Denise locked the front door of the salon.

'I'm afraid so,' she replied, practising her society smile and finding that, despite all her anguish, it came quite easily.

The reception at the hotel by the river was pretty well in full swing when she arrived, and soon her smile was working overtime, but two glasses of wine or champagne failed to drown her feelings of hurt depression, and neither had those that followed. After a while she thought it wise to ease herself out of the crowd and go to powder her nose and swallow an aspirin to curb her growing headache – then she could scan the morsels on the buffet table for fat-free mouthfuls that might soak up some of the alcohol that was slurping about in her stomach.

'What! Brian's not let you out on your own tonight, has he?' came a soft male Irish voice from behind her. 'I'd not be letting such a pretty one as you out of her cage so often, you might not want to come back in again.'

Such a patronising chat-up line would normally be parried with some icy repartee, but tonight even such a childishly phrased compliment seemed music to her ears. She turned her head to look up into the cool grey smiling eyes of her husband's solicitor, Donovan O'Shea. They'd met a few times in his office, and then she'd thought of him as a nice man, if a little bit aloof, but she'd never seen him at one of these gatherings before. Still, he was a friendly face, and there didn't seem too many of them about tonight. So she gave him back a half-encouraging smile – but the reference to Brian had touched a still sensitive nerve.

'Brian doesn't care what I'm up to these days. Work is his all-enduring passion, not me. Anyway, where's your pretty little cage-bird tonight, at home doing the ironing?' she responded, in a tone that was meant to be bright and cheerful, but even to her own ears it sounded more brittle than she'd intended.

O'Shea's face went blank and his eyes dulled. 'No such luck. I live alone. What would a pretty cage-bird want with the likes of me?'

Denise's eyes opened wide in surprise. If it wasn't for his beaky nose and hollow cheeks he'd be handsome enough, and there was a twinkle of humour in his eyes that might be fascinating if one stared at them for too long.

'Oh dear,' she sighed apologetically, 'I haven't said the wrong thing again, have I?'

'I shouldn't think so. Are you enjoying yourself?'

'Not really,' she replied, then she reddened slightly, because O'Shea was clearly looking down the front of her dress, but instead of feeling annoyed with him as she ought, she found that she was almost pleased, or at least relieved, that her charms were still good enough to be attractive to someone, and, as if in reward for giving her that very welcome boost to her confidence, she found herself instinctively leaning even closer to him, so that he could better see whatever he wanted to see. Why not indeed? It could do no harm. 'I'm only here to drum up business,' she admitted confidentially, to hide her embarrassment.

'So am I,' he whispered back in the same tone. That made them both laugh, and eased the tension.

'I didn't see you come in, have you just arrived?' she asked, anxious to keep the conversation going.

'About a half-hour ago, while you were talking to Councillor Adamson, and the skinny dumb blonde in the clingy dress whose name I can't remember, but who's

49

married to Jakes the scrap merchant, and has a laugh about as musical as bathwater draining down a plug-hole.'

Denise Labinski rocked a little on her heels as she giggled. 'That's Sharon. She's one of my new clients, and that dress really did come all the way from Paris – but it didn't cost a fortune I'm sorry to say. It's meant to show her figure off, both front and rear. I don't know if men like women's bums, but she must think they do, that's probably why she's not wearing any knickers underneath.'

'Good Lord. I hadn't noticed. I suppose it depends on the bum. How is the salon going?'

'Not as well as I'd like. It's hard work, that's why I'm so tired tonight. By the way, I've been meaning to ask you, how would I stand with the salon if anything happened to Brian? He's guaranteed the bank loan, but could he suddenly withdraw it, and leave me in the lurch?' Denise frowned down at the glass she was spinning between her fingers. It was empty now, and her mouth felt dry again, so she took up another from a passing tray, and sipped that.

O'Shea frowned, and put an arm out to shield Denise as a group of other guests

50

approached, and seemed likely to bump her.

'Why should anything happen to Brian? He's not ill, is he? He looked fit enough last time I saw him. As for the guarantee, you've no need to worry about that, the bank won't let him off the hook that easy.'

'Thank goodness for that. No, he's fine, but he's trodden on some toes badly enough for someone to make phone calls threatening to kill him.'

'Oh dear, but no doubt the company's solicitors will sort that out. If you're worried about the legal side of your bank loan, why don't you come and see me in my office some time. You're very welcome – anytime. Did you drive yourself here tonight, by the way?'

Denise nodded.

'Well, I don't want to be a kill-joy, but two glasses of champagne are enough to take most people up to the limit – so do be careful. Oh dear! It rather looks as though the Chairman of Everglides is heading this way. Between you and me I can't stand the fellow, so I shall promptly abandon you.'

Denise turned, and found the short plump Chairman approaching, staring at her with his small condescending eyes. The usual supercilious smile hovered round his lips.

'I'm so pleased to see you here, my dear,' the Chairman uttered silkily, reaching to touch her arm with his warm fingers. 'Are you enjoying yourself? I haven't seen Brian anywhere. Is he not with you?'

'Brian had some work to do,' she replied shortly, taking the opportunity to put her glass on the table and free herself from his clammy hand.

'Ah yes. A very hard-working man, is your husband, and a jolly good chap too. Now it would give me great pleasure to introduce you to my son. He's just home on leave from the Philippines. Naval attaché at the embassy, you know. The sea's been in our blood for generations. He's only a Commander now, but he'll be an Admiral like his grandfather one day. He's a fine figure of a man, isn't he?' He chuckled and waved a fat hand towards his approaching offspring. The son was of a seemingly different species of human to his father, being tall and egg-headed. He had black centre-parted hair, and his skin was surprisingly pale for a naval officer. Denise noted all this as she reached out to accept the son's proffered handshake, and managed to utter automatically the necessary words of, 'I'm pleased to meet you,' when in fact she felt completely the opposite. The recent boost to her self-confidence had soon flagged, and that niggling headache was back again, accompanied this time by a sickly feeling in her stomach. The champagne was affecting her brain too, and some of her words were not as sharp and precise as she would have liked them to be. If she didn't watch out all the catty gossips here would be labelling her a drunkard, and with that kind of stigma attached to her, the rich and the influential would definitely not frequent her salon. That thought made her straighten her back, and refuse any more champagne, and as soon as she reasonably could, she broke away from the Chairman and his pallid son, to join another group where she needed to do nothing more than smile and listen. Yet she had the distinct feeling that she was being watched.

Out of the corner of her eye she saw the group round the Chairman suddenly look in her direction. Had she upset them by not simpering at their condescending attention to her? All the faces in the room now seemed to be hostile or sneering at her. It really couldn't be so, she told herself, she must be imagining it. Then the thought suddenly came into her mind, as thoughts sometimes did when you were thinking of something else, that Brian's horrid attitude to her could only be explained by the fact that he now considered their marriage was over, and was planning to kick her out. Such ideas had crossed her mind before, but now they were back with a vengeance. What would she do then – with little or no money of her own? Her depression sank to an even lower level. There was not a friendly face in sight. She looked round for O'Shea, but he was nowhere to be seen. It was too early to leave, but after another half an hour she decided that enough was enough, she would have to go. She wanted to be somewhere where she could cry and be miserable all alone. The salon would be too cold – so she would have to creep up to her bedroom and there await the dismal future that was obviously to be her fate. Without drawing any more attention to herself than she had already, she made her way out of the room, and went to get her coat. It wasn't safe for her to drive, but the hotel reception desk would call a taxi for her.

Then Donovan O'Shea came out of the hotel's lounge bar, and came over to her with a smiling face that was so obviously pleased to see her that some of her depression immediately faded away, and she very nearly burst into tears there and then.

'You look really fed up, Denise. Had enough of it, have you?' He said cheerfully. 'I can't say I blame you. Did you show adequate appreciation for the honour of having LeClerc and his son deign to acknowledge your presence?'

Denise smiled back at him gratefully. 'He gave me the worst creeps I've had in years, and that son of his – when he touched me with his clammy hand, it sent shivers down my spine. He's weird.'

O'Shea chuckled. 'One mustn't gossip, but I have heard that the son is now *persona non grata* in the Philippines. An unhealthy interest in young boys, apparently.'

'Oh dear, how awful. I wish he hadn't touched me. It makes me feel dirty,' she said, giving a shiver. 'Well, Donovan O'Shea, I'm about to take your advice. I'm going to call a taxi. I'm not drunk, but I don't think I'm safe to drive.'

'Very wise, but you don't need to get a dirty, smelly old taxi. Let O'Shea drive you safely home. I should think we can get out of the car-park without being seen by any of those grotty gossips in there.'

Denise smiled sheepishly, and nodded gratefully at his polite concern for her well-being. 'That's very kind of you. Who cares about what gossips think, anyway?'

Outside, the cool fresh air made her head swim. She leaned back in the seat of O'Shea's car, and closed her eyes. She didn't want to go home to Brian and his nastiness yet, and her weakness for voicing some of her feeling without prior thought led her to utter the words, 'Can't we go somewhere and have a cup of coffee first, and just sit and talk to each other about something? Do you mind?'

'Not at all, but most of the cafés are shut now, and the ones that are still open won't be very nice. You could come to my place, if you don't mind that.'

Denise let her silence serve as a positive answer. Then the thought crossed her mind that O'Shea might have been lying in wait for her, knowing she'd drunk too much, and hoping he could get her on her own in his car. She'd been stupid not to have had a taxi, because now she had herself right open to possible sexual advances. Brian had not been forthcoming for ages, and was hardly earth-shattering when he did, but that was no excuse for getting herself involved with another man, and at a time like this too. It would be dangerous and could mean trouble. Still, she could hardly stop the car and get out now. That would be too rude, and it would hurt O'Shea's feelings too, for he was obviously a lonely man. Perhaps all he was after was a little old-fashioned innocent kissing and cuddling, and a bit of tender loving care. If he was, she might even go along with that a little, she'd had little enough tender loving care herself lately. It would depend on how he behaved. Then she realised that of course nothing untoward would happen – she was perfectly safe – because she was the wife of a valuable and influential client. One word from her to Brian might ruin O'Shea's practice in Cambridge. She could relax. She was perfectly safe.

But she wasn't.

No sooner had she turned in his hallway to allow him to take her coat from her, than his arms had come round her waist from behind, and he was kissing her neck passionately.

That was a great pity, because she liked his smiling eyes, and if he'd been more patient and less passionate she might have allowed him some small harmless favours. She

57

turned to face him, and gently pushed him away.

'You mustn't,' she said firmly, gazing sympathetically up into those bright grey eyes. Then more words came flooding out that would really dampen his ardour. 'Anyway, you can't. It's the wrong time of the month.'

She almost laughed as she felt the disappointment shudder through his body.

'No luck for the bloody Irish tonight, then,' he muttered grimly. 'I'll make some coffee. That'll take my mind off wicked thoughts, and then we can just sit and talk, damn it.'

Having solved that problem, Denise suddenly found that she was by no means so sure that that was what she really wanted. O'Shea desired her because she was still an attractive woman, while that beastly Brian, who was legally allowed to do anything he liked to her, just spurned her and wasn't interested. A feeling of hatred for Brian caused her fingers to clench in anger. He had no right to treat her like he did, yet he would be furious if his wife let another man touch her.

It would be a just revenge if she did let another man touch her – without Brian ever knowing, of course – but after what she had said to O'Shea, he would be as cold to her now as Brian had been. Could she tempt him into trying something again? Could she? Should she? Any signs of affection or appreciation would be better than nothing.

She kicked off her shoes, sat demurely in the middle of the long, softly-cushioned settee, and gave him a warm encouraging smile when he returned. Having put the coffee on a nearby table, O'Shea sat politely down beside her. She leaned a little towards him, and twisted slightly, so that he could see down the front of her dress again if he wanted to. That was about the only card she could play at the moment, without being downright brazen.

'You're not angry with me, are you?' she whispered softly, touching his hand sympathetically to make some sort of physical contact. She could almost feel his stare burning into her soft flesh, and then, thank heavens, he bent to kiss her lips, so she could gently return the pressure with just enough passion to suggest that more of the same would be quite acceptable. Her head started to swim and she closed her eyes. If O'Shea started doing anything now, she definitely wouldn't stop him, she decided. It wouldn't be fair on him for one thing – to stop him a second time. To hell with bloody Brian, she'd just lie back and enjoy whatever he did.

So she did not mind when O'Shea actually did take some tentative liberties. She did not mind either when a zip was eased down and the narrow sleeves of her dress were slipped from her arms, even if she did murmur a righteous, 'No,' as softly and unconvincingly as she could, and then look anxiously up at his face, in case he'd heard. The awe in his eyes as he looked down at her, was wonderful to behold. This was the adoration she craved. She was still a real woman, and she needed admiration and loving, and just now, she decided, she needed lots and lots of both. Danger and warning signals rose, but lacking clear definition, faded into her fast-growing desperate need for love and affection. Then her tormented mind blanked out all other thoughts, and she threw caution to the wind. She gently pulled herself away from him, and stood up to let her silky green dress slip to the floor. That surely, was more than just a hint that she had lied to him. She sank back into his eager fervent embraces.

'You're no lady, Denise. You'll never go to

heaven if you tell such lies,' he eventually whispered in her ear.

Denise giggled in girlish triumph, and gazed up at him with eyes that had trouble focusing. 'Well, you're no gentleman for finding out, but I claim I'm drunk and that you're taking advantage of me.'

'Do you want me to stop?'

'No! Not if you promise faithfully never to tell anyone.'

'I promise faithfully.'

'Good! Well, I'm floating on white fluffy clouds at the moment and I don't want to come down to earth until I have to.'

'But there's lots of storms and thunder and lightning coming your way now, I fear.'

'Lovely.'

Detective Chief Inspector Sidney James Walsh, head of the serious crime section of the Cambridgeshire Constabulary's Criminal Investigation Department, stepped into the legs of the white plastic boiler-type suit, then shrugged his broad shoulders to get his arms in the top part, before he could pull up the zip. It was a necessary chore, for no one, however exalted their rank, could go uninvited to the scene of a crime, not while the forensic department were still looking for, and collecting, evidence. That was Home Office regulations, and no one would be invited either, without them first donning the protective gear that would ensure that there was no contamination of the site by falling hair or any other such minute debris from body and clothes.

'You can see the vehicle tracks quite clearly, Sidney,' Dr Richard Packstone, the tall, grey-haired and bespectacled leader of the forensic team announced, pointing down over the long streams of white tape that marked out the areas which were not to be trodden on. 'A rapid acceleration from up there, under those trees. An impact on the front off-side with the dead man, which flung the body towards the hedge and probably rendered him unconscious. Then the vehicle braked sharply, backed the two off-side wheels over the man's torso, braked again, and then drove over him a second time before it went off. A cruel, callous and deliberate set of actions – there can be no doubt about that. It has all been photographed and videoed, but we'll do it all again in daylight, just to make sure we've missed nothing.'

'The vehicle was parked under those trees, was it? It wouldn't be easy for anyone to spot it against the dark background, yet the man walking up the track would be clearly silhouetted against the lamps in the lane back there,' Sidney Walsh muttered to himself. 'If that's how it all happened, then it's premeditated murder.' He could have added, as Packstone had done, the words cruel and callous, but such adjectives were unnecessary – all murders fell into those categories. He waited for the usual feelings of anger and revulsion to rise up within him, to drive a teeth-gritting determination to thwart the killer, and bring him or her to face the wrath of decent society, but this time those feelings did not come. He found himself looking down at the tyre tracks in the soft muddy soil with an indifference that not only surprised him, it also worried him. He knew why, but knowing why didn't really help. He'd had a tooth abscess for some time, which had ached a little occasionally, but as soon as his dentist had drilled out the root canals to allow it to drain and get better, the reverse had happened, and his whole jaw had suddenly started to swell. The pain had become so excruciating that aspirin could not ease it for long, and the antibiotics had not yet had time to work. The trouble was that a grown man like him could not admit that a mere toothache was unbearable, and so he was trying to work through it. It was hard going at times, because a headache came with the abscess pain, and so his brain didn't seem to want to work properly. His slow thinking betrayed him into asking an unnecessary question. 'You'll be able to work out the tyre manufacturer and wheel size from the tread pattern, won't you?' he asked rather sheepishly.

'Of course, and the vehicle manufacturer too. All the pertinent details are on computer. If we feed in the tyre size with the length of the wheelbase and the track width, then out will come the model, or those models nearest to it,' Packstone replied impatiently and signalled with a wave of his hand for the plastic sheet covering the body to be raised.

In the bright spotlights under the low tent Walsh stared down at the sprawled and crumpled body near his feet. The sight still engendered no wealth of emotion within him. Pathetic was the only word that came readily to his mind as he crouched down to study the victim with what he could only describe as professional detachment.

It was a lean, rather lined face, that

perhaps looked older than the dark hair showing under the woollen hat. The hair may, therefore, have been dyed. The skin was taut and appeared to be suntanned beneath the pallor of death. Though that might also be a make-up preparation, if the man had been so concerned about his appearance that he dyed his hair. Such matters would come out later in the pathologist's report, and might be useful if it was to be necessary to build up a picture of how this man's mind worked. The faded eyes stared sightlessly upwards, and if there was any impression to be drawn from them and the man's facial expression, then it was one of helplessness, as though the muscles of the face, so long used to controlling emotions, were now bewildered because there was no spirit left to tell them what to do. Possibly this man was a loner, going through life doing his own thing, but always fighting, pushing, controlling even, rather than enjoying the softness of pleasure, for pleasure's own sake. If that was a fair summing up, then it would be surprising if this man's passing into the nether regions of the next world were to bring great distress to those he'd left behind in this one.

Richard Packstone had obviously already

studied the dead man's face, and was finding that of the Chief Inspector more interesting, as Walsh found out when he looked up and discovered that he too was being scrutinised. There was something quizzical about Packstone's expression, as though a comment was expected. Had he missed something obvious? He hurriedly looked down again at the body. There was nothing that seemed to deserve any specific mention, nothing that warranted a question at this stage of the proceedings, yet there was still that strange expression on Packstone's face. A feeling of irritation came over him, as though he was being expected to join in some stupid guessing game. He muttered 'Thanks,' and started to turn away.

'Don't you want to know the time of death?' Packstone asked quietly.

'Of course I do,' Walsh replied sharply, turning back quickly, 'but whenever I ask that question I'm always told I'll have to wait for the pathologist's report. Is it different this time?'

'Just look at the watch on the man's right wrist,' Packstone suggested dryly.

Walsh glanced down. It was a very expensive watch but the glass was cracked, driven inwards by impact with the large jagged flint that was embedded there in the ground. He bent down to get a closer look. The sweeping second hand was still, so the impact had obviously jammed the mechanism. The other two hands, as far as he could see, indicated a time of five minutes to eight. He felt he could kick himself. He'd missed something that should have been obvious to anyone who was only even half awake. He heard himself mutter, 'But is it a plant?'

That question wasn't very well worded, but Packstone clearly knew what Walsh meant. More often in fiction than in reality, the time shown on a victim's watch is altered, before being *accidentally* broken. The purpose being to suggest a false time of death to coincide with a moment when the killer had a cast-iron alibi elsewhere. Even Chief Inspectors and forensic scientists read novels.

'I'm inclined to think it's genuine,' Packstone announced firmly, which was surprising, coming from someone who was usually noncommittal on anything until it had been fully examined at length, but that phlegmatic scientist had obviously thought this through. 'As I see it the man was probably jumping sideways to get out of the way, but he wasn't quick enough. The impact would have flung him back to the side of the track to roughly where he is now, and that right arm could well have landed hard enough on that stone, to smash the watch there and then. If the watch had been altered after the man was killed, then someone would have needed to have crouched down there, within the white tape area, and you'd have expected to see the toe marks of shoes, like the ones you've just made, but there aren't any. The stone's been deeply embedded where it is for a long time. No, I think it's genuine, but it won't tell you when he died, only when he was knocked down, but from your point of view that's more important. The time of death could be much later. In crushed chest cases like this, it's usually the internal haemorrhaging which actually causes the death. I might see things differently in daylight, but I doubt it.'

Walsh nodded, expressed his thanks for being allowed to view the scene before the pathologist had arrived, and walked carefully back down the track. Packstone was probably right. He usually was, but there was no point in flapping too much at this time of night. The man was dead, nothing was going to change that. It would be best to wait until tomorrow's daylight before starting an investigation. The initial check list of things to be done was routine common sense, and was simple interviewing. He and his team would have to talk to the man who found the body, the man's wife, his neighbours, friends and the people he worked with. Patient questioning and the promptings of gossips should bring forth news of any enmities or bad relationships, and when they'd got that sort of information, hopefully the pathologist's and the forensic evidence would also be available, then they could start the investigation proper.

'Has the dead man's wife turned up yet?' he asked the young constable who had been set the task of preventing any members of the public from going up the track.

'None of her neighbours know where she is. She might even be staying away from home,' was the reply.

The uniformed branch would keep a watch out for her while they guarded the site, so Walsh got in his car and drove home.

Maybe this would be a simple murder inquiry – if the wife had bumped her old man off and run away with her lover. Mind you, the cold-blooded running down of a husband with a car wasn't normally a woman's way of killing, neither for that matter, was it a man's. Motives were the important factors. Find a good motive and nine times out of ten you'd found the killer. The problem might then simply be proving it.

When evening faded into night the outside temperature, as usual, become cooler, which forced the damp clammy air to form a light mist, or a precipitating fog, as the shipping forecasts might have described it. That caused the street lamps to take on a rosy haze, and barely illuminate a dim world of tarmac roads, grey brick terraced houses and damp slate roofs. For the moment it seemed to have been deserted by all its human inhabitants, and most of the other kinds as well. Only one cat could be seen crouched on its haunches beneath a parked car, but it obviously deemed that the area was becoming much too crowded when a single cyclist without lights came pedalling down the street. It decided to dart across the road into the small front gardens on the other side. The cyclist wobbled, braked and slid off the saddle, then bumped the vehicle up the curb and pushed it into a dark passage that ran between the end of the terraced houses and the seven-foot-high perimeter brick wall of the factory. The features of the rider were indistinct under the cowl of a dark-coloured waterproof jacket. The bicycle seemed more difficult to control when being pushed than when being ridden, possibly because the heavy shopping bags hanging on each end of the handlebar, and the long bundle tied to the frame, made it top heavy. Still, it did not have to be pushed far. A few yards down the passage there was a wooden telegraph pole set up against the high wall, which seemed a convenient and sensible place to lean the cycle. After that the rider's actions seemed less rational and rather curious. The long bundle was untied from the frame, and in the process it unrolled into a large prayer-mat-sized piece of thick brown cord carpet. The time and place was hardly suited to the religious activities of any faith, but its true purpose was amply demonstrated when the rider climbed gingerly onto the bike saddle and reached up to throw the carpet lengthways over the sharp and jagged pieces of broken glass which had been set in the concrete on the top of the wall. The front wheel of the bike twisted sideways, and it would have toppled over had the rider not nimbly leapt to the ground. The shopping bags were taken off, and the handlebar was jammed between the wall and the post, firmly enough for the saddle to be a more stable part of a climbing frame, and the rider was soon up again, with a length of rope, to lower the shopping bags down the other side of the wall. That done, the loose end of the rope was taken round the telegraph pole and dropped over. The rider tentatively put hands onto the carpet, concerned, no doubt that the glass might pierce through and cut into flesh, but the carpet was tough and perhaps years of weathering had taken some of the keenness from the sharp edges, for the rider was able to balance on the top, swing round, and then drop lightly to the ground on the other side.

This was clearly a factory's lorry-loading area, and it was untidy, like most such places which were tucked away from the public gaze and free from concerns about the company's outward image. In one corner, near the gates, was a half-full rubbish skip, close to a rusty drum that had once been used as an incinerator, and leaning against the wall were several broken wooden pallets. The rider eagerly carried one to beneath where the two ends of the rope dangled over the wall. The pallet was about as high as the saddle on the bike, so, with the doubled rope to pull on, the return journey back over the wall was going to be quick and easy. So far so good. The rider then picked up the shopping bags and ran over to the main building. If the intention was to make an entry, then the rider was doomed to be disappointed. The thick steel roller shutter doors were bolted, presumably on the inside, as were the fire-exits, and several hours' work with oxy-acetylene equipment would have been needed to make any kind of entrance. Neither were there any windows, except for an inaccessible row set about twenty feet up. However, the rider's interest seemed to be on a couple of nine-inch square ventilation grills, set in the wall, only a little over head high. Two more of the broken pallets, leaned against the brickwork, made access to those easy. Now the contents of the shopping bags were revealed. A small crowbar, a funnel, a pair of three-litre plastic lemonade bottles, and surprisingly enough, a coiled six-foot length of ordinary garden hose. The crowbar, inserted into the gaps in the first grill, had enough leverage to snap away the cast iron and make a sizeable hole. The next job was a bit fiddly. Most of the length of hose had to be inserted into the ventilator hole, and while one hand firmly held the funnel in the outer end of the pipe, the contents of the first lemonade bottle could be carefully poured into the funnel, only it wasn't lemonade that could be heard spraying out of the other end of the pipe, inside the factory, it was petrol. Moving the pipe about ensured that as large an area as possible, hopefully of stored cardboard packing boxes, was being doused. The same procedure was carried out with the second bottle, through the other ventilator. The crowbar was slipped into a pocket, and the empty bottles could be squashed flat and pushed through the holes, with the garden pipe. There would be nothing left of those soon. Next came a fumbling in the waterproof jacket pocket for a cigarette lighter – and a packet of the joke kind of birthday cake candles with the saltpetre soaked wicks, the ones that even if you blow them out, immediately rekindle themselves. Four would be enough, each lined up to be lit in the left hand between thumb and forefinger. There was time to test them too. They were blown out, but seconds later the tiny flames returned. The first candle through the first hole was quite enough. There was a whoosh as the petrol vapour ignited, and a tongue of flame licked momentarily out the ventilator, causing the rider to step back in alarm. It seemed hardly worth throwing a candle into the other vent, but it was soon done, and then the rider ran back across the yard, in just a little bit of a panic, for now that the job was done, escape was the priority. Clearing the wall was easy, but was done a little too quickly, for one leg left the protection of the carpet and got rather deeply gashed by the glass, but the pain was minor and momentary. The carpet was hastily rolled up and the rope wrapped round it. There wasn't time to tie it on the frame, so it was tucked under an arm. The feeling of panic increased when it was realised the bike was facing in the wrong direction, but with a bit of a clatter, that was soon rectified. The rider hurriedly mounted, and pedalled quickly away from the scene.

Three

Denise Labinski's mind was full of wildly conflicting emotions when she arrived back home at half past three in the morning. To say that she was in a state of utter mental panic would not have been too far off the mark.

The warm happy afterglow of her sexual adventure with Donovan O'Shea had barely started to fade when an awful explanation of why he had so unexpectedly made her the object of his attentions suddenly occurred to her. She had believed herself safe alone with him at first, because she thought he would surely never have risked doing anything to offend an important client's wife, but he jolly well had. She'd got that well and truly wrong. But why? The answer was almost too horrid to contemplate, but she had to face up to it. O'Shea obviously hadn't been taking any risks, had he? Why? Because Brian must already have known what he was going to try and do with her. So Brian must have put O'Shea up to it, with bribes of money, or promises of future business. God! Brian would now have all the reason he needed to kick her out of the house without a penny. If she protested, he could shout from the roof-tops that she'd been unfaithful with the grinning, shameless O'Shea. She'd be called a slut, and her salon would be utterly ruined. How could two men be so cruel to someone who had tried so hard to make her marriage a success? O'Shea had wanted her to stay the whole night, but if her utter ruin was what he wanted, he would, wouldn't he?

With such awful thoughts in her mind, she couldn't get away from him quickly enough. She felt utterly sick and helpless. It was surely worse than the worst kind of gang-rape violations, to have been made love to so gently, tenderly and wonderfully, and then to find out that it was all a brutal callous trick. Could Brian really have bribed O'Shea to be that cruel to her? Oh yes indeed! To get what he wanted, Brian would do anything – and use anyone. She had insisted that O'Shea drive her to the hotel for her car, rather than let him drive her home, for Brian might be waiting there with a camera, for positive proof of her infidelity – as if he needed it now. At least, if she were in her own car, she could deny him that pleasure. O'Shea had pretended to be so upset and bewildered by her hurried exit, but he was obviously a past master in the art of cruel deception, and she couldn't trust him. He'd set a trap for her, and she had walked right into it.

Her mind was far too confused to think logically. She tried to persuade herself that she was wrong about O'Shea, but even if he hadn't done what he did for Brian, she might still be in serious trouble. Once a woman had let a man have sex with her he usually thought he could do it again, whenever he wished, and if she refused, he might demand her compliance as his price for keeping silence. Once in the claws of a blackmailer, anything might happen – he might force her to pose for dirty photographs, or even worse things. Why had she been so stupid as to think she might steal a few secret moments of happiness from this horrid world?

She uttered a prayer that Brian might have fallen asleep waiting for her, and that she could creep in without disturbing him. That would put off the evil moment, but tomorrow, all hell might be let loose.

So deep and worrying were all these

considerations that Denise did not see the police car which was parked to guard the end of the now deserted track.

She drove very slowly into the drive, hoping the crunching of gravel would not awaken her husband, or the dogs.

She wasn't really surprised to see the lounge lights still on as she crept softly over the shingle to the front door, with the key ready in her hand. It rather looked as though he was waiting for her, and that the music would have to be faced right now. She squared her shoulders bravely, but then she was startled by a male voice from some way behind her, which called out, 'Mrs Labinsky?' so loudly that it seemed that the whole neighbourhood must be roused. She spun round in alarm and received yet another shock – the sight of a uniformed police sergeant and a policewoman coming towards her. Her instinctive response was to hold up her hand.

'Shush,' she whispered, 'not so much noise. You'll wake my husband,' but now she was frowning. To humiliate her for staying out late Brian must have reported her to the police as being missing.

Possibly they'd been looking for her, or her car, for the last few hours, and now they'd be questioning her about where she had been and who she had been with. Well, she wouldn't play Brian's rotten game – she wouldn't bloody well tell them. 'It is very late. What on earth do you want?' she snapped angrily.

'I'm sorry, Mrs Labinski, but I'm afraid we have some bad news for you,' the Sergeant said hesitantly. 'Would you rather go in the house where you can sit down?'

'What bad news? Oh my God, it's not my Salon? There's not been a fire or a break-in, has there?'

The sergeant looked undecided for a moment, then turned to the slight young figure of his policewoman companion, clearly wanting her to take over and get this unpleasant task over as quickly as possible.

'Mrs Labinski,' the policewoman said in a surprisingly sweet voice, 'I'm afraid it's about your husband. Yesterday evening, we think it was while he was out walking his dogs, he was knocked down by a vehicle, and, er, sustained serious injuries, which subsequently proved fatal.'

Denise's mouth fell open in astonishment, and she shook her head vigorously in utter confusion, which set her long fair hair flying wildly.

'What? I don't understand,' she blurted out at last.

The policewoman took complete charge now. 'I'm sorry, but your husband is dead, I'm afraid, Mrs Labinski. Come now. I think it would be better if you went indoors and sat down.' She took the arm of a distinctly groggy Denise, and gently led her towards the house.

'I'll be in the car, if you need me,' the sergeant said gruffly, glad that his part in this tragic scene was over.

'Where are the dogs?' Denise asked plaintively. Her mind was a seething morass of confused thoughts as she slipped off her coat and sat gingerly on the settee in the lounge.

'The man in the bungalow next door is looking after them,' the waif-like, dark-haired young policewoman said briskly and competently. 'They'll all be all right, so I think it would be best to leave them until the morning. Now what about you? Can I get you a cup of coffee, perhaps, or maybe something stronger?'

Denise shook her bewildered head slowly. 'No thanks. I don't want anything. I just can't think properly – my mind's all fuzzed. You say Brian is dead. I can't believe it. I

82

just feel stunned.'

'You're bound to, under the circumstances. Is there a relative or friend you'd like to go to, or to come here and be with you? We can try and get them for you now, if you like.'

Again Denise shook her head.

'Well, do you think it might be better for you to go to bed? We can get your doctor to come out and give you a sedative to help you to sleep.'

Denise ignored that offer and stared helplessly down at her hands. 'It wouldn't have happened if he'd come with me, but he'd got some work to do. It's awful. I just don't understand it.'

Policewoman Mary Innes looked as sympathetic as she could manage, and decided to sit down as well. It looked as though this bereavement incident might go on for a while yet. Normally a grieving widow would already have burst into floods of tears, but this Labinski woman was too stunned yet for any such emotions to display themselves. Until she did, she must not be left on her own, that was what the counselling lecturers had all said, because unrelieved despair and distress could lead to dangerous suicidal feelings. Mrs Labinski showed no such signs, but she might yet do so. Conversation was needed, they could hardly just sit and stare at each other.

'Where did you go then?' Mary Innes asked politely.

Denise looked up sharply. 'A charity event, a sort of party – at the hotel by the river. I went home with, er, some friends afterwards, and we got talking, that's why I was so late getting back, but how on earth did Brian get run down? The dogs get walked on the green most nights, but that's only just across the lane.'

'It happened down that track. We don't yet know for sure how, but we're treating the incident as suspicious.'

'Suspicious? You mean you think he might have been killed deliberately? Oh, how awful.' Denise's eyes had become wide with horror and had now filled with tears. That was a good sign, tears were a woman's safety valve in times of stress.

'It might be so.' Mary said quietly. 'Did your husband have any enemies? Had anyone been threatening him?' Then to the policewoman's utter surprise, Denise's head began to nod.

'There was a man called Grimston – on the answerphone tape – something about

84

Brian having nearly killed his wife – he threatened to kill Brian – and he threatened me too – if I didn't get Brian to do something or other.'

Mary Innes's eyes lit up in sheer excitement. If she, a mere policewoman, were to come up with the name of a killer, a murderer, it would look mighty good on her records, and might even improve her chances of promotion, or getting a transfer to the CID, which was every young police officer's dream.

'May I play the tape?' she asked eagerly.

They played the tape twice, while Mary made notes, but the effort of listening exhausted Mrs Labinski. Her brain seemed to have gone soggy and unable to cope with all the crazy things that had been happening to her tonight. She sank back on the settee and closed her eyes. 'I think I'd like that cup of coffee, if you wouldn't mind,' she said drowsily.

Mary Innes went into the kitchen and after a little rummaging around, found the necessary ingredients, but when she returned to the lounge she found Mrs Labinski stretched out full length on the settee, fast asleep. She went upstairs and found a blanket to lay over the still figure, then she walked back into the kitchen, to use her radio phone to contact head-quarters, and to tell them that she had discovered that the previous afternoon a man called Grimston had threatened to beat the daylights out of Mr Brian Labinski, because some action taken by The Everglide Shoe Company, where Labinski worked, had caused Grimston's wife to have a heart attack.

To Mary Innes's mind it was obvious that this Grimston fellow had committed the crime, and that this case of murder was now virtually solved, save for some few minor irrelevant details, such as proof positive. Someone else would make the arrest, but hopefully that would not mean they took all the credit. In the meantime, there was little for her to do but make herself comfortable, keep awake, guard the sleeping newly widowed woman, and daydream about all the murder cases she would solve when she'd been made an Inspector in the CID.

The duty officer at Headquarters had certainly listened to the lowly police-woman's words with some interest, and he decided that such vital information, on what was already logged in that night's events register as a potentially very serious crime, should be passed on without delay. Not simply to the lightly-manned CID office, but directly and verbally to its most senior officer, so that it could be acted upon promptly, if that was deemed necessary.

All that was what one would expect from a keen and efficiently run modern police Constabulary, but it did result in Detective Chief Inspector Sidney Walsh being woken from a restless sleep, at the unsociable and unfashionable time of four-thirty in the morning.

Walsh lay for some moments in the darkened bedroom with the phone to his ear trying to gather his thoughts and force his brain into reluctant activity. Clearly he would need to gather his serious crime team together without delay, not a difficult task since that consisted only of himself and two others – then they could work out a sensible plan of action. He spoke quietly to the duty officer, so as not to wake his wife Gwen, who appeared to be still asleep beside him. 'Call Finch and Phipps for me please. Tell them to meet me in my office in half an hour, no, make that three-quarters of an hour, and then get someone to find out if we've anything on file about Everglide

Shoes and this Grimston fellow.'

At that time in the morning Walsh's office was almost as bleak and gloomy inside as the weather was outside, but matters of decor and style had little to do with the detection of serious crime, or those involved in it.

After Walsh had arrived, it was Detective Constable Brenda Phipps who was next to turn up. She was of medium height, in her late twenties, slim and very pretty, with unruly brown hair, and eyes of the same colour that glowed with energy and a zest for life. The word *elegant* might have been slipped in there somewhere too, had she not chosen to wear well-washed blue jeans, and a thick green woollen jumper that was loose and baggy from much use. Clearly, in her opinion, a call-out at that early hour warranted a scruffy comfort, rather than fashion and style, but that bothered Walsh no more than it did her, because they all had changes of clothes in the boots of their cars or office lockers, which would enable them to dress quickly enough for whatever occasion cropped up, be it following tracks across a ploughed field or merging in the most sophisticated of company.

Detective Sergeant Finch, however, when he came in a few moments later, seemed to have found the time to shower and shave, don a neat light-grey suit and find and sport a rather garishly coloured tie, which, even if it did nothing else, brightened up the drab office considerably. He was a fair-haired lean and lanky man, an inch or so over six feet tall. The impression that he might also be detached and languid, was at variance with the keen and intelligent look in his deep blue eyes.

'We've a new case,' Walsh announced bluntly, staring at his two assistants with tired eyes. This morning's aspirins had dulled the abscess pain, but not yet cleared the accompanying headache. 'I went to the scene of the crime last night, and the dead man's name is Labinski. It would seem that he was out walking his dogs yesterday evening, and got run down by a vehicle which, according to forensics' reading of the tracks, stopped, and then deliberately backed up over the body before driving off.' Walsh explained.

'Nasty,' said Brenda Phipps, twitching her lips into something like a cross between a grin and a mild sort of scowl, presumably to express her horror at such a cold-blooded method of extinguishing a human life. Quite why she said that, and made that face, she did not really know, for all murders were cold-blooded killings.

Reg Finch seemed anxious to have a point clarified, for he frowned across the desk at Walsh. 'Forensics' reading of the tracks? You were there, what's your opinion?' There was an element of surprise in his voice, because when it came to reading tracks in muddy ground Walsh was probably the most competent in the whole force, and usually the most enthusiastic. Many times in the past he had led his team across fields or through scrubby woodland, pointing now and then to bent grass stems or scuffed gravel, that to him were signs of the passing of feet. Rarely had such tracks played any significant part in their investigations, but, like all clues, they had been followed up patiently and meticulously, come rain or shine.

Walsh looked down at his hands, well aware of the surprise in Reg's voice. He knew that he had not studied the muddy marks on Labinski's body with the intensity that he would normally have done. He tried to recall the scene in his mind and follow again the sweep of Packstone's hand as the forensic scientist interpreted the various marks, but the mental pictures were blurred and indistinct.

'I saw nothing to make me disagree with their assessment of the situation,' he temporised sheepishly. 'Anyway, we've got two bits of useful information this time. The man's watch was broken in his fall, and the hands showed a time of five to eight. To all intents and purposes that seems genuine at the present moment, but forensic will be giving the watch special attention to see if there is any sign of it being tampered with. The other thing we now know is that someone by the name of Grimston had been making threatening telephone calls to Labinski. Some business disagreement, apparently.'

Brenda Phipps waved a hand aimlessly in the air. 'It doesn't sound as though this case is going to need a great deal of ingenuity on our behalf,' she exclaimed flippantly. 'I don't suppose a dozen witnesses have turned up as well, all telling the same story?'

Walsh's grimace was the nearest thing to a fleeting smile that he could manage at that moment. 'Not to my knowledge. However, from the tyre track measurements, Packstone's team have come up with the provisional suggestion that the murder vehicle was an old, short wheel-based Land-rover, but they're still checking on other makes. Anyway, this threatening phone call lead needs following up without delay. Would you go and see this Grimston fellow, Reg? Apparently he's a gamekeeper, somewhere out towards Barton. If he can't account for his whereabouts yesterday evening around eight o'clock, bring him in for questioning. You'd better take Arthur with you, the man has a reputation for being aggressive. Brenda, I'd like you to go to Labinski's business – Everglide Shoes, off the Newmarket Road, and find out just what the threatening phone calls were all about. I'll go and talk to Labinski's wife, if she's in a fit state to be interviewed, and the man who found the body; and I'll set Alison Knott organising the taking of statements from the houses in the vicinity. We can meet later on, when forensic have had time to firm up on their ideas. All right? Any questions?'

'Mrs Labinski had been out on the town last night, Mary said,' Detective Constable Arthur Bryant confided.

'Really,' Detective Sergeant Reg Finch

acknowledged vaguely, as he slowed the car on the main road to peer up yet another gap between the hedges, only to find again that it was an entrance to a field, rather than a track that might lead to a remote habitation. 'How about helping me find the way to this Grimston fellow's place, instead of just prattling on about nothing? Besides, how the devil do you know what this Mary Innes was up to while she was on duty last night?'

'Well, I sort of met her in the canteen before she went off duty this morning, didn't I?' Arthur's youthful chubby face wore a secretive, if somewhat guilty expression, not that his companion was in a position to observe it, or be particularly interested in it.

'She'll get herself into a load of trouble if it's found out that she gossips police business to any old Tom, Dick or Harry.'

'Hey, steady on, Reg. It's me she talked to. I'm not just any old body. She wouldn't gossip, honestly Reg, but we're sort of friends, you see. She's very clever, and I rather encourage her to talk to me. I can help her to look at police matters from different angles, you see. She'd love to work in CID, and she's got a lovely voice too. Slow down Reg, this might be the turning.

It says Private, and it's got massive old stone gateposts, so it ought to lead somewhere interesting.' Arthur leaned forward to peer up the flinty, rutted, hard-packed track.

Reg Finch drove slowly along the uneven surface of what apparently had once been a wide driveway through the woods, bordered, no doubt, by rhododendrons and random Scots pines. Now it was narrowed by the ferns, brambles and shrubs that together had tenaciously fought the foreign invaders for essential light and air-space. The main problem from Reg's point of view was keeping his wheels out of the deeper ruts, lest he lose his exhaust pipe on the ridge between them. There were occasional ominous scraping sounds as thorny tentacles brushed the car's side panels.

'Got a nice voice? What do you mean?' Reg asked curiously.

'She's a soprano. We belong to the Gilbert and Sullivan society – only in the chorus, of course, because our shift patterns mean we can't always get to rehearsals. This Grimston chap has got a bad reputation, Reg. He's been known to threaten trespassers with a shotgun.'

'That's why you're with me, Arthur. If he gets wild and starts shooting, it's your job to draw his fire – to give me time to run to safety. That's one of the privileges of being a Detective Sergeant, I suppose.' Reg announced with a bland smile.

'Very funny, but since we know he's an aggressive character, shouldn't we have an armed back-up team?'

Reg shrugged his shoulders. 'Doesn't it occur to you that every gamekeeper in the country probably has the same reputation? Think about it. The only contact he generally has with the public is when they're found trespassing on the private land which it's his job to guard. They may be innocent enough, and merely out for a pleasant walk in the countryside, but if he doesn't kick them off straight away with mild fleas in their ears, they and their townie friends will be back whenever it's a nice day, disturbing the game-birds, climbing trees, lighting picnic fires or throwing away the cigarette ends which could burn down a whole woodland, and destroy all the wild life of an entire area. As for shotguns, a gamekeeper is the one person in this country you shouldn't be surprised to see carrying a gun, and if you're like me, the very presence of a gun makes you feel threatened, even if it's not being pointed in your direction,' Reg admitted while carefully driving round a particularly large hole in the track.

'It sounds as though you're in favour of landowners stopping people enjoying the freedom of the countryside,' Arthur said cautiously.

'Not if a landowner is breaking the law. There isn't freedom in a town. You can't wander in and out of people's vegetable gardens, so why should anyone expect to do that out in the country where crops are growing? Ah! It looks as though we might have arrived, at last.'

The track had swung to the right, and the car had come out of the woods into a more open grassy space. On their left appeared the rambling overgrown ruins of a large old building. An ancient manor house, perhaps, or some rich man's nineteenth-century showpiece dwelling, that had failed to survive the transition into the harsher twentieth-century economic conditions. Reg Finch wound down his car window to get a better look. He was interested in history and had visited most of the important sites in and about Cambridge, but the existence of this ruin was new to him. He stared at the tall chimney-stacks, tufted in places with wispy rank grasses, and set starkly against the lighter sky, but any faint shadow of its former elegance and style was lost in the wild tangle of creeper and bramble that seemed determined to blot the remnants of the structure out of the visual landscape.

Reg, too, needed to blot it out of his mind, for just a little further on was a much smaller red-tiled building, perhaps the old stable block. It had glass in its small paned windows, and those windows were curtained on the inside, showing that it, unlike its once grand neighbour, was still inhabited. It too had creepers growing on its warm south-facing facade, although these were climbing roses that were budding but not yet in early bloom. A low rustic fence bounded a small front garden. Against the background of trees the whole scene had, with the judicious mental addition of summer leaves, a Constable quality about it, which was only marred by a number of modern vehicles parked on a nearby shingled area. An elderly, dark-green, canvas-backed Land-rover stood next to a more modern red two-door hatchback, and a blue moped leaned against the fence.

Reg Finch stopped the car and got out. That seemed a signal for two dogs to appear on the scene. Barking excitedly, the black retrievers dashed out from the side of the cottage and hurtled towards the tall grey-suited intruder, clearly intent on making a fearsome display of aggression which should, by rights and previous experience, result in the interloper beating an immediate terrified retreat. Arthur, indeed, after a moment's hesitation, decided to stay where he was in the car, and merely watch developments. Reg Finch, however, seemed totally unaware of the part he was supposed to play in the charade, and he strode forward to meet the dogs as if totally unconcerned. That was such an unexpected development that it took the dogs rather by surprise. Their growls and barking ceased and their headlong dash slowed to a cautious walk. When the fearless stranger then pointed a finger and imperiously snapped out the words 'Quiet!' and 'Down!', followed in a softer tone by, 'Come here!' their behaviour changed dramatically. Both looked round to see if they were being observed from the house, then, apparently finding no conflicting orders coming from that direction, their ears went back and their tails gave perfunctory wags and both wriggled on their haunches to Reg's feet making plaintive whining noises. When Reg bent down to pat their heads, they grovelled in an ecstasy of welcome, as if to someone who might have been their old long-lost best friend.

'Judy! Jason! Come here!' The voice came from a tall burly man with thinning fair hair who had just emerged from the front door. The light glinted ominously from the shiny black barrels of a shotgun held by the stock, in his right hand. The weapon was safe in its breech-open state, but the glint of brass showed that cartridges were loaded, and that it was ready for instant use. Reg heard a car door being slammed shut behind him, so he presumed that young Arthur Bryant was now out and about, and preparing himself to take some sort of suitable action if that shotgun looked as though it might actually be used. It was at that moment that Reg really did wish that there was an armed response unit behind him.

The dogs moved away from Reg Finch, but they didn't go far before they sank to the ground and started panting with open mouths, as though suddenly exhausted by an over-long walk.

'What do you want?' The man exclaimed loudly. He was frowning and looked tired, or possibly worried. The tone of his voice was certainly not friendly, but on the other hand, it could not be said that it was full of antagonism and aggression either. There was something in his manner, in his facial expression perhaps, that suggested the man was accustomed to being the lesser role in a landowner-servant relationship. A job like his probably necessitated that, as indeed do many others. The military and police being but two examples where the power of authority allows for the ordering of others. So this man's neutral attitude might be because he had not yet decided whether this visitor had any real power or authority. Reg Finch decided that adopting a confident but slightly patronising manner, might help achieve an easy co-operation.

'I'm a police officer,' Reg stated calmly, giving a mild emphasis to the word *officer*, 'and I'm wanting a word with a Gordon Grimston. Is that you by any chance?'

'Yes! I'm Gordon Grimston, but what the devil can you want with me?' came his cautious reply.

'Just a little of your time,' Reg went on quietly. 'I presume that if I were to ask you why you're holding that shotgun, you would tell me that you've just been cleaning it.

Well, if you take the cartridges out first you'll find it a lot easier to clean the barrels. I suggest that you unload it and put it away somewhere safe, then when you've done that, perhaps you'll be kind enough to answer a few questions.'

Grimston glowered thoughtfully at him for a few moments and started to chew his bottom lip. Whether he actually made a decision on how he would act, or had merely postponed the making of one, was not at all clear, but he did take out the bright-red cartridges and slip them into a pocket, then snap the barrels of the weapon into position. 'Let's have a look at your warrant card first,' he grunted.

Reg came closer and held the card out for the other to study. Grimston's eyes flickered from photo to face, stared at the constabulary crest, then read each word carefully.

'Can't afford to take chances – living in a lonely place like this. There's a lot of funny people about, you know,' he said eventually. 'You'd better come in. On your own though. There ain't enough room in here for your mate as well.' He turned in the narrow hallway and went into the room on the left. Reg called to tell Arthur to wait in the car, then followed Grimston in, with an air of self-confidence that wasn't, perhaps, quite as sound as it seemed.

The room to the left was in fact quite spacious. It had a stone floor covered with what once had been an expensive and colourful Persian carpet. Now it was worn in places, particularly where the flags were slightly uneven. There was an old three-piece suite with floral-patterned loose covers, a polished mahogany bureau on which stood a number of family photographs, and a low, glass-fronted bookcase. All was neat and looked immaculately clean, a sign, surely, of a woman's touch – not this man's.

'Sit yourself down. Now, what is it you want to ask me?' Grimston grunted.

Reg sat down on one of the armchairs, and found it surprisingly comfortable. 'Tell me where you were and what you were doing at eight o'clock yesterday evening,' he said calmly.

'That's easy. That's no problem,' came a girlish voice from the doorway.

Reg turned his head in surprise. A stout young woman in blue jeans and a colourful checked shirt, came into the room. Clearly she had just had a bath or shower, for her dark hair was still damp and lank. 'But what's he want to know for, Dad?' She went on truculently.

'Because he's a police officer, that's why. A detective sergeant too, no less,' Grimston growled.

'So what! Why's he asking you questions?'

'Don't know. He hasn't said yet.'

'Well, ask him then.'

Reg Finch grimaced. If he wasn't careful this girl's sudden interruption might easily lose him what control he did have over the interview. 'I'm asking questions because it is my duty to do so,' he said as pleasantly as he could, 'and it is your duty as citizens, to assist the police in their investigations. Now, would you please tell me where you were, and what you were doing at about eight o'clock yesterday evening?'

'Don't tell him, Dad, not until he tells you why he wants to know. He's got no right to barge into our home, demanding answers. This isn't Stalin's Russia,' Grimston's daughter declared passionately.

Reg felt irritated and looked questioningly at Grimston, who was himself frowning at the prospect of being forced into a confrontation with authority that he clearly did not want.

'Be quiet, girl. Don't interfere,' Grimston growled uneasily. 'I spent most of yesterday evening up at Addenbrooke's hospital. I would have been there at eight, certainly.'

'And I was with him, visiting my mum. She's in the intensive care ward. She's had a heart attack,' the daughter interrupted. 'What's it got to do with you, Sergeant?'

'You keep out of this, Tracy. If you can't keep bloody quiet, then bugger off, damn you. It's me he wants to question, not you, and I can speak for myself,' Grimston said angrily.

Reg Finch looked surprised. It sounded as though this Grimston might have a cast-iron alibi for the time Labinski was killed, for nurses on duty were a pretty wide awake lot, particularly on such a ward, and if he and his daughter really were there, there should be plenty of independent witnesses to back him up. Under these circumstances Reg could hardly arrest him on suspicion of murder, or take him into headquarters for questioning. He must check this alibi out first.

'You were at the hospital, you say?' he asked, just to make sure he'd heard the man right.

'That's right! We got there a bit before

eight, I reckon, and we stayed until ten, or thereabouts.'

'All right. We'll leave that for now, but there's another important matter. You made some pretty angry phone calls to a Mr Labinski yesterday. Why did you do that? What was that all about?' Reg asked curtly.

Grimston's face reddened angrily. 'You'd have been bloody mad too, if that bastard had done to your missus what he did to mine.'

'Which was what?'

'The bugger pulled the rug from under my wife's little business, didn't he? He conned her into doing only his work, because he was desperate for it. Now he's getting the stuff made in India and he don't need her no more. She's had to close the business down, and the shock and worry's give her a heart attack, hasn't it? You wouldn't treat a dog like he's treated my Tina. All she needed was some work to keep her going until something else turned up. That was the least he owed her. I wanted to talk to him reasonable like, but whenever I phoned, the bugger were never there.'

'I see. But you did threaten him, did you?'

'I suppose so, but what else could I do? It's been Tina's pride and joy, that little factory has. Her being her own boss and all. She's worked so hard to keep it going, and it's proper knocked the stuffing out of her. Our solicitor feller said he couldn't do anything because there weren't no contract, and nothing in writing.' Grimston's red face twisted with emotion, and his hands gesticulated helplessly. 'I've calmed down now, I have, but if I'd have got my hands round his bloody neck yesterday, I'd have rung it good and proper, that's for certain. Then you'd have been here after me for murdering the bleeder.'

'That's very honest of you to say that, because someone certainly seems to have felt like murdering him last night,' Reg said quietly. 'Labinski was run down and killed, we think by a short wheel-based Land-rover, possibly a similar model to the one parked outside here. Is that yours? Did you drive to the hospital in that last night?'

Grimston's mouth fell open in surprised shock, but his eyes flashed with an emotion that may or may not have been fear.

'I went to the hospital in the red car,' Grimston spluttered. Whether he was watching the performance of an excellent actor, Reg Finch could not be sure, but of one thing he was definitely certain:

Grimston was a very complex character, whose temper was probably always on a short fuse. Such a man could probably kill when he was in the blind heat of anger. Reg felt that he wanted to get away from that floral decorated room, with the glinting, menacing shotgun propped up against the wall, so he rose to his feet. 'This is a murder enquiry, and everything we are told must be checked out carefully,' he said bluntly. 'We will also need to examine your Land-rover. I'd like the keys for it, if you please, and I'd like to borrow this photograph of you both, for a while. I'll give you receipts. My assistant will stay here to ensure that you're not bothered by any of those funny people you're worried about. You are not under arrest, but I think it would be best if you didn't leave this place until we've confirmed that you were at the hospital last night, as you say you were.'

Four

Denise Labinski woke up feeling absolutely dreadful. Her mind was a whirling mass of confused thoughts and images, and uppermost in them were the vague memories of a horrid dream, which had recurred over and over again during the night. She had been resting peacefully on a white fluffy cloud, when several naked young men had appeared, and began pointing at her and taunting her. That awful fat Chairman had been there too, leering and jeering. Then an angry Brian had come, offering huge cheques to any who would brutally violate her. Suddenly a lean big-nosed man had turned up with a stick, and had beaten Brian about the head. Then the lean man picked her up, and rode off with her on his horse, towards a far distant black castle, but rather than being relieved at her rescue, she had been terribly afraid of more torments to come.

She shook her muddled head and rubbed her eyes. Some of that dream had surely echoed the living nightmare of last night's horrid thoughts, but nothing in her bewildered mind made real sense, except that Brian was dead. Brian was dead – wasn't he?

She stared up from the settee at the uniformed policewoman who had come as a replacement for Mary Innes. 'Is it true? Is my husband really dead?' she asked hoarsely.

'I'm afraid so, Mrs Labinski,' was the not unexpected reply.

Denise threw off the blanket and got to her feet, rocking somewhat unsteadily as she looked down in horror at the creased and crumpled silken dress that she'd worn at last night's reception. Her whole life was a crumpled mess now. Somehow she would have to try and sort it all out, but her brain refused to do any such serious thinking, and it was a relief to postpone the need, by deciding that having a bath was the most essential thing to do.

She stretched out her legs and let the warm water gradually creep up over her skin. Brian was dead. Brian was dead. Those words did not fill her with the grief and dismay that they ought, but why should they indeed? Brian hadn't loved her any more, if he ever had. His words and actions lately proved that. Her only true feelings were rather ones of relief. Yet money might – money would – be a problem, and she would have to ask O'Shea to help sort that out for her – but ask O'Shea? After last night?

Her over-stressed mind pushed the thoughts she couldn't cope with to one side, and trivial ones took over.

She was a widow now, and that word *widow* conjured up the vision of an elegant woman in a well-cut shimmering black satin hooded cloak, with sad eyes modestly downcast. That was obviously the sort of attitude that people would expect from her, and so that was how she must try to present herself. Maintaining it all the time would not be easy, and she would have to wear black clothes. Black, particularly silky and lacy black, could look absolutely stunning against an ivory white skin under an ambient light, but it hardly suited her colouring. A full-skirted dress, pulled in at the waist to emphasise the hips, with brief cap sleeves, a modest neckline, and a simple row of pearls sounded just the thing. She had nowhere near enough black clothes in her own wardrobe to last out a period of mourning, so she would definitely need more. That was at least a positive thought, and it made her feel more cheerful. Anyway, just how long did one have to mourn these days? She couldn't wear black all the time in the salon; black made for a sombre, gloomy atmosphere, and that would never do. Perhaps shades of grey, relieved with white. This widowhood business might prove a blessing in disguise. When the news of the tragedy got round, her name might be on everyone's lips, and people would come to the salon to express their sympathies. If they all bought things, then the salon would do well and make money, and then there would be nothing for her to worry about. Brian had guaranteed the bank loan on the salon, but how would that stand now that he had passed on? Yes, *passed on* was a better way of saying it than the word *died*. The house was in his name too, and he had other money in shares and things. She would have to force herself to go and see Donovan O'Shea sometime. When she did, she would act all haughty and cold, and pretend that nothing had ever happened between them, or even take one of the girls from the salon with her. That was the way to do it, but it could wait until she felt better. In the meantime she was in mourning.

She giggled as the choice of underwear sorted itself out quite naturally. She would mourn Brian today in the skimpiest black set that she had.

The face that looked back at her in the mirror looked awfully haggard and showed some dreadful signs of ageing in the wrinkles round her eyes. She still couldn't feel any real sorrow about Brian being dead. Did all widows really feel like that to start with? She mustn't let it show. She set about restoring the facial damage with professional care. She had nearly finished doing that when she decided that her work was too good, and had to clean it all off. She needed to look a little wan and haggard today. The choice of the right clothes from what there was in her wardrobe was much more difficult. A black tee-shirt was too casual, a black blouse fitted too well, so a looser fitting woollen jumper would have to do, that and a simple plain kneelength taffeta skirt. The combination made her look rather too young and innocent, but it reflected how she felt. From men she would certainly get looks of appreciation and sympathy, but women were harder to please and more critical. Nevertheless she swirled contentedly before the long mirror – if she left her hair loose and unadorned she would just about have achieved the right balance of effects. The open-eyed expressionless stare, which seemed to portray helpless bewilderment, was absolutely right, and needed only a few seconds practice. She must be careful what she said, and try to curb her tendency to prattle. A widow wouldn't prattle.

She went slowly downstairs to where the big wide world was probably awaiting her appearance.

Sure enough, there were a man and a woman sitting in the lounge – both rose as she came in. The man had a serious, interesting sort of rugged face, but there was no smile of welcome there. She must have missed seeing the appreciative lightening of his eyes.

'Mrs Labinski?' the man asked.

Denise nodded.

'I am Detective Chief Inspector Walsh, Cambridgeshire CID, and this is Detective Constable Knott,' he went on, indicating his stoutish companion with a wave of his hand. 'I know that you must be under tremendous strain at the moment, but if you feel well enough, it would be helpful if we could ask you a few straightforward questions.'

114

Denise focused her big sorrowful eyes on the questioner. 'Well, I'll do anything I can to help, of course,' she said bravely, 'but I'm not sure how sensible my answers will be. My mind is all mixed up, you see. I still can't believe that what happened really did happen.'

'That's understandable, but time is the great healer, they say. May we sit down please?' Walsh asked politely. This woman had the bewildered look of a child who had become separated from her parents on some crowded summer holiday beach.

'You really do understand, don't you? Yes, please do sit down,' Denise replied placidly.

'How long have you lived here in Cambridge?' Walsh asked.

'About six months. Before that we lived in Blackheath. We came here when Brian got appointed to the board of Everglide Shoes. The headhunters came after him, you know. Everglide's were in awful trouble, and they were desperate for someone who could pull them round. I didn't want to move really, but they made Brian such a good offer that we couldn't really refuse.'

'Had you been married long?'

'About two years. We met at a reception – when Prince Charles opened a new training

115

centre. Brian's first wife had left him years ago, because he was more interested in his work than in her. Well, he is, I mean was, a bit like that, but we got along really well. I had a salon in Blackheath that took up a lot of my time too, you know. The salon wasn't mine exactly, but I ran it, and did all the work. I own my own now,' Denise explained proudly.

'Any children?' the stoutish Alison Knott asked wryly.

The policewoman's voice sounded rather aggressive to Denise, as though it expressed an inexplicable personal dislike, but she was used to such things from other women, particularly those who were a bit overweight. It was understandable, so she shook her head mildly. 'We're both too busy, and it wouldn't be fair to have children if we couldn't give them the attention they deserve, but Brian already had one son by his first marriage. He's in his first year at university somewhere, I think.'

'We might need to talk to your husband's doctor and solicitor. Who would they be?'

'Dr Page, and Donovan O'Shea.'

'We know about the threatening phone calls, but had your husband made any other enemies in the past who might have felt antagonism to him?'

Denise wrinkled her nose and frowned. 'Not to my knowledge, but there must have been many people who hated him. He'd been involved in so many closures, mergers, and such things, and he often had to sack people who were not good at their jobs. That was Brian's job, and he did what he thought was right, but you can't tell the people who lost their jobs that though, can you? It's like this man Grimston. As I understand it, Brian had to close his wife's business, but I'm sure it was the right thing to do, and he couldn't possibly have known she had a weak heart, could he? It's a tough world. We all understand that, but that was no reason for Grimston to do what he did. People who are violent like that should be locked away, otherwise the public aren't safe, are they? He threatened me too, you know. As if I could make Brian change his mind.' Denise was a little surprised to hear herself talking on so long and defending Brian's behaviour, but a real widow would be expected to do that. As long as she didn't start prattling, everything would be fine.

Walsh frowned. 'We don't know that Grimston was responsible for what happened, and it may be that he could not have done it. We have an open mind at the moment, and must pursue all possibilities.'

Denise's eyes opened even wider and she looked shocked and agitated. 'But that's awful. The man said that he was going to kill Brian. You surely can't leave him free to roam about. He must be mad, and he might easily kill someone else.'

'Have no fear, we won't let that happen. Now tell us about yesterday evening, starting from the time you got home from your salon?' Walsh asked her.

'I got home about sixish, and went straight up to have a bath and change, because I was going to the charity reception at the riverside hotel. Brian came in at about seven, or just after. He was supposed to go with me, but he'd spent longer in India than he'd planned, and he didn't get back until yesterday morning. He said he'd got some work to do, which was a bit mean of him. So I went on my own, and left him to it. I called in at the salon first, so I must have got to the reception at about half-eight, I suppose. Afterwards I went to some friends' house, but I never thought I wouldn't see him alive again. I bet he wishes he'd come with me now, because then nothing like that would have happened, and he'd still be alive. Now

I've got to sort things out, and to be honest I don't quite know where to start. Brian looked after all our money matters, and I don't know if I'll have enough to live on. It's going to be awful too, being here on my own.'

'You've got your dogs,' Alison Knott suggested dryly.

'They're Brian's dogs, not mine. He always had to walk them when he was home. He hated it when they did what I told them to do; they never took much notice of him.'

Walsh glared in annoyance at Alison Knott's quite unnecessary interruption. The woman was obviously doing her best to control her shaken feelings. 'Many people in your position just put those sort of things in the hands of their solicitor, and go and stay at a hotel while he sorts it all out for them,' he suggested helpfully.

'That's a brilliant idea,' Denise said, far more enthusiastically than she actually felt. 'I think I'll do that. I'll ring and book myself into the hotel by the river. It's nice and quiet there.'

Walsh gave a grim smile and rose to his feet. 'I think we've troubled you enough for the moment. Anything else can wait. Will you be all right on your own? I can call the policewoman back for a while, if you like.'

'I'm sure I'll be all right, thank you.'

'What did you make of her, Alison? I rather got the feeling you didn't like her,' Walsh said as they walked down the shingled drive.

'I don't suppose I did, really. She's not a very bright woman, and probably she's mentally stuck in her teens, hence her girlish clothes, and the innocent pretty little girl act. The way she rolled those gooey eyes at you was quite sickening.'

'Really!' Walsh replied in surprise. The woman had certainly got nice eyes, and a nice figure too. She'd looked sad and bewildered, but under the circumstances that was only to be expected. He couldn't say that he'd noticed anything peculiar about her attitude and manner. Women were generally better than men at weighing up their own sex, but not always, sometimes they fell prey to instinctive likes and dislikes, which could cloud their judgement. He'd always thought of Alison Knott as being a down-to-earth and sensible person, and it was interesting to hear her views, but he didn't think he agreed with her this time. He winced as a particularly sharp twinge throbbed through into his headache. It seemed to be getting worse, not better. He needed to take more aspirins, and go somewhere quiet until they started to work. He could safely leave the rest of what he wanted to do to Alison. She was sensible enough.

'Well, when you've made sure that the house-to-house questioning is going according to plan, you can go and have a word with the man who found Labinski's body. Then you can find out whether you've summed his wife's character up correctly, by checking what you can of her story.'

The young receptionist in the Everglide Shoes front office looked tired and harassed when Detective Constable Brenda Phipps arrived, even though it was only a little after half past nine in the morning. The rubber plant and the two busy-lizzies on the glass-topped tables seemed to be drooping with fatigue too, as though worn out by some frenzied nocturnal activities. There was that sort of atmosphere about the place.

'I won't keep you a moment,' the flustered girl said hurriedly as she adjusted the microphone of her headset and then pro-ceeded to talk to it. 'I'm sorry, Mr LeClerc, but Mr Anderson hasn't arrived yet. No, he's not answering his mobile apparently, but they'll get him to ring you just as soon as he does come in. I'm sorry, Mr LeClerc, but I don't see what else I can do.' She pressed a switch, gave a heavy sigh and rubbed helplessly at her forehead. 'I can type, work the switchboard, speak French, and even bow and scrape with the best of them, but I can't bloody well work miracles,' she muttered to herself, then she straightened her back, and turned to her visitor once again. 'I'm sorry about that,' she said, giving a smile which, had it been reproduced on the face of an actress playing the part of a woman suffering the agonies of mediaeval torture, would have received an instant recommendation for the actress of the year award.

'I'm Detective Constable Phipps of the Cambridge Constabulary CID and I've come to see Mr LeClerc. He is expecting me,' Brenda announced seriously, a smile would have seemed out of place. She had changed the jeans and sweater for a more bland but business-like dark skirt and matching jacket. A red and white striped scarf round her neck added colour and a bit of elegance. The receptionist stared at her for a moment with a frown of interest creasing her forehead and an inquisitive glint in her eye.

'Which Mr LeClerc? Senior or junior?' She asked abruptly.

'Senior, I should think. Which ever one is the company chairman.'

That brought about a pressing of buttons and an announcement to somebody that Detective Phipps of the CID had arrived. 'He'll send someone down to show you the way to the boardroom in a minute. Have you come about the fire, or about Mr Labinski?' She asked tentatively.

'What fire?' Brenda replied cautiously.

'Didn't you know? Well there was a fire in the carton store last night. Pretty well all of our stock of empty boxes went up in flames. It isn't half a mess down there. That's what all the flap's about this morning, we've got to get new boxes from our supplier because there's some urgent orders to get out. The trouble is,' she confided, 'some people in this place think that all they have to do to solve problems is to shout out orders. You can say "I want this" or "I want that" as much as you like, but that don't actually make things happen, does it?'

Brenda Phipps ignored the question, and

asked one of her own. 'What's been the reaction here to the news of Mr Labinski's death?'

The girl looked down at her hands and shrugged her shoulders. 'Well, let me put it this way, there won't be many tears shed over him. The only one upset that I've heard of is his secretary Emily, but she's a bit of a wimp, and that might be put on for all I know.' The girl's face had a twisted smile on it when it was raised to look at the police visitor again. 'I shouldn't say this, I know, but you'll find out anyway, or you will if you do your job right, but down in dispatch they're running a book on which of our managers did it.'

'Really! Was he disliked that much?'

'Disliked? It weren't that, that didn't matter so much, but he was going to sack most of them, wasn't he? And where would they get other jobs, with the shoe industry being run down as it is? This part of the country used to be full of shoe companies, but where are they now? Gone, most of them. So they'll be on the scrap heap, good and proper, won't they?'

There was no time for Brenda to answer, for a tall young man with a crew-cut head of bright red hair appeared, to escort her upstairs to a long narrow room.

On the cream-painted wall at the far end was hung a large portrait in a dull gold frame, of a stiff and stern-faced man in dark Victorian clothing, but the room's really eye-catching feature for Brenda Phipps was not the long French-polished table and the chairs around it, which were upholstered with rich maroon velvet, but the glowing porcelain bowl on the table at the far end. She was fascinated with old porcelain, and had already acquired quite a large collection, much of which had originally been chipped or broken, and therefore cheap, but which had subsequently been so carefully and meticulously repaired and restored, that it would have taken a real expert to spot that they were not in original condition.

On a narrow sideboard was a tray of bottles and crystal glasses, but the short, plump, white-haired man sitting at the end of the table did not offer Brenda a choice of those, instead he merely rose to give a brief, polite handshake, and to indicate a chair near to his, for her to sit on.

'All of us are completely devastated by the sudden death of Brian Labinski, whom we held in the highest respect and esteem,' Mr

LeClerc senior pronounced solemnly, 'and we will, of course, help you with your inquiries in any way we can, my dear.'

Brenda Phipps nodded. 'Thank you. We may need to interview some of your staff later, but initially I'm interested in what had been going on between your company and a man called Grimston, who, we understand, had been making threatening phone calls to Mr Labinski.'

LeClerc nodded slowly. 'Our production director is the best man to tell you all about that. I'll get him here.'

While the summons was being made Brenda stared up at the portrait on the wall, and then at the face of LeClerc. The movements of her head were noticed, and as the Chairman put the phone down he gave a proud smile. 'I'm told there is a very strong likeness. He was my great-grandfather. He founded the company, way back in 1895. There aren't many family businesses still going after that many years, are there? My hope is that it will last at least another hundred. We produce high quality ladies fashion shoes, for the top end of the market, with a wider range of width fittings than most of our competitors, so we have survived where many have failed. Our products are expensive, of course, but people everywhere appreciate quality, and we sell quite a lot to Germany, Sweden and even to the USA,' he explained proudly. 'While we're waiting I can give you a little background information on Mr Grimston's wife. She runs, or ran, a little business just doing the subcontract work which the bigger shoe manufacturers put out when they are very busy. We used her quite a lot. The sales of shoes, sandals and boots tend to be a bit seasonal, you see, and because it's skilled work, you can't take just anyone on to do it. There used to be a lot of little businesses like hers, but they've nearly all gone now. It would appear that this Mrs Grimston was relying too much on what we sent her.' He held his hands out palm up and shrugged his shoulders. 'That's dangerous – having all your eggs in one basket – because we have our ups and downs too, like everyone else. She knew that. We're sorry, of course, if her business could not–' He was interrupted by a knock on the door. It opened and a worried-looking, middle-aged, bald-headed man with a bushy moustache came in. 'You wanted to see me, Mr LeClerc?' he said somewhat reluctantly.

LeClerc ignored him, and carried on speaking to Brenda. 'As I was saying. We are sorry if her business cannot continue, which I believe is the case. Right! Come in, George. This lady is a police officer, and she wants to know all about this silly business with the Grimstons, and how Brian Labinski was involved.'

George pulled out a chair near Brenda, and sat down rather wearily. 'Oh dear. Well, it's a sad little story really. Last week Brian phoned me from India, saying that I was to stop putting work out to sub-contractors immediately, and start running our own 'closing rooms' down. Closing rooms do the sewing, the decorations and that kind of operation on the shoe uppers,' he explained patiently.

'Did you tell Mrs Grimston what Brian had instructed you to do?' LeClerc demanded.

George looked down at his hands. 'Well no. He just said I must stop putting work out – so that's what I told the planning department to do. I didn't want to talk to her if I could avoid it. You see, not that long ago she'd had a lot of work offered to her by another company; but we were so busy then that we needed everything she could

128

produce, so Brian Labinski promised her that if she turned the other work down, he would keep her busy for at least six months, and after that, would give her at least four weeks notice if he had to cut the volume down. I didn't see that it was my job to tell her that Brian was going to go back on his word, so I just told planning not to send her any more work.'

'This agreement you say Brian made, was it in writing?' LeClerc wanted to know.

George shook his head. 'No, but I was there when Brian said it.'

'So you stopped her work. What happened next?'

'A couple of days or so later, Thursday I think it was, Tina Grimston phoned our planning department to find out what styles we were sending her for the next week, and then they told her she wasn't getting any more at all. She hit the roof, but there was nothing I could do about it. I told her that I was under orders, and the only person who could change my orders was Brian himself, when he got back from abroad. It was then that Tina Grimston's husband got involved and started phoning up and ranting and raving. I've never met him, but I think he must be mentally unstable. He said he'd been to see his solicitor, and that he was going to sue us for all sorts of damages. I ... we ... were very polite to him, but eventually he cottoned on that Brian was the only one who could change anything, but he couldn't talk to Brian, because Brian wasn't here. That was when he started leaving all those silly messages threatening violence. Oh dear, and it was all so unnecessary. We could so easily have given her a few more weeks' work. That's what I wanted to do, but Brian wouldn't have it. Now look what's happened. I suppose it's Grimston who's killed Brian, and it wouldn't have happened if he'd listened to me.' George looked quite distressed.

Suddenly the door burst open and a tall, egg-headed, angry-looking young man stormed in.

'Oh! So there you are, George,' he said furiously. 'What do you mean by going off? You must have known I would want you. I've had the carton maker on the phone. He can get us some in three days, but I told him that wasn't good enough. I want them tomorrow at the latest. He says his printing machines are tied up, but he could deliver some plain white boxes that he's got in stock this afternoon. We'll have to stick our own labels on them, but I thought that was a pretty good idea. So I want you to get some labels printed quickly.'

George rubbed his forehead, and his face showed barely contained exasperation. 'Listen, Mr LeClerc, he's just buggering you about. He's got the printing plates. We'd have to pick those up and take them to another printer, and by the time the new man had got his machines set up and running, the three days would be up anyway. We won't be any better off, and we'd still have the job of sticking the damn labels on. No, it's not a good idea.'

The younger LeClerc's face reddened angrily. He reached for a sherry bottle from the sideboard with hands that trembled, and poured its contents into a glass, but there wasn't much to pour – the bottle had been nearly empty. What there was, however, was swallowed in a gulp. 'Well I think it's a bloody good idea. All I seem to have had from you this morning, George, is a negative attitude. You're being defeatist, all the time. I'm trying to be positive, and I want those labels, and I want them quick. I'm the acting managing director now, so that's an order. Do you understand?'

While all this had been going on, Brenda

had taken the opportunity to get up and inspect the porcelain bowl. The inside design was of men seated round a checker-board, but it wasn't as old as she'd first thought, and the hand painting was not of the best quality, but otherwise, it wasn't a bad piece. She went quietly back to her chair.

The elder LeClerc, meanwhile, had been watching the interplay between the two men with intense interest. He turned now to Brenda Phipps to ask, 'Do we need George any more?'

She shook her head. She felt a wave of sympathy for the harassed George, but there was nothing she could do for him. 'But I will certainly need a full written statement from, er, George, later on.'

'That will be all then, thank you, George, and do try to be more co-operative in future,' the Chairman said silkily.

Brenda saw George's fingers clench into fists, but without a word he turned and strode out, followed by the younger LeClerc.

'Was that your son?' Brenda Phipps asked politely. It wasn't the sort of question that she should have been posing, for it had nothing really to do with her inquiries.

The Chairman, however, seemed to find nothing amiss with the question, and his face took on the appearance of pride. 'Yes, indeed. Isn't he a fine figure of a man? He's in the Navy, but you may have guessed that he was used to commanding people. He's got that easy confident air about him, hasn't he? It's fortunate that he was at home on leave just now. He's just the person to step into poor Labinski's shoes – temporarily, of course, at this stage, but I do hope it might give him a taste for the job. I can't think of anyone better suited for it.'

Brenda Phipps inclined her head to one side in an ambiguous gesture, that to a doting father might be interpreted as meaning wholehearted agreement, but to someone more sensitive, it might have suggested rather the opposite. It was necessary to get back to the task in hand. 'You must have known Mr Labinski quite well. What sort of person was he?'

'He was a very clever man. Very good at problem solving, or what these days they call trouble-shooting. George and Brian's predecessor had rather let things get out of hand, so there was a lot that needed sorting out.'

'Sorting out problems probably meant

that he had to tread on people's toes. Did he make any enemies here?'

The Chairman looked wary. 'Well, I don't know about making enemies. He had to be hard on people who were not, um, pulling their weight, of course. In that respect, I admit that I probably was not as helpful to him as I might have been. Being an old family business we rather look on our employees as family servants, and it took him a long time to make us realise that many people here were simply abusing our trust. So we let him have his own way eventually. He spent a lot of time with the senior staff, drawing up proper job descriptions and setting performance targets, then he told them that he'd give them three months to sort themselves out. Those that didn't would have to go.'

'When was this review due to take place?'

'Very soon.'

'So Mr Labinski's death may have had the effect of postponing the moment of truth, for some of them,' Brenda observed.

The Chairman shrugged his shoulders. 'Perhaps.'

'It would be an unusual motive for an unlawful killing, but there have been less plausible ones,' Brenda said thoughtfully. 'I think I'd better have the names and addresses of those who might be dismissed, so that we can start making enquiries about them.'

LeClerc senior looked shocked. 'But I thought that you were satisfied Grimston was Brian's killer, and were just tying up loose ends. Surely you don't really think that somebody here could have done anything so dreadful?'

'Grimston may be able to prove that he was somewhere else when Labinski was killed. At this point in time we mustn't take anything for granted.'

'Or leave a stone unturned,' LeClerc said, nodding wisely. 'I thought it was all cut and dried, but I'm obviously mistaken. I can't be certain that Brian's mind was totally made up about who would have to go, or when, but I'll have a list of the probables typed out for you this afternoon, which I trust will be treated in the highest confidence. Brian's secretary was unfortunately so upset by the awful news that she's had to go home to recover, but I trust she will not allow her personal grief to stand in the way of her loyalty to the company. I hope she will return this afternoon.'

'Thank you. Is there anything else you can

tell me about Mr Labinski?'

'Not a lot really. His father was a Polish Spitfire pilot during the war, one of the many who stayed on in this country. He read law at Durham University, and then qualified as an accountant. Most of his career then was doing special projects for a multi-national company, but it seems he'd got tired of the travelling. That's why I was able to prise him free to come here. He had a son by his first marriage, but I really can't tell you very much about his private life. He was reserved – a super-efficient cold fish, some might say.' He smiled a little maliciously. 'Still, he obviously had at least one weakness. Denise, his present wife, is a beautiful woman, but she's not very bright. Poor Brian never actually said so, but I think he realised that his marriage was a disaster. They had nothing at all in common intellectually. I know that Brian was looking out for a place in the Mediterranean – somewhere that he could one day retire to, and do the sailing, fishing and golf that he'd always wanted to do, but never found the time. That wife of his would never have fitted into that kind of scenario, and I'm sure he knew it. No sensible conversation at all. She likes the kind of parties where she can wear low-cut dresses, so that men can drool over her. Innocent enough. Lots of women like being admired, and that's all right, as long as they don't let it go too far. She was dressed like that last night, at the reception at the hotel near the river, and now I come to think of it, she was acting a bit strangely too. Rather tense and awkward, if you know what I mean. Brian's solicitor, the mad Irishman O'Shea, was there too, and giving her a lot of his attention,' he chuckled loudly. 'Mind you, they might have been talking business for all I know, but they certainly split up pretty sharpish when they saw me coming. Mighty suspicious, so I kept half an eye on them during the evening. They don't know it, but I saw them sneak out together. Maybe she was going to draw up a new will with him, or was he an old will going to draw up her?' he sniggered, and tapped his nose suggestively.

'Might I have one of your catalogues, please?' Brenda asked coolly, ignoring the older man's adolescent humour.

'Of course, my dear,' LeClerc said, reaching out for one of the glossy brochures that lay on the table, and handing it to her. She stood up, and slipped that, with some

137

care, into her voluminous bag. It had occurred to her that it was very convenient that the young LeClerc was around when Labinski died. Everglides could perhaps now become a family concern again. That glossy brochure bore the older man's fingerprints. They might come in useful if forensic were to come up with any from Labinski's killer on a Land-rover. Asking officially for a tentative suspect's fingerprints made such people think that they were actually being accused of a crime, and they could get very upset, so, if one could, it was much better to get them surreptitiously. 'By the way, I collect unusual wine labels too; may I have that empty bottle for my collection?' A surprised look sufficed for affirmation, so that went into the bag as well.

George's office was very untidy. There were bits of shoes on the desk, on the cabinets, even on the floor. On the wall, though, were some photos of a cricket team posing before a clubhouse, and, being used as a paperweight on the desk, was a cricket ball which had been mounted onto a polished wooden plinth. It wasn't difficult to guess what one of this man's other interests was.

He looked grey and tired as he read quickly through the statement that he had dictated to her, and then he signed it with a flourish, and handed it across the desk to Brenda. She folded it carefully, plain paper wasn't the best for secretly recording fingerprints, but that would have to do.

'You must have hated Mr Labinski,' Brenda suggested innocently.

George looked at her glumly, but slowly shook his head. 'No, not really. I admired him in a way. He came in and immediately started doing lots of the things we had tried to do, but couldn't. LeClerc still wanted it to be a family firm, with him as Big Daddy, you see, and if we wanted to change anything then we couldn't, because things had to be done the way they always had; and we couldn't sack anyone either, because they were old family servants. He wanted profits, but didn't want changes – until the bank gave him an ultimatum. They threatened to foreclose on the loans and overdraft, if changes weren't made. So Labinski came in, and was given a free hand. With the bank behind him, he could afford to ignore LeClerc when he moaned.'

'It was Labinski who thought of buying from India, was it?' Brenda probed further.

'Yes and no. We'd tried it a few years ago, but it all went wrong. The quality was terrible and deliveries always late, you see. It was Brian who had the idea of buying a factory out there, and controlling the quality and delivery with our own people, and it was he who persuaded the bank to come up with the money.'

'What will the bank think now, if Labinski's not here?' Brenda asked shrewdly.

'As long as the plans he made are carried out, I wouldn't have thought they'd be that bothered. Labinski had done the worst bit, even a burke like young LeClerc can't go too far wrong doing the rest. See this?' he held out an expensive-looking real leather shoe upper in a nice shade of green, complete, except for the sole and heel. 'It's not just the cheaper labour costs. We can buy this in from India, all cut and sewn, for less than just the leather itself would cost in this country. You'd have thought with all the sheep and cattle in this country, we'd be swimming in cheap leather, but not a bit of it. Folk don't like the smell from tanners, and new EEC regulations about this and that have just about killed off the industry in Britain. In fact, the way we're going on we soon won't have any manufacturing

140

industry left at all. Poor Brian Labinski. He'll miss out on all his profit-sharing bonuses, and share options. I don't know all the details, but a bloke like him wouldn't have come to a grotty place like this unless there was big money being offered. Now it'll all go to restore the LeClerc family fortunes instead, until LeClerc junior gets his dirty hands on it, then it won't last five minutes. He's the one I hate. A bigger, jumped-up, self-opinionated, evil, little prig, I have never met before, or want to. He's the one that should have been bumped off, not Brian. Still, it's never too late to hope. He might trip over his big feet tomorrow, and break his bloody neck.'

Five

Reg Finch knocked on the varnished mahogany door which bore the word 'Registrar', and went straight in. He felt a little impatient, for finding one's way around the administration wing of a hospital as large as Addenbrooke's in Cambridge seemed to take an inordinately long time, yet it was very necessary. Finding out what he wanted could not be done by telephone – for reasons of security. After all, any Tom, Dick or Harry could ring up asking questions, and say they were the police. So, inquiries had to be made in person, with an authentic warrant card handy to prove one's identity. Then he might expect co-operation, provided he was pleasant and polite, and did not display too much impatience.

'Good morning. I'm Detective Sergeant Finch,' Reg announced, beaming out his best pleasant and polite smile.

The woman seated before a computer keyboard had brown hair cut rather severely

143

short, and wore a long green denim dress, with pretty flowers embroidered on the sleeves and collar. Her face seemed vaguely familiar. She looked up and stared suspiciously at him for a moment through heavy, thick-lensed spectacles. He seemed to meet whatever the criteria of her examination demanded, for her lips slowly relaxed into a smile.

'So, you're a policeman, are you? I saw you at the archaeological society meeting a couple of months ago, when the chap gave a talk on stone tools and gave a demonstration of flint knapping.'

Reg Finch's smile broadened into a big grin. 'I remember you quite clearly now. You gave him a piece of elastoplast when he cut his finger, and you asked him whether his anti-tetanus injections were up to date. He was quite embarrassed, I think.'

'So I did. You want to talk to Nurse Blackett in intensive care, do you?'

'Yes, please, if it was she who was looking after a heart attack victim named Mrs Grimston yesterday evening.'

'It was. She'll be back on duty in ten minutes or so. I think I'd better walk down there with you, to signify to all and sundry that you have official approval. Don't worry,

I can spare the time. My boss is in a meeting – in fact he's always in meetings.' She checked to make sure that her photographed identity pass was in position on her left lapel, and ushered Finch out of the office door, which she then locked behind her.

Finch was obviously being accorded a bit of VIP treatment, probably because of that archaeological society meeting, but it suited his purpose, and he was quite happy to listen as the secretary recounted other clever comments she'd made at other meetings, while the two of them strode along the maze of interconnecting corridors. He was taken to a rest room near the intensive care ward, where its supporting staff could have their tea breaks with a little privacy from patients and public.

Nurse Blackett was a heavily built, dark-haired, competent-looking woman with a ready smile, bright brown eyes, and she answered, as the identity card clipped to the pocket of her uniform clearly stated, to the name of Ruth.

'I suppose with a name like Ruth Blackett you must often get called Nancy. "Jib-booms and bobstays", "shiver my timbers", and all that sort of thing,' Reg observed with a humorous smile.

Nurse Blackett's response was a blank look of utter incomprehension. 'Eh?' she replied suspiciously and stared keenly at his face, perhaps looking for signs of senile dementia.

'You know – *Swallows and Amazons* – Arthur Ransome's books?' But Reg was only making matters worse. This woman had obviously never as a child sailed in her imagination to Wild Cat Island, climbed Kanchenjunga, or hoisted a pirates' flag on a tall lone pine, but she had clearly decided that Reg's problem was simple common lunacy, not senile dementia. She edged her chair a little further away from him, just to be on the safe side, and set about humouring the patient, as a good nurse should, until the men in white coats could be summoned with straightjackets.

'Very likely,' she said soothingly. 'Now, I'm sure you must be very thirsty. Just you sit here for a few minutes, and I'll fetch you a nice cup of tea.' She rose to her feet, intending at least to get some assistance.

'Hold it. I don't want anything to drink, thank you,' Reg exclaimed in exasperation. 'Now, I understand that you were on duty yesterday evening, looking after Mrs Tina

Grimston. I'd like you to tell me whether this man and this young woman came to visit her, and if so, when they arrived and when they left.' He took Grimston's photograph, still in its black wooden frame, from his leather briefcase, and held it out for Nurse Blackett to peruse. She seemed more at ease, now that he was behaving and talking in a recognisably sensible manner, so she took the photo tentatively from his hand and studied it.

'That,' she said positively, pointing at the figure of Grimston, 'is the man who said he was her husband, and the girl he had with him was, I think, his daughter, but I'm not sure if she was Mrs Grimston's daughter as well, though. Yes, they both came to visit yesterday evening. As to the time they got here, I can't be certain off hand, but it'll be noted on the patient's record. Everything that happens in here gets noted on the records, however insignificant,' she explained.

'The times could be very important. May we go and see what you wrote?' Reg asked.

Nurse Blackett nodded. She was only too willing to leave the isolation of the rest room for the more populated and safer area of the ward.

147

'This is Mrs Grimston,' she said quietly, when they stood at the foot of the bed in which a very pale woman lay helplessly prone, tethered to a range of mechanical, softly-bleeping or flashing gadgets by a maze of wires and plastic tubes. She glanced down at the clipboard of notes. The words and figures there were incomprehensible to Reg, but obviously told her some sort of story. 'She's doing all right. She's probably out of danger now, unless there's a sudden relapse. The doctor will most likely have her moved to an intermediate ward later on today, to free this bed up.' She flipped back the top sheet, and then another. 'Yes, there we are. 'Husband and daughter, 20.05 hours'. That means five past eight in the evening, and left at 21.55 hours – or five to ten. Now, at 21.27 hours, some other woman came as well, but they're only allowed two visitors at a time, and we're very strict on that, so the daughter went off somewhere. I don't know who the other woman was, a friend perhaps.'

'You're very precise with your recording of events, is that usual?' Reg asked.

'In intensive care it is. Visitors can be a pain or a blessing. Mr Grimston visited in the afternoon for a short time as well, and

Mrs Grimston's heartbeat rate and blood pressure eased. She relaxed, in other words. His presence clearly brought her a sense of security, and a contact with her real life, and that's got to be good for the patient. In those cases visitors can stay as long as they want, so long as they don't get in the way, or stop the patients getting the sleep they need.'

'You're obviously very observant. How would you assess Mr Grimston's state of mind last night? Was he excited? Did he show signs of having been under stress, perhaps?'

'You're a right funny detective, you are,' the nurse observed scornfully. 'Of course he was stressed. All the visitors who come here are worried and stressed. Wouldn't you be, if your wife had nearly died and was in a place like this? They also look relieved, or even happy, when they're told their loved ones are off the danger list. What is certain, from what I've seen, is that he's devoted to his wife, and she to him.'

'I see,' Reg said quietly. 'Thank you for being so helpful. I need to make what you've told me official, by getting it down in writing, in the form of a statement. It's not complicated, and you're obviously busy, so if I write it out for you, would you sign it?'

Nurse Blackett nodded, but when Reg brought her the draft, a quarter of an hour or so later, she read it through with great care before appending her signature. Even as he passed through the exit door he heard Nurse Ruth Blackett's voice, in an over-loud *sotto voce* saying to someone, 'He's a right weirdo, he is. He wanted to call me Nancy, would you believe?'

Richard Packstone, the forensic scientist, was looking tired, Walsh thought, as he sat down in the glass-partitioned office set in the corner of the long, low laboratory. Packstone's hair was more white than grey these days, a sure sign of his advancing years. How far those years had advanced in his case was a matter of conjecture, for no one liked to ask such questions of a man who had, it seemed, always been there, doing that job. But time marched on remorselessly, and one day Packstone must retire. Walsh liked Packstone, and the thought of him leaving was quite depressing. After his wife had died some years earlier Packstone's whole life had become virtually hinged around the problems of forensic work, but without them and the companionship of his fellow scientists, there would be little to stimulate his powerful mind when he did retire. The prospect of becoming old was quite appalling.

'Come on, Sidney,' Packstone said impatiently. 'I haven't got all day. If you're going to try and put me under pressure, then I'll tell you here and now that it won't work. I've two people off on holiday and one on a refresher course, and I also want to be there myself when the pathologist does his postmortem this afternoon. So, nothing is going to get done as quickly as you or I would like, but what I am prepared to discuss with you is the priority I give your work.'

Walsh wrenched his mind back to realities. 'Everything to do with the Labinski investigation is a priority at the moment,' he said, 'and since we have a suspect already with this Grimston fellow, I need some things clarified pretty quickly. Firstly, Labinski's watch. Had it been tampered with, or is the time it stopped an accurate indication of the moment that he was run down?'

Packstone nodded. 'I had anticipated the importance of that.' He got up and went to the door. 'Roger, can you spare a moment?' he called.

A young ginger-haired man came over.

'Roger is our clocks and watches expert,' Packstone explained. 'Tell Sidney what you think about the Labinski timepiece.'

'Well, as you know by the maker's name, it's a very expensive watch. The damage is not as bad as it might appear. However, it is quite clear that the crushing of the glass jammed the hands down against the face, preventing any further movement. The question I've been asked is whether the glass was broken by Labinski's initial fall, or whether it was deliberately broken afterwards,' Roger explained, rather un-necessarily. 'I studied carefully the scratches on the glass,' he went on, 'and the profile of the stone embedded in the track, and I came to the conclusion that there could have been only one impact. That glass is pretty tough – if it hadn't been broken by the first impact, then the only way it could have been done afterwards would have been by stamping down very hard on the man's wrist, and that would have impressed the strap deeply into the flesh, and there was no indication of that. Besides, we know the driver did not get out of the vehicle, or he'd have left footmarks – but to be on the safe side, I checked the back for fingerprint smears. When you turn the side knob to reset the hands, the forefinger slides on that part of the back plate. Such a smear doesn't last long, because of the movement of the watch against the flesh of the wrist, but in this case there would have been no such movements, so if it had been altered, there should have been a fingertip smear, and there wasn't. So,' Roger smiled, 'I conclude that the watch had not been altered or adjusted at that particular time.'

'But what you can't tell us is whether the watch, at that moment, was showing true Greenwich Mean Time,' Packstone commented.

'True,' Roger agreed, but he nevertheless shook his head. 'Watches of that quality go on for years without losing more than the odd second. He was a businessman, wasn't he? I can't see him having a watch that didn't tell the right time.'

'Well, there you are, Sidney,' Packstone said when Roger had gone. 'I'm pretty sure that the time on the watch will fit in with the lower end of the pathologist's estimate of when the man died, give or take a half-hour or so, because death was probably not instantaneous.'

'Your Roger sounded convinced,' Walsh

acknowledged thoughtfully, 'but the time of death could be a very important factor in this case. However, let's get on. I ought to attend the autopsy myself, but it's pretty obvious that most of it will be about internal injuries resulting from the vehicle's wheels. That'll all be highly technical medical jargon, and way above my head. My main concern is whether the pathologist will go along with your interpretation of the sequence of the wheel tracks, and agree that it was deliberate and not accidental.'

'So I'm unreliable now, am I? Perhaps you think I'm too old to do my job right, and should be pensioned off?' There was no anger in Packstone's voice, in fact there was more humour in it than anything else.

'I have no doubts about what you tell me, Richard, but if the pathologist interprets things in a different way, the coroner might say that I should be looking for a hit-and-run driver rather than a cold-blooded murderer, and that makes a difference to what resources I can put on the case.'

'Have no fear. I personally will dance attendance on the pathologist for you. We have the photos and the traces on the man's clothing, and logical reasoning is, well, logical reasoning, after all is said and done.'

'Right. So the next priority, as far as I am concerned, is Grimston's Land-rover.'

'Of course it is. When Reg Finch rang through I sent young Albert Steddings out with the trailer, to bring it in. He's confirmed by phone that Grimston's tyres are the makes that we're after. When it's in the garage we can soon see if the degree of wear, embedded stones and cuts, tie up exactly with the tracks we recorded last night, but to be one hundred per cent certain, we'll need to find traces of Labinski and his clothing on the front of the vehicle, and such work is the area in which I've got a backlog. I honestly can't make any promises about when we'll be able to get around to it.'

'If the tyres match with that amount of detail, then we've surely identified the murder weapon. I'm not too bothered about body impact traces. That can come later, when we have a case to present in court, but it's much more important to me for you to work on the inside of the cab, especially the driver's seat. My problem is going to be finding out who was behind the steering wheel last night, and proving it,' Walsh explained frankly.

Packstone frowned. 'But if this Grimston

had been making threats of violence, and we can prove the vehicle was his, then surely it was him driving it. I thought this case was pretty well cut and dried.'

'Unfortunately it's anything but cut and dried. According to Reg Finch, at the time when Labinski's watch stopped working, Grimston was visiting his wife in the intensive care ward at Addenbrooke's Hospital. He was seen, identified, and logged on the patient's records by the nurse on duty. His daughter was with him too. Unless there's something very wrong with that damned watch of Labinski's, there's no way that Grimston could have killed Labinski.'

Packstone sat quietly for a few moments, apparently looking down at his long bony fingers, which were idly twisting and stretching a rubber band, but in fact his eyes were probably not even focused on anything at all. 'What you're saying then, Sidney, is that if our time of death is correct, then somebody else took and deliberately used Grimston's Land-rover to commit a murder, with the hope no doubt, of him being blamed for it. That's nasty. Right, I'll put someone to work on the driver's position just as soon as one of them finishes the job they're doing,' Packstone promised.

'Thanks very much,' Walsh said smiling ruefully, and then instinctively, without thinking, because if he had thought about it he would certainly not have said anything, 'We're all getting older, I'm afraid, Richard. Have you ever given thought to what you'll do when you give up work?'

He was surprised when Packstone grinned back at him broadly. 'At one time the prospect worried me, so I used to try not to think about it. It seemed that whatever you did, when you got to a certain age you were discarded and ignored by the rest of the world, because you were of no more use, but since then I've had offers of lecture tours, consultancies, and even a publisher wanting a book about my more gory experiences. I'll probably be busier retired than I am now, so I think I'll put it off as long as I can. Why? I'd always thought of you as a fixture in this Constabulary. Are you thinking of chucking it in, Sidney?'

'Of course not. I don't know why I asked really. Just interested I suppose,' Walsh said hurriedly.

It was quiet and peaceful in the long college room. Which was as one ought to expect in an establishment dedicated to the stimulation and development of mental activity. The fine oil paintings on the long wall, and over the carved marble fireplace at the far end, might have been specifically chosen to enhance that quality of the atmosphere, but that was not in fact so. The valuable art collection acquired by Cambridge's Downing College over the years was not intended for display in some sterile soulless gallery, they were to enhance the walls of the apartments of those fellows and dons in residence, and by long tradition, in order to prevent any one of them hogging the most popular, every month or so they were changed around. Professor Edwin Hughes, whose apartment this was, had one of his favourite paintings back, and hanging in the prime spot, in the middle of the long wall, opposite the two stone-mullioned windows – a large oil painting of an early nineteenth-century naval battle. Two ships of the line were engaged in a ding-dong exchange of broadsides. Both were heeling under a full set of billowing sail, many of which had been rent and torn by flying shot. There was no doubt about which was getting the upper hand. The one flying the British flag showed puffs of smoke as each of its guns still fired, whereas the one with the French tricolour was replying with only a few scattered shots, because its main yard had crashed to the deck, smothering most of its broadside cannon under a tangle of sails, rope and broken spars. If the viewer stood a few paces back, then the dark clouds seemed to be racing along in the cold grey sky, and the ships heaved and swayed as the wind blew spume from the tops of the driving waves, but closer, where the short, bald-headed, rotund professor was actually standing, the amount of detail was quite extraordinary. Tiny British seamen were already at the gun tackles, even as they recoiled from their firing. Other figures held swabs and rammers at the ready and small boys ran with more shot and charges. Blue-coated officers on the quarterdeck peered through telescopes, or pointed hands to direct those of the crew heaving on sheets or clew-lines, and two doughty grey-haired men stood solidly and impassively at the massive wheel, staring intently forward as the fluttering foresails warned of the danger of the ship being taken aback. On the French ship there was panic and confusion. Figures frantically wielded axes trying to cut away the wreckage that smothered the main deck.

The wheel was shattered, its attendants lying sprawled and helpless with many others that were dead or wounded. Where guns would still bear, they were manned by tired and dogged crews that were already short-handed.

The professor reluctantly turned away from viewing it to face the young girl seated in one of his deep red leather armchairs near the window, who had been reading from a sheaf of handwritten papers.

'You are rather implying, Tracey, that just because Agricola was his father-in-law, Tacitus would have inherited Agricola's campaign records and diaries, if there were any. That may be true, of course, but there may well have been surviving sons to inherit such personal property. Besides, Tacitus and his wife were not living in Rome when Agricola was supposedly murdered, so it is much more likely that his things were dispersed among those of his immediate family. The only reference he ever makes to his actual sources, is in the section about a possible invasion of Ireland, when he writes, *'I have often heard Agricola say.'* Which suggests he either made notes of his dinner table conversations, or that he was relying solely on his memory.'

That was, one might have thought, a reasonable enough comment in a discussion on classical Roman authors, but its effects in this case were unusual. The girl let the sheets of paper slip off her lap to the floor, dabbed at her eyes with a screwed-up piece of damp pink tissue, and started to sob.

'Come, come, now, Tracey. Your essay is really quite good. It is not like you to be upset by minor constructive criticisms,' the professor said peevishly. 'The whole point of these supervisions is to stimulate your logical thoughts by examining the merits of different points of view. If you favour any one in particular, you must naturally be prepared to support your opinions with rational argument.'

The girl was shaking her head slowly. 'It's not that, professor,' she mumbled.

Hughes stood looking down at the girl and frowned. Normally a crying girl or woman engendered some feelings of sympathy in a man, but this Tracey Grimston's tears roused in him only feelings of irritation, and he was puzzled to understand why. She was pretty enough, in a way, and as well-endowed as most girls of her age, but the truth was – he did not really like her. Still, she was his pupil, a human being, and clearly in some distress.

He reluctantly sat down in the chair opposite her and leaned forward. 'Come now. Tell me what it is that troubles you. It will go no further. You can trust me.' His own voice surprised him, the tone he had used was full of genuine-sounding sympathy. It must have surprised the girl too, or perhaps it contained feelings that she was not used to hearing expressed, for she immediately looked up suspiciously and scanned his face through tear-filled eyes, for signs of falsehood or sarcasm.

It was clear that this girl had a barrier between her inner feelings and the outside world, that he had for a brief moment seen through; now he was intrigued to learn why the barrier was there.

'Yes, you can trust me,' he said quietly, as though in answer to those unexpressed questions in her eyes. Her eyes still showed doubt, but also possibly hope, and after another long-drawn-out, miserable sniff, she started talking.

'My mum's had a heart attack,' she blurted out suddenly.

Hughes frowned. Such an incident might exacerbate a problem, but it would not be the cause of this one. 'I'm very sorry to hear that. How is she?'

'She's getting over it. They're moving her out of intensive care today, but–' The super-absorbent tissue that the makers claimed would still be soaking up when all others had failed, was by now itself so saturated that it was disintegrating, and on the next dab a piece came away and was left on her cheek. She did not seem to realise it.

'But?' Hughes prompted.

'But the police came this morning.' Gradually the story, as far as Tracey Grimston knew it, unfolded. 'I'm sure they had come to arrest my dad, but when he told them that he was at the hospital with me, it rather took them aback, because the taller one then went off to check what dad said with the hospital.'

'Can you describe this taller policeman? He wasn't in uniform, I presume,' Hughes asked diffidently.

'No, he wore a grey suit and a fancy tie. He was a sergeant I think. Tall, thinnish, with fair hair and blue eyes.'

Hughes nodded. He'd had some dealings in the past with Cambridgeshire Constabulary's Criminal Investigation Department, or at least, its serious crime team, and could recognise Detective Sergeant Finch from the girl's description. To Tracey Grimston the police were obviously an enemy, but an interesting little plan was forming in his mind which might be spoiled if she thought he had a foot in their camp. So he must appear neutral. 'What happened next?'

'The other man hung around, until a trailer came to take away dad's old Land-rover.' She looked down at her hands. 'I had to come away too then, because of lectures, but I didn't like leaving my dad there on his own. He can't cope with things sometimes, and gets aggressive. I worry about him, and I feel so helpless too – not knowing what's really going on.'

Hughes pulled on one of his many chins with his fingers. Having such a father might be embarrassing to a young girl, however much she loved him, and it must have affected her school friendships and social life. That might be one cause of her mental barrier. 'I didn't realise that your family lived so close. You're a first-year student; are you in residence like all the others, or do you have a concession to live at home?'

Tracey had almost stopped crying now. An occasional wipe with the back of her hand sufficed to dry her eyes, one of which caused the flake of tissue to fall into her lap.

'I live in college. I thought the independence would do me good, but I only need to sleep, or eat in hall, for four nights each week. I've got a little moped for transport, so it's quite convenient really.'

'Did you sleep in college last night?'

Tracey nodded.

'Did you go to the hospital with your father, or did you meet him there?' Hughes went on.

The girl frowned a little, but replied. 'I met him in the car-park, and before you ask, we got there about eight and left about ten. That's what the police wanted to know.'

'Bear with me. Did your father drive this Land-rover of his to the hospital?'

'No, he was in mum's car.'

'Interesting. Very interesting,' Hughes mused softly.

'How so?'

'Well, if things are as you say they are, then we can presume that the man who died was killed roughly between eight and ten last night, while you and your father were at the hospital, otherwise I am sure that he would be under temporary guard, or "helping the police with their inquiries", as I believe they say when they are interrogating a suspect,' Hughes explained patiently.

'So?'

'You say you feel helpless, but I don't see why that should be. It seems to me that you are in an ideal position to assist in the solving of this problem – if you are prepared to pit your wits against those of a killer. It could be an interesting diversion, and I would be happy to assist you, if you would like. Come now, instead of moping aimlessly about and feeling miserable with yourself, why don't you and I join forces and make our own detective team, and do a bit of harmless investigation ourselves?'

The girl's eyes opened in surprise. 'But how can we know what's going on? The police won't tell us,' she protested.

'True, but we can work some things out for ourselves, by just using logic, Tracey. Clearly the killer has tried to put the blame on your father. He or she has failed, because your father was fortunate enough to be somewhere where there were witnesses at the crucial time, but that person must have known that your father had been making threatening phone calls. The list of such people may or may not be a long one, but that person must surely be on it. When you next talk to your father, find out from him how many threatening calls he made, and to

166

whom. Write the details down, and that will provide the basis of our first suspect list.'

'I suppose I could, but I can't see how that will help much. Even if we knew the names of the people my dad had spoken to, we still wouldn't know who they'd told about it.'

'We could only find that out by asking them, Tracey,' Hughes said, smiling cheerfully at the prospect of doing a little Sherlock Holmes sleuthing, 'but that is only one of the things that you need to do. The key to this mystery,' he went on, dramatically waving a hand in the air, 'must be the key.'

Tracey's face went blank. 'I don't understand.'

'After your father had left to go to the hospital last night, someone must have gone to your house and driven the Land-rover away. If the police are so interested in your father's Land-rover, then surely a vehicle like that was used in the murder. Now, if you know a lot about car electrics and can get under the bonnet, you might get it started, but if that had happened I would have thought your neighbours would have seen something going on, and raised the alarm. Under normal circumstances, one can't start a car without an ignition key, so that's your other task – finding out who, other than your father, had access to the Land-rover's keys. If there's a common name on the two lists, then it ought to be the name of the guilty party.'

Tracey looked at him in astonishment, and her mouth momentarily gaped open, but she recovered her composure quickly. 'Our nearest neighbours are the best part of a mile away, I'm afraid, so they can't help,' she replied calmly. 'Your logic is like a sword, it's sharp and keen, but the world is not so black or white. I'm sure there's an over-simplification in what you say. It sounds too easy.'

Hughes blinked at her comments on his use of logic. 'The best plans are simple, but are sometimes difficult to put into practice. It might not be easy, but that's no reason for not giving it a try. So, rather than feeling depressed, you should count your blessings. Your mother may have had a heart attack, but she's getting over it. Someone may have tried to blame your father for a murder he could not have committed, but has clearly failed. Now you have the chance of an adventure, for the likes of which Enid Blyton and her Famous Five would have given their eye-teeth. So, are you prepared to give it a go?'

Tracey Grimston actually smiled at Hughes's demonstrable enthusiasm, which seemed to her not unlike that of a child anticipating some extra special treat. Her face became quite animated as she said, 'I don't seem to have much option, do I? I've been thinking about dad's car keys though. My mum probably had one on her key ring too, so I'm wondering if whoever locked the factory up after she collapsed, used her keys. Dad didn't lock up because he went to the hospital with her in the ambulance. Probably it was Shirley – she's one of the factory women, but I'll find out.'

'See, you're getting the hang of detective work already, but you told me earlier that your father wasn't very good under pressure. What did you mean by that?' Hughes asked.

Tracey's face looked sad. 'Dad was a marine in the Falklands war. I don't know what happened exactly. A bomb or shell exploded too near him, and it somehow affected his brain, I think. When he got discharged the gamekeeping job seemed the ideal thing for him. One of the officers in his regiment found it for him. Then my real mother died, and I had to go and live with my grandmother. Dad was left alone and had to look after himself, until he met Tina, and got married again, so I came back to live with them in the cottage. They are ever so happy together, or they were.'

'It sounds as though your life so far has not been a bed of roses,' Hughes said sympathetically.

'You could say that,' the girl responded bitterly. The girl's barriers had not come completely down yet, but Hughes felt that he had made some progress. Perhaps by the time she left the university in two years' time, he might have succeeded in making her a much more well-balanced member of society than she had been when she arrived, and that was what it was all about.

'Excellent, well you'd better go off and start your sleuthing now. Hold your head high, pull your shoulders back, and look the world straight in the eye, and come and see me tomorrow.'

After the girl had left, Hughes sat quietly in his chair thinking. Young people sometimes had over-fertile imaginations and could invent some highly incredible stories, just to draw attention to themselves. It would be as well to make a few simple checks, just to make sure that he had not been listening to a tale that fell into that category. The local newspaper contained a story on page three, about the suspicious death of a man who had been run down by a vehicle. On page four, five lines of a column sufficed to announce the closure of a small shoe-related company run by a Mrs Grimston, that had regrettably made ten people redundant. The easiest way to have set his mind at rest would have been to ring Detective Chief Inspector Walsh, and talk to him, but that might sound as if he were interfering in matters that should not concern him. However there was one other thing he could check on. He went out of his rooms, down the stairs and across the quadrangle, to the porters' lodge. At a certain time in the evening the great wrought-iron gates of the College were closed, and then entry could only be made through the lodge itself. First-year students who turned up later than the prescribed hour had to explain themselves. Hughes flicked back the pages of the register, and there it was written. At 10.20pm Tracey Grimston had signed in late, the reason given: visiting mother in hospital.

That confirmed his general feeling that the girl had been telling him the truth. In that case, the next few days might just bring the opportunity for some amateur detective work, which would be a lot more interesting for him than the usual mundane college routine.

When the front door closed behind her police visitors, in spite of her protestations that she was all right and could look after herself, Denise Labinski suddenly felt very tired and lethargic. The effort of acting how she thought a proper widow would talk or behave had drained away what energy and spirit she did have left after the traumas of the last twenty-four hours. She wandered through the downstairs rooms trying to compose her mind. She ought to ring and book a room at the hotel, like the Chief Inspector had suggested, but somehow her body did not quite seem to want to do what her brain was telling it.

She decided that she could ring and see O'Shea too – if she wanted – for obviously there could be no risk of blackmail from him now, not with Brian dead. She would only talk to him of money matters though, nothing else, and it would be with such an icy glint in her eye that he would instantly know she would stand no nonsense from him. Those thoughts made her feel much better, for a while, but she still did not ring either of them. Eventually, when she did make the effort to telephone someone, it was her assistant at the salon. Somehow or other that woman had already learned of the dreadful news, and was full of sympathy and assurances that all was in safe hands, and that she, Denise, had no need to worry about anything, until she'd got herself properly sorted out. But the news that she was not needed only added to her feeling of depression. The world had no need of her for the moment, and so she sat in the lounge and sobbed for a while.

A picture suddenly came vividly into her mind, from a programme she had seen recently on the television about the life of Maria Callas. In one film clip that dark-haired woman with the amazingly large black eyes had sung of her misery and distress in such a rich melancholy voice that half the audience had been in tears, and the rest were biting their lips to hold them back. What the words being sung were, or whether they were from Tosca or Fidelio, she did not know, and it was of no consequence. That was the scene that should be played out for her. She held her head in one hand and held the other limply out in a gesture of despair. To release her beloved husband from torture and a cruel death she had no choice but to helplessly submit to the evil demands of the wicked Count, who was mad with desire for her. That wasn't quite right – perhaps it should be that she was preparing to kill herself with the jewelled dagger she clasped to her breast, rather than surrender to the horrid advances of the gross and hideous commander of the castle. The audience would be so touched by her sad, brave pathos that they too would all be sobbing and weeping into their handkerchiefs. She turned her head up to stare blindly up at the ceiling, and heaven, and raised her other hand beseechingly. Now those thousands of captivated watchers would be unable to hold back the feelings of sympathy that overwhelmed their hearts. She maintained the pose for several minutes, but then the admiring audience suddenly vanished, and the feeling of rejection and loneliness came back with a vengeance. So she wiped her eyes with the backs of her hands and decided that she really would phone the hotel by the river, and make a reservation. Then she would definitely go upstairs and pack a suitcase. In the hotel there would be people who would fuss about her well-being, and later perhaps she would walk to the salon and make sure for herself that everything there was as it should be. That was being brave and positive. She got up to do just that, and that was when the front-door bell rang.

Who could it be? A neighbour perhaps, to express sympathy and offer condolences. She opened the inner porch door. Through the crinkly glass of the outer door she could see a shape, and it appeared to be dressed in dark blue or black. She frowned, obviously the police were back to continue their questioning, but having already opened the inner door she could hardly pretend that she wasn't at home. She twisted the catch and pulled the door open, but there was nobody standing there. She leaned forward to peer outside, then a hand suddenly appeared holding something small and blue, and a fine jet of tear gas was sprayed at her face. It was meant for her eyes, and enough got there to make Denise scream with pain, and instinctively bring up both hands to ward off the mist that was being remorselessly aimed at her. Blindly she turned and staggered back indoors, still screaming hoarsely, because the mist was in her throat too. A hand grasped her shoulder, but she shook that off. Then another grabbed the waist band of her skirt, and she was brought to a sudden jerking stop. In sheer panic she wrenched herself forward with all her strength, and the tearing of buttons, seams or zips gave her a chance to break away, but when the remnant of the skirt had slipped to her knees, she was brought crashing down to the carpeted lounge floor. Her hands could do nothing to break her fall, because they were still tightly held to her eyes. Then her assailant landed on her back, and the weight drove all the air from her lungs. As she fought gaspingly for breath, she dimly realised that her jumper was being pulled up over her face. Her hands tried to wrench the woollen garment down, but her assailant had already grabbed her wrists and was trying to twist them behind her back, and by doing that actually pulled the jumper off her face again, which was not what the assailant obviously wanted. To keep that sweater over the struggling woman's head, it was first necessary to pull the victim's arms from the sleeves, and after much twisting and pushing, that was finally achieved. Now the sweater stayed where it was wanted, while

Denise's hands could be held firmly behind her back. The attacker then looked round anxiously for something with which to tie them, but there was nothing handy, except the thin strap of the black bra round Denise's back. That would have to do. It was grasped and viciously pulled. The back clip gave way easily enough, but the straps were deceptively strong. Denise screamed repeatedly as the thin material cut deep into her flesh, for it needed several hefty tugs before the skimpy garment would come free, and could then be used to tie her hands. The removal of that garment convinced Denise that she was about to be brutally raped. Hoarsely and desperately she cried out. 'Please don't hurt me. I'll let you do anything. Honestly. Please. Please,' into the muffling folds of the sweater.

Her pleas had no effect on her silent attacker, and what she dreaded now appeared about to happen. Those ruthless hands grabbed at her hips, and her tights were wrenched off too.

Denise went rigid with terror. When the man had finished with her she might be brutally kicked, tortured and beaten, or maybe he would just kill her. 'Please don't hurt me. Please,' she whimpered plaintively, but she became totally bewildered as to what her fate was to be when her feet were tied and her ankles brought up to be knotted to her hands, leaving her with an arched back, trussed up like a lamb for the slaughter. An unfortunate phrase, which fortunately did not come into her mind, because that was already numbed by the pains which wracked her body and still burned in her tear-stricken eyes.

She was therefore unaware that her attacker had risen, and was pulling on gloves. After a quick look round the room, that person went off into another, apparently searching for something. It was not a long search, for that something was soon found, on the desk in the lately-deceased Brian Labinski's study at the back of house. In the lounge Denise had fallen on her side, but was still sobbing and shivering with terror. The sweater still safely covered her face, however, and her pathetic trembling must have twanged some strings of compassion, for the attacker fetched a coat from the hall and tossed it over the whimpering woman's body, then turned up the central heating thermostat on the wall, before carefully closing the inner hall door and opening the outer one. It was clearly dangerous out in the big wide world, and it was necessary to hurry. The outer door was pulled to as the attacker left, but not with enough force to close the latch.

Six

Jamie Hamilton, the old-age pensioner who lived alone in the little bungalow next door to the much newer and grander Labinski residence, was feeling a bit peeved. It was one thing to help out a neighbour when they were in trouble, but it was quite another for that favour to just go on and on without a word. One felt one was being taken advantage of. Sure, poor Mrs Labinski must have been very upset over her husband's sudden death, but one would have thought that she was starting to get over it by now, and would have come over to do something about her two dogs. If she couldn't look after them properly herself, then she'd have to put them into kennels or something. Mind you, he'd never thought it right for dogs to be shut up in the house all day, like these two had been, while their owners were away at work. It wasn't fair on them. He liked dogs, usually, but these two were a pain in the neck. They wandered around as though they owned the place, plonking themselves on his chairs and his bed, getting hairs all over everything, and when he spoke sharply to them, they just looked at him as though he were a piece of dirt, and took no notice. They'd also turned their noses up when he'd given them some sausages and baked beans to eat, so, out of the kindness of his heart, he'd found a bit of rope for leads and had walked them all the way in the drizzly rain up to the shops on the other side of the green, and spent some of his meagre pension buying two big tins of dog food for them. They'd eaten the stuff, but he couldn't keep on doing that, he couldn't afford it. Money was tight enough as it was.

It was starting to get dark when his patience finally gave way. If the mountain wasn't going to come to Mohammed, then he'd have to go to her. The dogs were asleep on the spare bed, so he slipped on his thick windcheater, put the Yale lock catch up on front door, and closed it quietly behind him. He crunched down the Labinski gravel drive, wondering why people who were obviously not short of a bob or two and could afford to buy such posh houses, didn't have proper drives of tarmac or concrete, like anyone with any sense would have. Both cars were there, and there were lights on in the house. He pressed the door bell, and heard it ring inside. No one came. He rang it again, getting more impatient and angry each time it was ignored. He bent to peer in through the letterbox, and then realised what he ought to have spotted in the first place – that the front door was not properly closed. Under these circumstances he felt he'd every right to go in, provided he shouted and called out. Possibly she didn't want the dogs back, and was pretending she wasn't in, hoping he'd go away, but tough luck on her, he wasn't going to. Those damned dogs were not staying another night with him.

'Hello there,' he shouted out, as he opened the inner door. If that wasn't loud enough to warn those within of a visitor, the breeze caught the outer door, and slammed it shut with such a noise that must surely have been heard throughout the house. It was so warm in this place that it was like walking into a tropical greenhouse. In the silence after the slam he thought he'd heard what sounded like a cry or a whimper. Perhaps she'd had an accident, or a heart attack, or something. He hurried through into the lounge, and found Denise Labinski lying trussed up on the floor.

It had been countless hours since her attacker had left her with streaming eyes, tied up, hooded with her sweater and partly covered with a coat, and all that time had been one of pain and utter misery. Writhing and tugging at her bonds had merely tightened them even more. Her almost constant tears had long since washed away much of the pain from her eyes, but with so many other pains coming to replace it, that relief was hardly noticeable. Her fear was that she had been forgotten, and would lie there helpless and alone for ever and ever. Mercifully, mental exhaustion drove her into a coma-like sleep for some of the time, from which the noise of the front door bell had roused her, and set her once again screaming for help.

Hamilton looked down at the bound figure with astonishment. Hurriedly he knelt down and pulled the sweater off Denise's face, at the same time freeing her tousled long fair hair. Her reddened eyes peered up at her rescuer from her swollen, bloated face. They saw male trousers and shoes, and suddenly she had that desperate fear again, thinking that perhaps her attacker had returned to continue to torture her. Her hoarse throat gasped out the words, 'Who is it?'

Hamilton was shocked and bewildered at the fear in her voice. 'It's me, of course. From next door. I got your dogs. What yer doing down there?' he asked in astonishment.

'Thank God it's you. Please help me. Untie me,' she cried urgently.

Hamilton was in for some more shocks – for when he pulled the coat from over her he saw that she really was bound up, and that she had hardly any clothes on. Shaking his head in confusion, he knelt down to untie her bonds. It was difficult, his fingers were stiff and awkward, and anyway the knots were too tight, so he fumbled for his pocket knife, and started sawing at her bonds. The extra pressure made Denise cry out again with the pain, but eventually he managed to free her ankles from her wrists, and could slowly straighten her legs. She groaned in relief. He then freed her ankles and set about the black bra – that had dug into the flesh of her wrists, and was much more difficult to cut, but eventually he was successful. She rolled in writhing agony onto her back, rubbing wildly at her wrists, crying out from new pains, as the blood started to flow and circulate again.

Hamilton stood there in shock, with his mouth open, just staring down at her near-nakedness. All the women he'd ever known would have instantly covered themselves from his gaze, pains or no pains, but eventually the realisation that the girl was in too much discomfort to worry about mere modesty penetrated through his strange mental paralysis. He got his hands under her arms, and managed to half lift and half drag the crying woman to the settee. She clung tightly to his arm. 'Please don't leave me,' she whimpered desperately.

'What's been going on here?' he asked hoarsely, shaking his head in confusion.

'I, er, I–' she mouthed from dry, parched lips.

'Thirsty? I'll get a drink. I won't go away.'

She let go of his arm and he stood up to look round, dragging off his thick jacket at the same time because it was so hot in that room. There were bottles and glasses on a nearby table. He tipped clear gin in a large crystal tumbler and topped it with tonic, and took it to her. It was a pretty stiff drink, but it would do her good.

Her hands were too unsteady to hold it, so he had to pour the contents slowly into her mouth. She spluttered a few times as the pungent liquor bit at her throat, but she was too hot and thirsty to worry about what the drink contained, and soon the glass was empty. Gradually the alcohol started to act as a mental painkiller, and she mouthed for more. Her aches were easing a little as the minutes went by, and her shrill crying had quietened to mere whimpers.

Jamie picked up his coat from the floor and draped it over her, more to hide his own embarrassment than hers. 'Cover yourself up, girl,' he grunted, and went to refill the glass. He took a quick sip of it himself while he was there, but he wasn't that keen on gin.

'That's better, ain't it? We don't want no more crying, do we?' He spoke to her as though he might have been talking to a child, and slipped unknowingly into the role that her tortured mind had already given him, a father-figure comforting a hurt child.

'I'm sorry, but I do hurt all over,' she cried hoarsely, pushing his coat petulantly off her hot body to the floor, and rubbing vigorously again at her aching wrists as best she could.

Jamie's head buzzed violently. If what she wanted was massaging, he'd try a bit of that himself. With a fast beating heart he reached down to rub at a calf muscle, expecting any moment for his hand to be angrily brushed aside, but, instead, his clumsy attentions seemed most welcome, so he boldly moved up to tackle the warm sweaty flesh of a thigh.

'What happened?' he grunted as he stared down at the scanty wisp of black lace that was all she still wore, the likes of which he'd only ever seen before on dummies in shop windows.

'I opened the front door, and something awful was squirted in my eyes,' she explained, speaking slowly because of the soreness in her throat and the swimming of her head. 'Oh God, did it hurt? I tried to run away, but he caught hold of my skirt. Then something gave way and I did get free for a bit, but then I fell over, and he was on top of me, pulling my jumper over my head so I couldn't see his face – as if I could with all the pain in my eyes. I tried hard to fight him off, but he was far too strong. He just tore my clothes off, and used them to tie me up, I think. He was a brute, and he really really did hurt me.'

'Poor thing. Did you know his voice? Did he, er, do anything to you?'

'No. I thought he was going to rape and kill me, but he didn't, thank God. When he'd tied me up, he went away, but I know who it must have been. That man Grimston, the one who killed Brian. He said on the phone he'd work me over if Brian didn't do what he wanted.'

'Who? Grimston? Here, I'd better call the police, and get a doctor to you.'

He was shocked and surprised when she suddenly jerked upright, shaking her head wildly. 'No. No. Just look at me. I can't have people come here seeing me like this. I must look dreadful. My eyes must be all red, they're so sore, and I'm as weak as a kitten too, and I ache all over.'

Hamilton shrugged his lean shoulders. Looks wouldn't have bothered him in such a state, but women always did have funny ideas. 'You oughter be in bed then,' he muttered helpfully.

'Yes. Yes. In a little while, but can I have another of those drinks first, please? Make it a strong one. I think they're doing me good.' Not since her wild silly teens had she drunk to get drunk, but now it was different, if drink could blot away the horrid world that tormented her so, then she wanted to drink until she was senseless.

Hamilton poured her another stiff dose of gin. The bottle had been nearly full, and was now half empty. What she'd already had would have put many men on their backsides and senseless in the gutter – so it ought to be killing her pain, and it would sure make her sleep well. He needed something for himself too. He felt he was going half mad, what with all the long-forgotten thoughts the sight of her body had sent rushing through his old brain. He'd have liked to have got his hands at the other end of her, but them things hadn't been tied up, so he hadn't dared to. He took a long swig of whisky, straight from the bottle.

When she eventually finished sipping the drink, she tried to stand, but her legs would not support her, and she needed Hamilton's assistance to totter unsteadily up the stairs.

There were still some aches left in her body, but the gin was rapidly numbing those pains away too, and it had nearly cleared her head of the memories of her horrid mental traumas as well, leaving just the whoozy wild and silly feelings you got when you'd had one or two too many.

In the cream and pink bedroom Jamie Hamilton pulled back the sheets and covers, and reluctantly helped to lay her down with her head on the pillows. It seemed that his adventure with this woman's wonderful body was coming to an end. Then he saw a chance of keeping it going for longer, and maybe to do what downstairs he had so desperately wanted to do.

'It's mighty sore – here – where them straps dug in,' he grunted anxiously, touching with his fingers the reddened weals over her shoulders and round her ribs. 'I'd best put ointment on.'

'I might have died if you hadn't come to rescue me. Thank you ever so much,' Denise muttered gratefully.

'If you'd had your dogs, it mightn't have happened. Ointment'll make you better,' he mumbled as he hobbled stiffly off to search the bathroom cabinet.

Denise's eyes were closed when he got back, but nevertheless he started to anoint those pinkish weals anyway.

'That's much, much better,' she murmured contentedly as the cool ointment was smeared on her sore skin. Her head was swimming and quite out of control, but the rough touch of his hands suddenly brought back an old memory so vividly that she actually giggled out loud. She'd only been about twelve, and Jacky, the older boy from next door, had heard her weeping in the tool shed at the end of the garden, because those at school had ganged up on her and called her flat-chested.

'It ain't nothing to worry at, them's only silly kids,' that Jacky had said. 'They've started, but what they need's is a bit of massage, regular like, to get them really going. You can't do it yourself though, that don't work.' Denise smiled broadly at the memory of his eager young face. Every day for nearly a whole term Jacky had done her a favour with his rough hands, although by then, as payment for giving up so much of his valuable time, they were doing other things besides, until his mum had caught him at it. Perhaps Jacky had been right. In which case there were quite a few since then who had enjoyed the fruits of his labours.

Then Denise suddenly stiffened in surprise. These rough hands were not just soothing pain away any more, they were doing what Jacky had done. There could be no doubt about it.

'Gently!' she admonished automatically, as she so often had done in her wild youth to impatient boys. The gin had made her so very silly, because she was giggling as though it were one huge joke, instead of saying 'no' quite firmly, and brushing his hands away. She couldn't have done that anyway – her arms had gone strangely limp, and would not move. She peered up at the aged wrinkled face of the old man, and saw his staring eyes and slightly open panting mouth. She knew what that meant, he was roused. She laughed again, because it was incredible to think that her body had the power to do that to someone so old and ancient. She closed her eyes and her numb body seemed to float about the room. It was a pity he wasn't young and handsome. The knight in shining armour, the handsome Arab sheikh, and others who were in the business of rescuing lovely maidens, after they had ridden into the sunset, out of sight of all the viewers, surely then stopped and demanded their maiden's favours as their just reward. This old man might try the same thing. She had no strength left in her to resist him if he did. What if he had a heart attack at the crucial moment? She bit back another giggle, but this time it was one emotional strain too many for her overwrought mind. It decided enough was more than enough for one day. Her brain promptly switched itself off. She fell fast asleep and started snoring lightly.

Hamilton frowned down at her with very mixed emotions. He did not immediately stop what he was doing, but he knew that this fantastic dream was at its end, and he did not quite know how he could go back to his empty life and leave it all behind. He reluctantly stood up, and stared intently down, trying to imprint every detail of this wonderful image into his brain. Then he pulled the bed covers over her, turned about, and went downstairs.

He found the room thermostat, set it at a more sensible level, and poured himself another large whisky. Such luxuries did not come his way too often, and after what he'd been through, he needed it badly. In fact he slipped the half empty bottle into a pocket of his coat for later. She couldn't object to that – after all, as she had said, he might have saved her life. Then he picked up the phone and dialled the police, where his message, it seemed, caused a little consternation.

He touched nothing else, but leaned back into the cushions of the settee, sipping his drink, and waiting for the door bell to ring.

When it did, he opened the door to admit two worried-looking uniformed police officers. The younger one introduced herself as Policewoman Innes, and went on to ask, 'What on earth has been going on? We thought Mrs Labinski was going into a hotel. Where is she now?'

'I don't know nothing about hotels, but she's asleep upstairs, poor kid,' Jamie Hamilton grunted, as he led the way back into the lounge.

'So! What happened? How did you get involved?' the older one, the sergeant, demanded.

Jamie didn't hurry to reply, he took another sip of his drink first. 'I took her dogs in last night, didn't I? Well, she ain't been to collect them, so I came here to see what she's doing with them. I rang the bell. Then I saw the front door weren't properly shut.'

'The front door wasn't properly shut,' the sergeant repeated, as he wrote in his notebook.

'That's what I said. So I pushed it open, and called out. I thought I heard a cry, so I went in, and she was all tied up with a coat over her, and a woolly jumper on her head. Right there on the floor, just where you're standing.'

'Jumper over her head,' the sergeant muttered.

'How was she tied?' the policewoman asked.

'Hands behind her back. Ankles tied

together, and pulled up to her hands. Trussed up like a pig, she was. Don't know how long. Must've been hours.'

'What was she tied with?'

'Her hands – with that black thing there. I had to cut it with me knife.' He pointed to where the ruined garment still lay. 'The bugger, he'd just ripped it off her, she said, and there's deep marks on her too – where it dug in. Them other stocking things was what bound her feet.'

'He? Did she see him?' The sergeant asked urgently.

Hamilton shook his head. 'Says not. Said she opened the door, and got sprayed in the eyes. Tear gas, I reckon. Could smell something even when I come in. Then he pulled that jumper over her head – so's she couldn't see him. He didn't say nothing, but she reckons she knows who it was. That gamekeeper fellow, Grimston. He killed her husband, didn't he? And he said he'd work her over too. Seems like he did. Terrified the poor girl must have been, and where were you bloody lot when she needed help? Nowhere. You useless gits.'

'Was she er ... raped, do you know?' The sergeant asked, ignoring the previous remarks.

'Said not, but how would I know? Wouldn't be surprised. She's a good looker. The sooner you get that Grimston behind bars the sooner folks can sleep safe at night.'

The sergeant shrugged his shoulders. 'It's not as simple as that. If she says she didn't see him, we can't arrest him without proof. Anyway, he might be a burglar. Have you checked? Is there anything missing?'

'How the bloody hell would I know? I ain't been in here before. Ain't you even going to arrest this Grimston? He killed her hubby, and he's bloody dangerous. He's got to be put away.' The whisky was making Hamilton aggressive, but he finished the glass in one gulp.

The sergeant shrugged his shoulders and shook his head. 'It's all up to the CID. They're the ones in charge of this case.'

Jamie's head had started to swim. He'd had more than enough excitement for one day, but his spirit was roused by such complacency, and he could not allow it to pass without protest. 'It's bloody typical, ain't it? You lot make me sick. You leaves the poor girl defenceless, then you stand there and say you can't do nothing when a bloody killer comes in and tortures her. You ain't got no guts, you lot,' he shouted.

197

'Steady on. You'll wake her,' Policewoman Innes said urgently.

Jamie guffawed scornfully. 'Wake her? That's a bloody joke. She's downed near half a bottle of gin. Right blotto, she is.'

'I think you've had too much to drink too, Mr Hamilton. It's understandable, after the shock of finding her like that, but you'd best go home and sleep it off, before you say something that'll get you into real trouble.'

Hamilton picked up his coat. 'So I bloody will then, but I'm bringing her bloody dogs back. You can have the bleeders. They'll look after her better than what you lot did.'

'You'd best see him home safely, and bring the dogs back, Sarg,' Mary Innes suggested helpfully. 'The last thing we want is for him to trip over something and break his neck. I'll just pop upstairs and see if she's all right.'

Sidney Walsh felt so unwell that evening that he actually considered cancelling the meeting that he'd arranged in his office with Brenda Phipps and Reg Finch. The aspirins were now having almost no noticeable effect, and all he really wanted to do was go home and curl up in a corner somewhere until the pain in his head went away, but

198

pride, or sheer stupidity, wouldn't let him give in to such feelings. The result was that he was now leaning forward with his elbows on his desk, holding his head in his hands, trying to stop the pulsating throbs within from bursting his skull apart, while pretending that he was listening intently to what was being said.

Reg Finch was finishing the account of his visit to the hospital. '...with nurse Blackett being so positive, and that being confirmed by two of the other nurses there,' he went on, 'there was little else for me to do but get it tied up with official statements, and get the hell out of there. I don't like hospitals at the best of times.'

'Me neither,' Walsh grunted emphatically.

'Anyway, if Labinski died when forensic say he did, then Grimston's not our man. He's got a cast-iron alibi.'

'Did you go back and get a statement from Grimston?' Walsh asked doggedly.

Reg shook his head. 'It didn't seem to be worth while just then. We haven't had time to think through the ramifications of Grimston's alibi yet, and we might learn something from what forensic can tell us about his Landrover.'

There was a knock at the door, and Alison

Knott came in, with a notebook grasped in her hand. 'Are you ready for me yet?' she inquired.

'Not yet, but sit down, Alison. We won't keep you a moment,' Walsh replied gloomily, while lightly rubbing his sore jaw. 'I doubt if forensic will be able to tell us much that's useful about the Land-rover yet, Reg. Their preliminary comments on the driver's position are that the seat had been moved back as far as it would go, and that the wheel and gear knob had been wiped with an oily rag. So we won't even have an estimate of the driver's height. They've found some faint smears of a thin oil on the passenger seat that they can't yet explain, neither can they tell us whether the wires to the ignition switch have been tampered with. Those wires aren't easy to get at, but they are the oldfashioned push-on connectors,' he added bluntly, and then he turned to Alison. 'Well, what did your house-to-house inquiries come up with?'

'Not a great deal I'm afraid, Sir. First we did the five other new executive houses next to Labinski's, at the bottom of the lane, then worked back past the six older bungalows, to where it joins the main road. There's a cluster of houses there too, so we did those as well and some more towards the village, but we weren't getting anything positive at all, except a bit of stick for asking those along the main road whether they'd seen any Landrovers. 'About one a minute,' they'd say, because it's very busy along there, even at night. So I didn't bother going into the village itself. The people in the houses nearest Labinski's knew his wife better than they knew him. Generally they liked her, because she always had time for a chat, but some of them said she prattled on too much about her private life for their liking, and they all took whatever she said with a big pinch of salt. One day everything would be fine, and the next she'd be moaning about how unkind her husband was. She'd told most of them about Grimston's threatening weekend phone calls too, but they hadn't taken her seriously,' Alison explained.

'What about the chap who found Labinski's body? Had he remembered anything new?' Walsh asked hopefully.

'I left him until last, because people were saying that he was a bit snappy and aggressive. So I thought I'd wait until there was someone within easy call before I spoke to him, but I needn't have bothered, he was all right with me. He was a bit curt, and would hardly string more than three or four words together, but I felt sorry for him. He's just another lonely old man, who might get upset if his space or independence was threatened. He'd got Labinski's dogs there, and he wished he hadn't taken them in. 'Getting hairs everywhere,' he moaned. Ex-army chap – with lots of mementoes and medals lying about, and he didn't like Labinski because he was snooty, but said his wife was all right. He didn't have anything to add to the statement he'd made yesterday.'

'Thanks, Alison. Still, it's all good background stuff, and it might come in useful later,' Walsh conceded, but he had hoped for something more positive from her. His disappointment must have shown on his face, because as Alison rose to leave, Brenda commented. 'You can't win them all, Chief.'

'True! So how did you get on, Brenda?'

'Not too bad,' she said brightly, trying to bring a little animation into the proceedings. 'The shoe company has been in financial trouble for some time, and the board, or rather, their bank, decided to bring in a 'top dog' manager, to sort it all out, and Labinski was their man. He'd bags of experience troubleshooting for a big international company and, it seems, he didn't come cheap. I don't know the details, but there was a five-year contract which included share options and bonuses when the company was making big profits again. The plans to do that had been made, and were being put into operation. The bulk of their production will now be done in India, with just enough finishing work left in the UK to justify a 'Made in Britain' label. Something like ninety per cent of the production workers will be made redundant, and a hell of a lot of the management staff too.' Brenda looked as if she did not quite approve of the interaction of free markets within a world economy. 'That's why Labinski wouldn't honour his promise to keep Mrs Grimston's little factory unit going, even for a few weeks, because then there might be trouble with the unions.'

'There's nothing in the papers. Have these redundancies been officially announced yet?' Reg asked her.

'I think that's going to be done tomorrow, but everyone appears to know anyway. You could cut the atmosphere there with a knife. They all seem to hate Labinski, I don't mean dislike, I mean hate, but before I go on, you may not have spotted it on the occurrences schedule for yesterday, but last night there was a fire in the shoe factory's packing department. I thought that might be too much of a coincidence, so I sent Arthur to look into it. He hasn't come back to me—'

'Hold on a minute, Brenda. You realise you're broadening the horizons of this whole business, away from its being just a simple petty revenge killing,' Walsh grunted grimly.

Brenda shrugged her slim shoulders a little irritably. 'I can't help that. What I can say is that there's a whole lot of people other than Grimston who won't be at all unhappy that Labinski's dead. Whether hatred or dislike is an adequate murder motive or not is another question, but we can't ignore the fact that it might be. I haven't finished yet either. The Chairman's son is at home on leave from the Navy, and he's standing in for Labinski, and he's determined to put the rest of Labinski's plans into operation. A more slimy, cold, supercilious toad than him, you can't imagine,' she went on, twisting her pretty features into an expression of disgust that surprised her two companions with its intensity, 'but being a family firm, it seems to me that the father and son will save millions because of Labinski's death. Do you not see? Labinski had done all the hard work of organising and planning, and now, with him dead, there'll be no need to pay him his bonuses and share options. Is that a good motive for murder? I think so. Those two need looking into very closely. What else did I learn?' She flipped through her notebook. 'Ah yes. A bit of gossip. The Chairman said that Mrs Labinski was just a pretty prattling blonde with a good figure, and that Labinski was showing signs of regretting his marriage to her. We ought to look into that too, I think. Both of the LeClercs were at the same reception that Mrs Labinski attended last night, and they thought she was drinking more than normal, and that her behaviour was unusually tense and nervous. Labinski's solicitor was there too, and according to LeClerc, they actually left together. That's another thing that needs checking out. Perhaps she knew Labinski was going to dump her, and took the opportunity to bump her old man off, hoping the blame would fall on Grimston, because of his stupid threats.'

Walsh forced his reluctant brain to work for a moment and almost groaned with the effort. 'So the LeClercs are on the list, and Mrs Labinski. How many managers at the shoe company are to be made redundant? Do they go on the list too?' he asked reluctantly.

Brenda held up a typed sheet of paper. 'Yes. Six of them. I went back later and got this from Labinski's secretary. She hadn't been there in the morning. It seems she was the only one to be sorry about Labinski, and at least her eyes were red. She said he demanded efficiency, but if he got it, he was pleasant enough.'

'Right. We'd better look at Brenda's list and decide who's going to work on what tomorrow.'

At that moment, however, there was a knock on the door, and Detective Constable Arthur Bryant came in.

'I'm sorry to interrupt you all, but I don't know if the fire at the shoe company is important to your discussions or not,' he said rather sheepishly.

'Neither do we, but now you're here, what have you found out?' Brenda demanded curtly.

'Not a lot. The fire chief says it was almost

certainly petrol poured in through a wall ventilator. The sprinklers worked, but some idiot had put all the big cartons on the top shelves, so all the boxes below were kept nice and dry and must have burned like billyho. I went round with Martin from forensic, and we reckon someone had got in over the back wall where a pallet had been used as a ladder. The wall's topped with broken glass, but someone had laid a bit of cord carpet over it, because we found some stiffish brown fibres. It was a good idea to cover the jagged glass, but it didn't quite work. It seems the intruder must have cut himself on a jagged bit. A leg probably, because there was snag of blue jean thread, with just a smudge of blood on it. That's it, I'm afraid. Not much help, unless you know someone with a gash in their leg and a pair of torn jeans, who likes brown cord carpet in their house,' he announced with a chuckle and a smile. The faces before him stared back impassively.

'Thank you, Arthur,' Walsh said politely, and as the door closed again he went on, 'Now, this list of Brenda's.'

'Hold on, boss. Just a minute. There's more to all this than Brenda's list,' Reg protested. 'If we're not careful, we're going to start chasing rainbows. Motives are one thing, but unless there's the means and the opportunity to go with them, they're useless; and the means of killing in this instance, was Grimston's Land-rover. That's the murder weapon and that's what we ought to be concentrating on – finding out who had the keys and who could have driven it.'

'Don't give us lectures, Reg. We're not stupid,' Brenda snapped angrily. 'Of course the killer had access to the Land-rover, that's obvious, but it was an old one, wasn't it? Any damned fool with a bit of wire could start one of those. Crikey, you've only got to look at all the young kids who go off joy-riding in the very latest models fitted with super dooper locks, they don't seem to have much of a problem getting into cars and driving them away. I think we would be wrong to limit our investigations only to people with access to Grimston's keys, which is what Reg obviously thinks we should do.'

Reg Finch flushed and his eyes glinted with annoyance. 'Perhaps my lecture wasn't long enough then,' he said coldly. 'The killer was not only able to drive the Landrover away, he or she also seems to have known that Grimston had made threats to Labinski, and that he would be leaving his cottage and the Land-rover unattended while he went to the hospital. That person also knew that Labinski would be taking his dogs for a walk down that track at about the time he did. Unless, of course, you're suggesting that it all must be a coincidence, Brenda.'

'I never said anything about coincidences, but isn't it also obvious that a lot of the people on this shoe company list would have known about Labinski and his dogs, and about Mrs Grimston's heart attack? All we've got to do is find one of them who hasn't got a cast-iron alibi, then we'll probably have found our killer,' Brenda's lips were tight with annoyance.

Walsh's stomach felt sick, as well as his head. This meeting was getting out of control. He was surprised and dismayed, because he had thought that his team would always work well together. Now these two assistants, who he also thought of as friends as well as compatriots, were starting to fight like cat and dog. He struggled to force his mind to think, to come up with an investigational plan that would enthuse these two on whom he relied so much, but his brain wouldn't work – so his instincts led him to temporise. 'There is something in what each of you says. I can see no reason why we can't have parallel investigations for a few days, as long as you both agree to co-operate.'

'That's fair enough by me, but what line are you going to work on then, Chief?' Brenda asked with the sweet smile a cat might have on its face before extending its claws to scratch the full length of a friendly arm.

Walsh really tensed up now. It was one thing for these two to bicker between themselves, but quite another for one of them to start making digs at him. Headache or no headache, he needed to defend his position and status. Once again his subconscious, or his trained instincts, came to his rescue.

'This inquiry isn't a day old yet, and it's much too early to have pet theories, but Grimston is still the prime suspect in my mind. He must have known Labinski was just back in England. He couldn't get him on the phone, so it stands to reason that he would have gone out to Labinski's home to try and talk to him there. Perhaps when he saw Labinski walking his dogs something snapped in Grimston's mind, and he ran him down. That's obvious, but the alibi, on the face of it, says no. I'm going to check that alibi out thoroughly. That's one thing. Next, because the majority of murders are committed by a partner for domestic reasons, I'm going to work on the betting man's choice, the statistical favourite, Labinski's wife. Perhaps his solicitor will tell me that Labinski was already a very wealthy man. Maybe some gossips will name a lover too, so I'm going to try and break her alibi, as well as Grimston's,' he blurted out, but he'd had as much as he could stand tonight. He said words to that effect as he got to his feet. 'We'll meet again tomorrow, and compare notes; then we'll firm up on our future plans. Right!'

It had not been a good meeting. There should have been a properly agreed plan, with each person quite clear what they, and each other, had to do. Instead they were all going to play with their own pet theories, which probably meant that a lot of time would be wasted. It couldn't go on like that. He, Walsh, had better buckle down and get himself sorted out.

If you couldn't cope with an urgent problem yourself, then it was sometimes best to swallow one's pride, and seek help from someone who could. When he drove away from headquarters that evening, he had decided what he must do. Slowly and carefully, because, with the pain pulsating in his head as it was, he was probably more of a danger on the road than any drunk driver, he drove to his doctor's surgery.

'What can I do for you?' that worthy man asked, looking with professional interest at Walsh's drawn and tired face.

'Abscess,' Walsh grunted, pointing at his swollen cheek.

'I can see that,' the doctor said, reaching out to touch the infected area.

'It's the bottom tooth, third from the left. It hardly hurt at all, or not much, until the dentist drilled out the root canals to drain it. Now it hurts like hell. I went back yesterday morning, and he opened it up again, but that hasn't done much good,' Walsh explained plaintively. 'He gave me some antibiotics, and said take aspirin for the pain. I'm taking two every two hours. It eases the pain a bit, but it doesn't last long, and with a headache like I've got now, I just can't think straight, and I've got to think straight in my job.' He would have liked to have asked, like a child might ask, for the doctor to please take the pain away, but it was humiliating enough for any grown man to have to admit that pain really hurt.

The doctor nodded slowly and surprisingly took up Walsh's hands, to peer at the tips of his fingers. 'The trouble is,' he said confidentially, 'that we're getting older all the time, and our bodies start playing up. Now, you don't come and see me very often, so while you're here I'm going to check your blood pressure. Roll your sleeve up. Are you still smoking a pipe? You ought to try and cut it out really.'

Walsh blinked in irritation and simply nodded – one didn't argue with a doctor when it came to one's health. Anyway, he hadn't smoked his pipe for two days now. He couldn't grip it between his teeth properly because of the pain in his jaw, and so part of his problem might be withdrawal symptoms. He didn't mention that, of course. Instead he slipped off his jacket and allowed the wide canvas thing to be wrapped round his arm and pumped up.

'That's all right. I might have known it really, but I also want to take a sample of your blood. Your fingernails look a little pale, and that could mean you've gone a bit anaemic. Lack of iron in the blood makes you feel tired and lethargic, and it also means your antibodies – your immune systems – aren't as active as they should be. That makes you more susceptible to all the little infections that you would normally brush off easily. I'll have the results of your blood test in a few days, but in the meantime it wouldn't do you any harm to take some iron tablets, or vitamin pills with a high iron content. You can get them from the chemist. Now, there's not much I can do about your abscess, I'm afraid. The antibiotics will sort that out in two days or so probably,' he turned away and started tapping at the keyboard of his computer system, 'but I can give you some painkillers that are stronger than aspirin, and the effects will last longer. Take two, four times a day. They might make you drowsy, so watch your driving. You'll feel better in a few days.'

As the machine whirred to print out the prescription, Walsh expressed his thanks, and ventured to ask. 'How is it that you doctors always seem so cool, clear-headed and wide awake?'

The doctor smiled grimly. 'An optical illusion, I can assure you. In a place like this we always get every bug that's going around

214

– we can't avoid it, but it's part of our training, never to let the bloody patients know that they're getting us down.'

'I'd better try and do the same with my bloody customers then, I suppose,' Walsh said dismally. So, he might feel better in a few days. That was nice to know, but somehow he'd got to survive them. That was going to be the big problem.

Seven

Back in his bungalow, and now without those dratted dogs, Jamie Hamilton sat down in his favourite chair and put his aching head in his hands.

The vision of the woman next door lying on the bed swam before his eyes, and the feel of her flesh was still warm on the palm of his hand. How lovely she had been, but those red weals round her shoulders showed how much she had suffered. His jaw gritted and his mind became a blazing inferno of blind anger at the thought of the man who had so callously tortured and tormented that poor trusting young girl. So she didn't see his face – was that any reason why he should get away with his crimes? If someone didn't do something it meant that each and every day that woman would live in the constant fear of the evil brute coming back to do the same thing all over again. It should never have happened in the first place. The police should already have put Grimston safely away for killing her husband.

Everyone knew that's what he said he'd do. She'd never be safe with him still at large. If she had been his wife or daughter, and anyone had threatened to hurt her, he would have been round there like a shot, and beaten the bugger into pulp with his own bare hands. He probably couldn't do that now, not to a much younger and stronger man, but something must be done to shield her from the bastard.

Not once had that young girl even tried to hide her sore body from his gaze, so much had she trusted him, and old as he was, that trust must not be betrayed. It was up to him to find a way of removing the threat that hung over her young life.

In his mind the vivid vision of the girl lying on the bed changed as suddenly as if a child's kaleidoscope had been turned, to be replaced by other images of a much different nature, which although greyer and older, were still clear in many details. They were of tanks and guns, planes and the sounds of explosions, bullets and mud, and dead bodies lying in their last stiff agonies.

The officer with the tired red eyes laid the map out on the bonnet of the Bedford truck, and pointed to a spot with a grimy finger. 'They've got a man holed up in this red-brick cottage. He's a danger to anything that moves, and he's holding up the advance. Take him out, Hamilton. Eliminate him. Any questions?'

'Yes, sir. No, sir.'

When Hamilton stood up in his little room, his face had changed. His eyes had become icy cold and his jaw was hard and determined.

In his spare room he knelt down and reached under the bed for an old brown army kitbag, which still showed his painted initials and army number, and a long narrow green canvas bag which held his most valued possession, his secret and very special souvenir of his world war – a Lee-Enfield rifle, or more specifically a No. 4, Mk 1(T).

It may not have been used for more than fifty years, but its condition showed that it had not been neglected. The wood still gleamed and the black metal shone dully, yet a good clean was always the right thing before a battle. 'Look after your rifle,' they used to say, 'and it will look after you,' and good advice that had been. His headache seemed to have gone, now that he was faced with a task worthy of his attention. He cleared the kitchen table, laid on it some old newspapers, and set about stripping and cleaning the parts. An old pair of underpants, cut into strips, sufficed in lieu of flannel for the pull-through, and it took several passes before the inside of the barrel, with its long lazy spirals, met his meticulous standards. The all-important bolt was given special attention. Then it could slide in freely, and be snapped back in its place. There were rounds still in the magazine, which was foolish – they could weaken the spring. Now he could check the safety catch, and work the bolt to empty the magazine. Unloaded, and with the stock held comfortably to his chin, he could line up the sights on a spot on the wall, and pull the trigger. For an ordinary soldier, that was all that was needed, but Jamie Hamilton had been no ordinary soldier. He had been someone special. He had been a sniper. That rifle was for a marksman, and it was as yet incomplete.

He climbed the loft ladder into the roof-space for a dusty flat wooden box. In it was a 3-power No. 32 telescopic sight, and with that on the rifle, properly zeroed, in his prime Hamilton would have clipped a target bull at 500 yards, nine times out of ten. Hamilton was nearly ready for action.

He and this rifle had become inseparable companions in those last years of the war, so much so that when the end came, to have parted with it would have been like betraying and deserting a true old friend. When he'd been demobbed, he'd done a costly deal with a mate in the armoury, to fiddle the records so that he could keep it.

The ten cartridges of match-grade ammunition were wiped with an oily rag and pressed carefully into the magazine, and the bolt action checked again.

The other thing to come out of the kitbag was a strange rolled up garment. He spread it out over the table. It was his old sniper's Ghillie suit. He'd preferred using that to the more common Denison smock, which although wind and waterproof to some extent, had only a painted camouflage. The Ghillie suit was a long one-piece grey linen overall, on which had been sewn a fine netting. Depending on the local cover, leaves and grasses would be pushed or tied in that netting, until the wearer blended so well into the background that he became well nigh invisible. As its name implied, adorned no doubt with sprigs of gorse and heather, the highland Ghillie would have worn such a thing as he crawled and stalked into rifle range of the wary and proud monarchs of the glen. So too had Hamilton once stalked Germans. Common soldiers he'd generally ignored. They had not been worth the risk of betraying his position. He had always been after more important prey: tank commanders, gun layers, officers with maps – anything to disrupt their command and weaken their fighting potential.

Headache, whisky and wisps of black lace – with the years – seemed to have faded away. Now there was just the waiting, until it was time to go into action.

There must have been some deterioration in the match-grade propellant of the cartridges, but there was nothing he could do about that. With all the current restrictions on the owning of firearms, and this one being as illegal as you could get, it would be impossible for him to get new ammunition. The years would have affected the sight's alignment too, and it ought to be properly zeroed again, but there was no use in worrying over something about which one could do nothing, and in truth, in his now very unstable mind, the more than fifty years was only as yesterday, so there was really no problem.

With the old man's cold eyes and hard jaw,

and that menacing weapon, who could doubt that years ago they had been a lethal combination?

Killing in those days had been a duty, the victims unreal, impersonal, people-shaped blobs, who were potential threats to him and his mates. The simple philosophy of the real infantry war needed no long moral debates of arguments for and against. You kept your eyes open, your head down, aimed true and killed whoever it was, before he killed you. Then, give or take the odd bomb or shell, which no one could foretell, you might be lucky, and be one of those who survived.

That had all been a long time ago, when Hamilton was young and tough, and fighting with good mates as constant companions. Now he was old and alone. He read, watched TV, pottered in the garden and went on long walks in the woods simply to fill his day and keep fit enough to look after himself and hold on to his independence, but like so many who have outlived much-loved partners and friends, and whose near relations have spread far out into the big wide world, such loneliness could act like a slowly growing cancer. The human contact from official carers of the elderly would be rejected if it was offered patronisingly, as it often was, with the childish words and over-familiarity which sickened the stomachs of those who had been adult so long. That could mean a mind turning in on itself, which would only have hastened the destruction of essential brain cells.

In eras past, or even now in some primitive tribal societies, Hamilton would have had a place, by right, in the councils of the elder wise men, and would be involved in the running of the society he still lived in. There his views would be heard and considered, and youngsters would gather round him as the light faded to learn the wisdom of knacks and tricks of the trade, and would surely listen with respect when he told his tales of the daring deeds of his own youth. Unfortunately Hamilton lived in an advanced western society that demonstrably had no use for him after the age of sixty or so, while those still younger in years carried on the largely self-imposed routines of a media- and computer-wrapped civilisation, leavened only by the repetition of World Cups, Test Matches, Olympiads and such visual events. He, and many thousands of others, were expected to confine themselves to their tiny patches, and be as little a burden on society's scarce resources as possible. The suggestion that the patience and wisdom of the aged ought somehow be used to influence the behaviour of the growing number of disadvantaged and loveless children who thieved, mugged and drugged away their youth, has few adherents among those professionally concerned. So, those aged minds, without intent or purpose, were left to slowly grind themselves into abject senility.

Jamie Hamilton had already progressed some way along that path, but too sudden stimulations of an elderly brain can be dangerous, and Denise Labinski's bare flesh had roused and shaken Hamilton's mind so violently that evening, that memory and reality had coagulated into one single confused state, with the only two clear pictures now regularly repeating themselves. That of a bound, near naked woman, who writhed in agony, and whose face now seemed like that of his long dead wife, and that of the officer who gave his orders identifying a specific target – and that target, in the red-brick cottage, was the gamekeeper – Gordon Grimston.

It must have occurred to even Hamilton's

confused mind, that he might walk up to that cottage with rifle in hand, and warn or scare the bloody villain into abject repentance and a promise to behave. That might indeed have been an option – if the evil had still been merely a threat. But when that threat had already been actioned once, with the violent torture of the girl, and might yet be repeated, there could be no such forgiveness. Besides, he was a sniper, not a bloody religious copper or padre. He'd had his orders, and they must be carried out.

So, it was a very dangerous and half-mad man who sat that evening in his chair, with his rifle lying across his knees, staring at the flames of a gas fire, dreaming of bare limbs and scanty underwear, and planning ways of getting to a spot about five or six hundred yards from a red-brick country cottage, where he could kill without being seen.

The black-garbed witches must have been stirring their boiling brew and uttering their evil curses more vigorously than usual, that dark night.

When the car had pulled up onto the grassy verge and its headlights had dimmed, what little light there was left came mostly from the big old house on the other side of the high wooden fence.

Surprisingly, the driver's face was hooded with what was probably a most uncomfortable garment, a stocking mask in which eye-holes had been cut. However, that individual opened the car door and got out holding a long curved crowbar. The fence planks were overlapping and securely nailed vertically onto solid horizontal bars; so it took some time, and physical effort, to lever and prise the first plank off, and it was necessary to remove two more before there was a gap through which it was possible to squeeze. Hurriedly the crowbar was cast into the back of the car, and two wine bottles were snatched from the front seat. The figure squeezed through the gap in the fence and forced a way through the clinging branches of shrubs and bushes to the back of the big house. There was a side door, with a cat flap cut in the bottom, but the figure was really looking for open windows. There was only one, a casement, open barely two or three inches, and from the ground the gap almost seemed too narrow to throw one of these bottles through, but there was no other choice and besides there was a need to hurry. Tension and fear was bringing on a feeling of panic, and at any moment someone might appear and give the alarm, or call the police. The cloth stuffed in the top of the first bottle stank of petrol fumes, as was only to be expected, since that was what filled the bottle. A flick with the cigarette lighter set the cloth flaming. The arm went back and the bottle was flung high at that window. It hit the wall first, but thankfully it then ricocheted inside, where, presumably it smashed, because there was a high-pitched scream, and a sudden outward gush of flame and burning debris, one piece of which sailed through the air like a slow comet trailing sparks, only this was going down not up, and it landed on the back of the figure's throwing hand. The figure stared at it, mesmerised and spellbound, until the sharp pain of burning brought it to its senses. It was flicked irritably off, but this was no time to be hanging about staring. The second Molotov cocktail was hurriedly lit, and thrust through the cat flap. There was no sound of breaking glass in there, but the figure did not wait to see what would be the result, instead it dashed off back the way it had come, or nearly so, for the newly created gap in the fence was no longer where it should have been. There was no time to look for it, and near to utter panic the figure scrambled over the solid wooden planks, getting a handful of splinters as a just punishment. It ran back to the car, jumped in, slammed the door, and accelerated away. Leaving behind the LeClerc family residence, which was already blazing like some mediaeval pine torch.

Eight

Sidney Walsh was up and about quite early the next morning. The new painkillers had worked well enough to give him nearly a full night's sleep, the first now for several days, and as a result he felt somewhat better – not a lot – but definitely better. The swelling of his jaw still felt enormous to him, but in the mirror, as he shaved the tender area with great care, there was scarcely any outward sign. The effects of last night's pills, though, were fast wearing off, and soon the throbbing pains returned to both his face and head. He took the next dose of tablets with his coffee and round of toast, but he hadn't really felt like eating anything – the painkillers or the antibiotics, or the combination of both, had caused mild constipation and a sickly, bloated stomach. He looked at his watch. Time was getting on and he couldn't wait for the renewed relief to take effect first, there was too much for him to do.

'Must you go in today, Sidney?' his wife

Gwen asked anxiously. 'You really don't look well at all.'

'Bless you. You're the only one who ever notices when I'm out of sorts. It's not too bad now when the painkillers are working, but it's damned near unbearable when they're not. I can't afford to miss a day at the moment, this new case is still developing.'

He'd been informed yesterday evening of the assault on Mrs Labinski, but with her being effectively under police guard, and reported as being fast asleep and likely to remain so, it would have been a waste of time for him, or any of his CID team, to have rushed down there. However, he had intended to make the Labinski residence his first port of call anyway. It was important to question her again as soon as possible. If, as it would appear, her husband's killer had returned, forced an entry and assaulted the wife, then there might be vital clues lying about that just might help make sense out of confusion.

After that he would drive steadily to Grimston's cottage, timing the journey accurately, and then go on to the hospital doing the same thing. One of the forensic team had already done that, but he needed to satisfy himself of the validity of Grimston's alibi. A few minutes outside the time-scale might make all the difference between a successful prosecution for murder, or no prosecution at all. Not that he could make the decision to take a case, good or bad, to court. That was the Crown Prosecution Service's prerogative, and as more often than not these days, whatever they did, they would make a mess of it.

Denise Labinski had recovered remarkably well from her frightening experiences of yesterday, and the soporific effects of too much gin had gone, leaving only the merest of hangovers. She had bathed and washed her hair; and had obviously decided that her looks were now presentable enough to be viewed by the a wider public, for by the time that Walsh arrived she was downstairs, garbed in a pretty quilted housecoat, having an animated natter over a cup of coffee with a distinctly tired-looking Policewoman Mary Innes.

Walsh listened as Denise recounted the story of her misadventure. It tended to ramble, and be so heavily interspersed with *horribles* and *awfuls* that it might easily have been part of a heroine's torment in some cheap romance, but he was given a brief glimpse of a reddish weal on one shoulder and similar marks on her wrists, and so there could be no real doubt of the basic facts of what she was saying.

'This Hamilton is the same man who found your husband's body, then. What was his reason for coming round yesterday?' Walsh inquired.

'He'd been looking after the dogs for me,' she said brightly, waving a hand at the two animals sprawled on the carpet, one of which lifted its head for a moment. 'I think he was worried in case he got landed with them permanently, and he wanted to know what I was going to do with them. It was jolly lucky for me that he came when he did. I was only hanging on by the skin of my teeth. A few minutes longer, and I might have died. He's not a bad old chap to have around in an emergency.'

'Huh!' retorted Mary Innes. 'I thought he was a foulmouthed bad-tempered old bu ... beggar. He'd been at your whisky when we got here last night, and he could hardly stand upright. The sergeant had to help him home, and got a clout on the ear for his pains.'

Denise shook her head with a puzzled

frown. 'Oh dear. I know that his wife died many years ago, and that he's very lonely; so I always stop and have a little chat with him when ever I see him. He's always been pleasant enough to me.'

'So, after your attacker threw the coat over you, you heard nothing more?' Walsh asked thoughtfully.

'No, but for some reason he turned the central heating up too. It was like a Turkish bath, under that thick coat,' Denise admitted ruefully.

'Did you hear him going into any of the other rooms in the house? I know you think your attacker was just after getting at you, but is there anything missing? He might have been a burglar as well,' Walsh reasoned patiently.

'I'd thought of that too, Sir,' Mary Innes announced, rubbing at her dark eyes which really seemed much too big for her small, pale, oval face. 'We were going to have a good look round when we'd finished our coffees.'

'Well, let's do it now then. All right, Mrs Labinski?' Walsh asked with a smile, and surprised himself by adopting a tone in his voice that one might use when talking to a temperamental young child, such was the effect that Denise Labinski had on him.

They wandered slowly through the spacious rooms. None of the furniture or pictures, Walsh noticed, drew the appreciative eye. They were all of good quality certainly, but blandly modern, and the ornaments fell into the same category.

Mrs Labinski kept saying, 'Yes, this is as it should be. Nothing missing here.' Jewel boxes, expensive videorecorders, TVs, and music decks, the usual booty for sneak thieves and robbers, were untouched. In one of the bedrooms a much-travelled and labelled suitcase lay open and half unpacked on the floor, but it was downstairs, in the small study with its desk and bookshelves, and the long view of a lawn with an as yet immature shrubbery, that something was just not quite right.

'I'm not allowed in here, so I don't know what should or shouldn't be,' Denise explained with a pouting bottom lip.

'He was a businessman, Sir. So there ought to be a briefcase somewhere, but I haven't seen one,' Mary Innes observed seriously.

'Well I'm sure he had one with him when he came home. He must have, because he said he'd got work to do. It was a black case, but I don't know where he put it, or where it is now,' Denise admitted, shaking her head and still damp hair earnestly.

'It might still be in his car. We'll have a look out there in a little while. Now what are your plans, Mrs Labinski? As you can imagine, we're more than a little worried about your safety now,' Walsh announced seriously.

Denise looked rather pleased at that. 'I've got to dry my hair and finish dressing, and pack a couple of suitcases – that won't take me long. Then we're going to lock the house up, and Mary's going to drive with me in my car to take the dogs to the kennels. They'll be much happier there, and then she's going with me to the hotel by the river. So I should be all right this time, thank you very much.'

'Don't forget that your solicitor is desperate for you to ring him. Three times he phoned yesterday evening, and I sort of promised him you would, as soon as you woke up,' Mary added, with a frown and a yawn.

Denise frowned too, but with an added grimace. 'He can wait. I'll ring him from the hotel.'

'Right then, Mrs Labinski, while you

finish getting dressed, we'll check out your husband's Jaguar. I'll put it away in the garage for you too, if there's room in there.'

On the desk was a bunch of keys with the appropriate badge, but they found no black briefcase in the boot of the expensive car, or inside it on any of the seats. Big as the garage was, it needed the waif-like Mary Innes, with both hands held warningly just apart, before Walsh could edge the long car up to the far brick wall, and make enough room for the doors to be closed.

'Someone from forensic came here last night, Mary. Did he find anything useful?'

'Only smudges on the door handles.'

'You've been on duty a long time, and you must be very tired, do you mind seeing Mrs Labinsky settled?' Walsh asked considerately.

'Oh no. Besides, they're short of people who've done the course on bereavement counselling. Anyway, this is much more interesting than I normally get to do. It's a funny business, isn't it, Sir? Nothing missing but a briefcase? That rather ties the husband's killer to his business environment, rather than to some gamekeeper's, doesn't it?'

Walsh looked down at her with more

interest. She was so petite that she could only just have met the very minimum of the Constabulary's height requirements, but she was obviously very keen. 'You don't go along with the idea of some opportunist young male sneak-thief then, or of someone taking revenge on her because of what her husband did or didn't do?'

Mary shook her head. 'I can't see any of those types putting a coat over her, and then turning the central heating up so that she didn't get cold. Neither, frankly, can I see many of those types stripping the clothes off her, and not taking the chance of, well, doing things to her. She's got the kind of body men rave about.' Then an idea struck her. 'Unless, of course, someone did rape her, and she's just too embarrassed or frightened to say so.'

'Possibly, but she didn't hold back on any of the other intimate details of what happened to her. If anything like that had occurred, I'd have thought we would have had at least a hint.'

'Possibly, but I think she sometimes lives in a fantasy world, in which she's surrounded by ardent admirers. Things that aren't nice, like the death of her husband, or yesterday's assault, would soon get blotted out by some new event. So as long as a rapist was gentle and didn't actually hurt her, I don't think it would worry her that much. She'd probably think he could hardly be blamed for finding her irresistible, and feel sorry for him.'

Walsh chuckled. 'Well, her attacker wasn't very gentle with her though, was he? Alison Knott said something much like you about her yesterday, but aren't you being a bit hard on her, just because she is an attractive woman? She certainly has a butterfly mind, which doubtless goes a bit haywire when she's under the kind of stress that she's been under lately, but I don't think she's stupid, not by a long chalk. Let's give her the benefit of the doubt, and assume that she is telling the truth, and that there was no rape. What does that suggest about her attacker?'

'That it wasn't a man, I suppose,' she said hesitantly. 'So, it must have been a woman, and probably someone Mrs Labinski actually knows or might have recognised. Hence the CS gas spray, and all that business about pulling the sweater over her eyes. That was to make sure that she didn't see who it was,' Mary Innes added, her large dark eyes looking up at Walsh's face anxiously, clearly worried that what she had said might be scorned and derided as nonsense, coming from one so junior. But there was no such expression on his face, and she felt emboldened enough to go on and explain more of her ideas. 'There's an element of panic about this incident too, Sir, which rather suggests that her attacker didn't have the time to think it all through properly. Otherwise she'd have come prepared with proper lengths of cords to tie Mrs Labinski up with, and even a proper hood to pull over her head.'

'You're doing very well, but there's more to be gleaned from what we've been told. Go on – if you can,' Walsh said encouragingly. With his head clearer than it had been for days, he could even venture a slight smile for this eager young policewoman.

'Well,' Mary went on, her eyes narrowed by the effort of deep concentration. 'Whoever this woman attacker was, it wasn't Labinski's killer, because she obviously didn't find out that he was dead until yesterday morning, hence the panic. Presumably there's something in the missing briefcase that's so important that she's prepared to take some risks to keep it secret.'

'That's excellent, but you've still missed a few points that might be important as well. Who is the one person in the world who you might expect to know just what Labinski had in his briefcase, other than himself, of course?' he asked her seriously.

Her puzzled frown cleared suddenly. 'Good lord,' she said in a voice full of awe. 'His private secretary, of course. Damn! I should have thought of that.'

Walsh chuckled. 'We can surely presume that Mrs Labinski had met her, and might recognise her again. We could surmise too, that this private secretary might live alone, possibly in an area of the town where she feels nervous and vulnerable, and is scared to go out at night. Why else would she feel the need to carry a personal defence CS gas spray in her handbag? She's probably been abroad in recent months too – unless she's got access to police equipment. You can't legally buy those gas sprays in this country yet, if that is what she used on Mrs Labinski, but you can buy them easily enough on the Continent. So, do we have a relationship of some sort between Labinski and his secretary? Fascinating, isn't it? Particularly if his wife has found out. What would she do about that, do you think?'

There was no time for Mary to answer, because he shrugged his shoulders, and went on speaking. 'You must keep all this to yourself, young lady. None of it's for common gossip. If any of it turns out to be right, then it's good logical deduction. If it's wrong, then it's an over-use of the imagination, and just wild speculation.' He took a few steps towards his car, then stopped and turned round. 'I think you're wasted on the beat, Mary Innes. It's review time in a month or so, and I can ask to see your file if I want. Would you be interested in CID work?' The look of delight on her face was enough of an answer. 'I'm not promising anything, because I can't. It depends on what vacancies might come up, but if you keep your nose clean doing what you're doing, I'll see what can be done.'

He had driven out on to the lane when a thought struck him, and he stopped the car. That pensioner – Hamilton – might just have seen something yesterday that might help with the identification of Mrs Labinski's attacker. The sergeant should have already asked such questions, and included the appropriate answers in his report, but it would do no harm to meet the old fellow himself.

The bungalow was pebble-dashed and small, with metal window-frames. At a guess, it was at least thirty or forty years old, and probably unmodernised inside. The hedges and garden were not so much overgrown as just neglected – as though the owner was too weak or had not the time to ever finish properly whatever work he'd started. That was typical of a man getting old, trying to go through all the motions of a long-standing routine, but gradually slipping further behind. Things were probably the same inside, certainly the net curtains were more grey than white, unless it was the windows that needed cleaning. It was very sad, Walsh thought as he rang the front-door bell. It must be so very bewildering for people who were once bright and active, to find themselves gradually becoming unable to cope with the everyday essentials of life. It would, and must, come to all who lived long enough. How would he, Walsh, cope, when the time came?

There was no one coming to answer the door, so presumably the old man was out, probably seeking human contact to break his loneliness, and to have a scene change from the prison-like interior of his own

244

home. Further up the narrow drive stood an ancient Morris Traveller that, although rusty, looked as if it was still in use – certainly its windscreen displayed a valid tax disc. In fact, even further up there was the untidy stripped wreck of another car of the same make, which presumably had been cannibalised for the spares which kept the other on the road, but it was fairly obvious that the time was not too far distant when even the most brilliant of mechanics would be unable to keep that particular vehicle roadworthy. If he could not afford a replacement, then some of this man's independence would have gone for ever.

Walsh walked gloomily back to his car. His headache was starting to return, and clear thinking was getting difficult again, but before he set off there was something much more important to do. He used his radio phone to contact Brenda Phipps. 'Are you at the shoe company, Brenda?' he asked.

The reply of 'Yes, but I'll ring you back in a moment,' was curt, so presumably their conversation could be overheard. Phones had that disadvantage.

In less than a minute Brenda had rung him back. 'I'm outside in the car-park now, Chief. There's too many big ears inside there. What did you want?'

Walsh briefly explained the deductive reasoning that pointed a suspicious finger at Labinski's secretary as possibly being Mrs Labinski's attacker.

'That's not such a daft idea,' Brenda Phipps replied in soothing tones. 'Her eyes were quite red when I saw her yesterday afternoon. If she'd stepped forward immediately after having used her CS spray, instead of back, as the instruction on those things say you should, she could well have walked into the mist and got some of the gas in her own eyes. Her name's Emily something. I'll find out what I can about her. When do you want to pounce and make a confrontation?'

'Not while she's at work, certainly. There's no panic. Some time this evening, after we've had our progress meeting.'

'We might need to search her place for Labinski's briefcase. We'd be stumped if we can't find that. I'd better organise a search warrant as well.'

'Do that then.'

Walsh set out two iron tablets, two painkillers and an antibiotic on the passenger seat beside him, filled a cup of coffee from his emergency thermos, and proceeded to swallow the pills one by one. That done, he made a note of the time, and drove away.

He was beginning to wish that he had not said anything to Mary Innes about the CID. If she and Arthur Bryant were too friendly he wouldn't have her in his department. In his experience that sort of thing always led to trouble. Still, it was part of his job to find and nurture talent in the Constabulary, if he found it anywhere, and so that's what he would do, but just how he would do it in this case needed a bit of thinking about.

Reg Finch was unable to make an early start on his chosen line of inquiry. There was some work to do in his office on other cases that could not be left. Then he saw the name LeClerc come up in an item about a house fire, as he scanned through the on-line computer screen which displayed, in chronological sequence, all the reported incidents and activities that had taken place in the Constabulary's area during the previous night. The link with Labinski's death and the arson attack at the shoe factory were obvious enough, so he decided to make LeClerc's house his first port of call, before going on to talk to Gordon

Grimston. As the latter task would again involve the questioning of a person with a known aggressive personality, he must needs take someone with him as witness and moral support, so he asked the stout but sensible Alison Knott to go along with him this time.

The scene of the house fire was all mess and confusion. A good half of the roof had burned and collapsed before the fire had been brought under control. The charred rafters seemed bare and stark against the grey sky, and faint wafts of smoke still exuded from the lower rooms, where a gang of firefighters could be seen poking about in the debris. Scenes of fires were for specialists: those individuals to whom the dismal picture of charred wood and smokeblackened walls told a full and interesting story. So, Reg and Alison sought out the fire-brigade expert, who was only too pleased to point out the salient features.

'Two petrol bombs,' he explained. 'One of them was thrown through a cat flap in the downstairs door. That room was tiled, so it never got much of a hold. However, the one that went through that window,' he pointed to the blackened upper frame that somehow had survived the blaze, 'burst in the bedroom where a man was sleeping. Wicked that. If he survives, which isn't by any means certain, he'll be scarred for the rest of his life. The fire-bomber stood about here, I reckon. He must have had a good throwing arm – that gap's not very wide, and it was just about here where we found what was probably some of the wadding fuse. Your forensic man's got that under safekeeping. When the bottle burst it must have been flung straight back out of the window to here, where the arsonist must have been standing. It might even have landed on him and burned him, which would be ironic, wouldn't it? Anyway, your job should be easy enough. There's umpteen footprints in the shrubbery there, and tyre tracks too, on the verge outside. Your forensic man's been busy making plaster casts.'

'I don't think our task is easy at all, Alison,' Reg mused. 'On his first job the arsonist used brown cord carpet to climb over a glass-topped wall, and he probably cut his leg too. Now on this one he uses petrol bombs, might have burned himself, and he's left a load of footprints, but how the devil do we find him out of all the hundreds of thousands of people who live on our patch?'

When Reg Finch and Alison Knott arrived at Grimston's cottage, they found they had a different kind of problem. It was one which occurred quite frequently when police visits were made on spec – without prior arrangement with the other party. Having rapped loudly on the front door of the red-brick country cottage, and having peered through the net-curtained windows, Reg deduced that Grimston and his dogs were not there. The small red car was parked outside though, so if, in the absence of the Land-rover which was still in police custody, that was Grimston's only mechanised transport, it was reasonable to assume that the gamekeeper had gone somewhere on foot, with his dogs, and was thus probably not far away.

'What are we going to do now?' Alison Knott asked impatiently. Reg Finch gave a wry smile. 'We'll have to hang on for a while. You can bet your bottom dollar that if we went now, he'd turn up just as soon as we'd gone out of sight. It's annoying, but I can't get on with what I want to do without finding out from Grimston who he phoned with his dire threats about Labinski's future well-being – or unwell-being – as things turned out. Pig-headed and big-mouthed is our friend Grimston, and stupid too, for thinking that a tough cookie like Labinski would be scared by his bully boy tactics.'

'So your theory is that because Grimston was making all these threats, someone else with a motive jumped on the bandwagon and killed Labinski, hoping that Grimston would take the blame and the flak,' Alison Knott mused as the two of them walked towards the ruin of the old country house. 'It seems to me that there's plenty of people with the hate motive – all those who'll be loosing their jobs at the factory. Wouldn't it be as well to work from that angle?'

'Brenda's doing that, but that's too broad a brush for my liking. Besides the motive you've got to have the means, and in this case the means means having access to Grimston's Land-rover keys, which is the other thing I want to question him about,' Reg explained. 'I ought to have done that yesterday, but probing into his alibi took priority over anything else.' They had reached what had been the front steps of the ruin. Reg walked up three of the crumbling stone slabs, and looked round to see what the view from the big house might have been. The woods stretched out on both his left and his right, in more or less straight perspective lines, funnelling the vision to the wide area in between. Once, no doubt, there had been a closely-shaven lawn in the foreground, park-like grazing in the middle ground, and in the far distance, a mile or two away, a background of woods and rolling hills. It was a very fine picture, and it did not need a great deal of imagination to be able to visualise how it might have been, even if both lawn and park had long since been erased by the plough, for in their place there was a broad swathe of shimmering green winter wheat, broken only in its bland uniformity by a few scattered hardwood trees, that might just be survivors of the original park. He scanned the edges of the field and woods for signs of movement, dogs or human, but could see none, not even when he'd climbed to the topmost step. He looked through the space behind him, where there had once been an imposing front door. The hall had been tiled, in fact it still was tiled, because through the moss and rotting vegetation, there were glimpses of green streaked marble. The other down-stairs rooms must have had wooden floors, long since devoured by worm and rot, since the levels dropped away into a tangled damp mass of brambles and shrubby growth. It was a depressing place. A once fine house, warm and dry, that had rung with the sounds of life and laughter, now callously unwanted and abandoned, and too young by many centuries to be awarded the dubious dignity of a Heritage site, with its infill of shingle paths and neat mown grassy plots between its stark walls.

With nothing else to do they wandered round the back of the house, where the desolation was perhaps even more complete. There was no sign at all of a terrace or formal garden. All was scrubby bramble, with birch and deciduous saplings fighting out their primeval wars at a snail's pace, for the domination of space and light, and the right to live long and strong, or die weak and young.

It was then that Reg heard the throbbing of a car engine, and Detective Chief Inspector Sidney Walsh drove up.

'Hello, you two,' Walsh muttered conversationally, as he noted the time in his notebook and then peered at that part of the ordnance survey map he'd loosely folded to be uppermost. 'It's barely two miles from Labinski's house, as the crow flies, but it's taken me twelve minutes by road. There's 'no quicker route, not by car, anyway.'

'A motorbike might be quicker, Sir,' Alison Knott suggested helpfully.

'It's a Land-rover we're worried about, not a motorbike,' Walsh replied, looking at her sharply. 'What are you both doing here?'

'I'm after Grimston's threatening phone calls, and his car keys, but the beggar's not here,' Reg explained ruefully.

'From what you said of him yesterday I'd rather gathered he doesn't like company. He's probably got a packed lunch and intends to keep well out of the way, somewhere in the woods. You may well be wasting your time hanging about here, but if you're interested in his car keys, why not have a word with his daughter. She'll probably be able to tell you what you want to know. Right, what's the time? I'm off to the hospital now. My problem is keeping my speed down to that of a clapped-out old Land-rover. I'll see you later.'

'He seems a bit brighter today. He's been in a right miserable mood lately,' Reg observed, as Walsh's car disappeared down the track through the trees.

'That's not surprising, Reg. Didn't you see the swelling on his left cheek? That's a tooth abscess. My dad had one. He said it was like

254

a dozen pneumatic drills going on in his head, all at the same time. He'd never known pain like it,' Alison explained.

Reg Finch looked thoughtful. He'd not noticed a swelling jaw. Still, there was nothing he could do about that now. 'Come on. The boss is right. Let's go back into town and see if we've better luck with Grimston's daughter. Her college might know where she is.'

Reg Finch walked on his own across the wide, rather misty green grassy expanse of Parker's Piece. He hardly needed Alison's support to interview a harmless young female student. He crossed St Andrew's Street and went into Downing College's porter's lodge.

The bowler-hatted, black-suited porter watched his face with interest as he showed his identification card and then made his request to be told the possible whereabouts of student Tracey Grimston. The porter's reply was surprising. 'I've been asked to inform Professor Hughes if anyone from the police inquires about Miss Grimston's movements, Sir. So I'm sure you won't mind if I do that,' and he turned away to use a telephone. 'The Professor would be pleased if you would spare him a moment of your time. He's in his rooms. You know the way, I believe.'

'There's something about her that I can't readily explain, Sergeant,' the professor explained. 'An underlying hardness in her personality. Anyway, they're clearly a very close family unit. She's obviously quite devoted to her father, yet at the same time, she's ashamed of him. She was very upset when it seemed that he was a prime murder suspect, so to divert her mind I suggested that she and I might do some investigations of our own, with the object of trying to clear his name ourselves, a task, which on reflection, was hardly practical. What really concerned me most though, was the unhappy feeling that she, herself, might be capable of such a deed, if it was against someone who threatened her family, and that concern is heightened by your presence here, making inquiries about her. If, without breaching any confidences, Sergeant, you can set my mind at rest, I'd be very much obliged.'

Reg Finch hesitated. Hughes was as trustworthy as any man could be, but such information as Reg had was governed by strict rules of secrecy, yet by picking the right words, some non-committal comments might be made. 'The time of Labinski's death seems to fall into a period with fairly tight limits, and during that period it would appear that both Grimston and his daughter were at the hospital visiting Mrs Grimston, who was in intensive care. My interest in Tracey Grimston is because I can't get hold of her father just at the moment, and I want details of his phone calls, recent visitors and car keys. I thought she might be able to help me.'

Hughes nodded approvingly. 'So we may not be clasping a viper to our college bosom, then. That's nice to know, but you are after just the same sort of information that I told her we would need if we were going to become active Sherlock Holmeses, although, of course, not being police officers, the following up of any clues we found would be difficult, if not impossible. There's an element of anti-authority about her attitude to life – so frankly, I doubt if she would co-operate with you willingly, even if you did speak to her. I feared I might fall into that same category too, but obviously I didn't, because she wrote all the answers out for me last night, but, as I said, our facilities for following them up are rather limited.'

'But mine aren't though,' Reg exclaimed quickly. 'If you've got all that information, that's just what I need.'

'I didn't throw it away, because I did think it might come in useful. The list of phone calls, she said, was a bit vague, because her father couldn't really remember what he did with any clarity,' he said as he reached in a bureau drawer and drew out two hand-written sheets of paper, which he then handed to Reg.

Reg Finch scanned through the words quickly. 'Ah!' he said a few times. 'This, professor, is going to be a great help. Thank you very much indeed.' Some few moments had to be given to those polite platitudes which would hopefully mask a rather rude and hurried exit, but even as his long legs took him striding across the expanse of damp grass back to Headquarters, he was using his radio phone to talk to Walsh.

'Boss? It's Reg. I've had a real slice of luck. There's three Land-rover keys. Mr and Mrs have one each and a spare used to hang on the wall in the cottage, but that seems to have gone missing. Now, after Mrs Grimston had her heart attack one of the women in her little factory used her keys to lock up, and that was the same woman who went to visit Mrs Grimston in the hospital that night. That's when she gave them back, apparently. I've got her name, and I'm going to see her now. Interesting, isn't it? There's another thing too. Grimston said he spoke to his solicitor about the shoe company's broken promises. Well, guess who that solicitor was? O'Shea no less. He's Labinski's solicitor too, isn't he? And he actually visited Grimston's cottage on the Saturday morning, so he could have pinched that spare Land-rover key. You said you were going to see him, and I hope you are. If what LeClerc told Brenda about O'Shea and Mrs Labinski going off together the night her husband died is true, then some very interesting possibilities rear their ugly heads.'

O'Shea, the solicitor, had his offices above a little row of shops in Jesus Lane. He shared an entrance and a common landing with an accountant and a chiropodist. *Donovan O'Shea – Wills, Probate, Conveyancing, Litigation,* were the words acidly etched in smoky letters, on the glass door panel.

'Good day to you, Inspector,' O'Shea said brightly, leaning over a desk cluttered with pink tape-tied files, to briefly shake the hand of his visitor. 'I do beg your pardon – Chief Inspector. So you're the detective who the grapevine says always gets his man, even if the Crown Prosecution Service does let him off your hook too often. I don't think we've met before, but never mind, it's a pleasure that's better late than never. Donovan O'Shea is at your service, and how can he help?'

Walsh looked at the lean face and bony nose, and the bright, Irish, intelligent, piercing eyes, so typical of the fearless adventurous race which had once helped build an empire for the British. They were better friends than enemies, if you could ever really know which it was they were. It was wise to be cautious, particularly when faced with over-fulsome compliments. 'You've had some dealings recently with the Grimstons. Would you tell me about them?' Walsh asked shortly.

O'Shea seemed a little surprised at that question, and needed a moment or two to get his thoughts in order. 'I helped them with a lease some years ago, so they weren't actually active clients. I had a phone call from Mrs Grimston, last Thursday, in the afternoon. Very upset she was, because her only customer wasn't giving her any more work, and without it, she was in such deep financial trouble that she didn't see how she could carry her business on. There were no written contracts, so frankly I didn't see that there was much I could really do, except give her good advice.'

'Which was?'

'That calling in the Receiver ought to be the very last resort, and that she should do everything in her power to try and find other work first, and maybe even go and talk to her main customer in person, to see if she could persuade them to change their minds. That obviously helped her to think constructively, so she spent the rest of that day and all day Friday, phoning everyone in the industry who might have work to put out. Unfortunately she wasn't successful, and when I spoke to them a day or so later it was clear that they could not afford to carry on, so I gave them the name of an Official Receiver to ring first thing on the Monday morning. It was a great shame. I hate to see people who work as hard as she did, miss out.'

'So do I, but you said you spoke to them a day or so later. That wasn't a phone call, was it? You drove out to their cottage on the Saturday morning and talked to them in person. I don't think I've ever heard of a solicitor working on a Saturday morning before. Why did the Grimstons get such special treatment?'

O'Shea's eyes glinted, but he responded readily and promptly enough. 'Because I'm just a simple human Irish idiot, and I felt sympathetic enough to go through all the pros and cons with them, face to face, to make sure they really understood what would have to happen. They're broke, so I shan't be charging them for my time, either. Maybe St Peter will give me a brownie point for it sometime, it wouldn't go amiss.'

'I hope he does, but didn't you feel a bit awkward with the Grimstons, knowing that it was another client, Brian Labinski, who was putting her out of business? Whose interests were you really furthering?'

'It wasn't Labinski who was putting her out of business, it was the shoe company. They are an entirely different legal entity. You know that. There was no conflict of interest on my part.'

'You weren't involved with the legalities of the Indian factory acquisition then?' Walsh asked. There was no sign of this quick-tongued fellow going onto the defensive, but there was no harm in keeping the pressure on.

'My. My. We have done our homework, haven't we? No, I've never ever acted for Everglide Shoes. That would have been a conflict of interests. It was Brian Labinski who was my client.'

'You obviously helped draw up his five-year contract then. I can get all the details from the company if I have to, but with your client the subject of a murder inquiry there's no breach of confidence on your part by talking to me. Tell me the financial details.'

'They're simple enough. A salary of two hundred thousand a year, twenty per cent of all net profits after tax over half a million, and an option to buy a large block of shares at a notional value, if he achieved all the set targets within the first three years.'

'Real fat cat stuff. Would he have achieved his targets, do you think?'

'Without a doubt. He's the only man I know of to have worked out how to handle the fluctuating pound sterling to his advantage when exporting, but that's irrelevant. All I can say is that, as a businessman, I think he was absolutely brilliant,' O'Shea acknowledged admiringly.

'But Labinski's dead now, and all those bonuses and profits sound nice on paper, but they had yet to be earned. So, what value is that five-year contract to his estate and beneficiaries now?'

O'Shea pulled on his jaw thoughtfully for some moments before replying. 'Not a lot.'

'You were obviously deep in Labinski's confidence. Tell me, had he set out his plans for getting all these profits over the next few years in the kind of written detail that somebody else, of lesser ability, could follow and bring into being?' Walsh asked curtly.

'He did talk to me in confidence, but making plans like his is one thing, making them work and bringing them into reality, is an entirely different matter. That needs a cold, ruthless, unshakeable determination. Brian had it. I've not met many like him.'

'But buying the India factory was the most difficult bit, surely?' Walsh interrupted sharply.

'True, that will bring the company back into profitability, and if that was all there was to it, then, yes, I suppose even an idiot could run the place, but Brian had plans for subsequent takeovers and acquisitions that even the board knew nothing about yet.'

'The younger LeClerc's a naval officer, at home on leave – could he do it?'

O'Shea's eyes lit up and he gave a cackle

of nervous laughter. 'You must be joking. He's about as thick as two and half short planks. It's only nepotism and an old school tie that got him a commission in the first place. Mind you, his daddy will need to find something for his dear son to do. The grapevine has it that there's a few more abused young boys in Manila than there used to be. If the young LeClerc recovers from these burns the local radio news says he's got, I doubt he'll ever go back there. He might be a long time behind bars if he does. That's by the way, and whether it's true or not, I don't know, or care,' he admitted, and then waved a bony finger accusingly at Walsh. 'But you were really asking me if I thought the LeClercs could now put Brian's plans into effect themselves, and therefore killed Brian to save having to pay out millions in bonuses. Well, I'd say that I wouldn't put it past them, but the nub of that question is, do they know they're not as clever as they think they are? They own a garage in the Fens, with a Rover dealership, that's just about on its last legs too, so business acumen in this generation of their family is noticeably lacking. Do they know it though? I don't know. I pass. Ask me another question – like who was it who tried to kill *them* last night, and I'll tell you I haven't a clue.'

Walsh blinked at the Irishman's erratic replies. If he was getting rattled it might be worth trying out the idea that Labinski might have been having an affair with his secretary. If he had really been in the dead man's confidence, he might very well know.

'Right! So Labinski is a hard man,' Walsh said thoughtfully, 'and he's presumably got a fair bit of money tucked away already, but his marriage hadn't worked out the way he had hoped, had it? He'd been looking at alternative female companions, so, what had he done about it? Anything?'

'Jesus. You damn near know everything. All right, just before he went to India he did come in asking for a temporary new will to be drawn up as a stopgap measure, while he got some things in his life sorted out. In the existing will everything went to Denise, except a hundred thousand to that son of his who won't have anything to do with him. But, in the new will everything went to the son, except for the house and a hundred thousand to Denise, and a hundred thousand to a lady of whom I know nothing, but whose name he would fill in later. I know your next question. Yes, the new will was typed out while he was away, and no, he never had time to come in and sign it. He was to come in the day after he died to do that, and at the same time discuss a legal separation from his wife Denise.'

'Did his wife know what was going on?'

'I don't know for sure, but she must have realised that something was wrong. Brian was no great actor, and his attitude to her must have become harder, and colder too, probably. Something was worrying her while he was away, because she was asking me how she stood with her salon, if anything happened to him, but to find out what was in her mind, you ought to ask the people who knew her better than I. According to Brian, she'd sometimes rattle out the most intimate details to anyone with the time to listen. It used to make him furious.'

'I thought I was asking one of those she talked to, and who knew her well. You left the reception together the night her husband died, but she didn't get home till gone three in the morning. A healthy man like you, and a beautiful woman like her, wouldn't have spent all that time alone just talking about the weather.' Walsh went on, speaking hesitantly, because the throbbing headache had come on again. There were more questions he wanted answers to, but it was difficult finding the right words with which to phrase them, and the words that were coming together were rather too blunt and stark, but they came out anyway. 'How long have the two of you been lovers? Mighty convenient, don't you think, that your lover's husband suddenly dies, leaving her still a wealthy woman, when just another few days might have seen the bulk of those riches slip out of her fingers. Would it bother you to have a prattling wife who likes playing salons? Did you take the spare keys to Grimston's Land-rover. Did Denise ring you that evening to tell you that Brian was back home, and when he'd be taking his dogs for a walk?'

'That's enough, Inspector. I'll answer no more questions from you, except in court,' O'Shea thundered, his lean face all red and angry. 'By Christ, if you weren't a bloody copper I'd come round there and ram your front teeth right down your rotten throat.'

Walsh walked slowly back along Jesus Lane towards HQ and his office. He would have had a lot to think about if he could only think clearly, and now there was a message via his radio phone. The Chief Constable wanted to see him urgently. Was there no peace for the wicked? Was O'Shea's reaction to his too-taunting questions one of an offended honest man, or that of a devious killer, trying to act as an innocent man should? Was he hoping to get his hands on some of the wealth that would shortly come the way of an attractive newly-made widow?

Nine

Shirley lived in a row of red-brick, red-tiled terraced houses, that might even be called a row of picturesque cottages, because they were quite old, and were just off the main street of the ancient village. The tiny front garden of the second one from the left was shingled all over, but a few yellow tulips in pots added a little colour. Many of the other cottages had been double-glazed with modern white plastic frames, Reg Finch observed, but this one still had its original sash windows, and they were smart and neatly painted.

The woman who answered the door to his knock had short dark hair, sharp brown eyes, and was tall and lanky, but not quite so tall and lanky as Reg was himself.

'We'd like to ask you a few questions. May we come in, please?' Reg asked politely, having explained that he and Alison were police officers and displaying their identity cards in case that assertion might be disputed or doubted.

The woman stared at them both impassively for a moment, then nodded and stepped back so that they could enter, indicating with a jab of a finger, that they should enter the front parlour.

Inside that small room all was not merely neat and clean, it was spotless and immaculate. The wooden furniture was not of particularly good quality, but it glowed with the kind of shine only achieved with real bees' wax, and elbow grease. There were only two easy chairs. Shirley sat in one, and Reg in the other, so Alison perched herself on a low footstool.

'I believe you worked for Mrs Grimston until recently, at the little factory unit by the garage near the church,' Reg said mildly, to start the interview off. The woman merely nodded, as yet she had not spoken a word or changed her impassive expression.

'On Monday, after Mrs Grimston had had her unfortunate heart attack and was taken into hospital, you took charge of her keys, is that correct?' he went on.

At last Shirley showed signs of being mentally alive. She seemed to frown in puzzlement and surprise, then relax considerably.

'That's right. She'd left them on her desk

272

in the office, which ain't surprising, because she was all upset that the shoe company was closing us down. They hadn't no right to do it. We'd worked our socks off, the bastards. Tina's lucky she ain't dead. If I hadn't been there to give her first aid, she would've been too. It's the company what's to blame. God, wouldn't I make them suffer if I had the chance? So, what about her keys? I had to use hers to lock up, 'cos I gave my set to the Receiver's man, didn't I? So, what's the matter? I always opened up and locked up when Tina weren't there.'

'So, what did you do with her keys? Did you go out to their cottage that night to give them back?'

Shirley looked really puzzled now. 'Course not. Why'd I want to do that? I know'd she weren't there. I give her them back when I went up the hospital to see her, didn't I? What the hell's going on? I've had her keys dozens of times when she's forgot them. So what? You ain't thinking I've been and gone and nicked things out of her cottage, are you? You ain't got that from her – I know you ain't. She'd trust me with every penny she's got. We're friends, see. We've been real good friends for years.'

Reg found Alison Knott's hand poking at

his shoulder. He looked round and discovered her frowning and staring intently, first at the carpet and then at the woman's right leg, where a wide strip of plaster showed beneath her brown tights. Alison wouldn't do that without good reason. A brown cord carpet, and a cut leg? Then the penny dropped.

'Real good friends, are you? Well, I've got a lot of time for that sort of thing,' Reg said slowly. 'If a real friend of yours gets into trouble, there's nothing you wouldn't do to help. Is that right?'

Shirley nodded vigorously. 'Too right.'

'And if some rotten beggar pulled a fast one on your real friend and left her in the lurch, then by God, you'd want to get even with them somehow, wouldn't you?'

'You bet.'

'You bet, all right, but it's one thing to set fire to a factory that's deserted and where there's no one to get hurt – we know you did that, because we've got bits of this same carpet that you threw over the glass on the wall. Did you realise that you left some of your blood on the wall when you cut your leg. But to then go on and hurl petrol bombs into a house where people were fast asleep is going much too far. That's nigh on cold-blooded murder – burning people alive.'

Shirley's jaw fell open with shock and fear at this totally unexpected verbal attack. 'I ain't bombed no houses with people in them,' she cried out hoarsely in horror. 'I ain't done nuthin like that. Bloody hell! You can't pin that on me, you can't. Okay, so I did set fire to the bloody factory. Yes! I admit it. It didn't burn down like I wanted it to, but it ain't no more than what they deserve – but by Christ, I ain't done nothing else, and you can't say as I did.'

'Oh come on,' Alison interposed quickly, because Reg seemed to have run out of steam, and the pressure needed to be kept on. This woman had already admitted to the arson attack at the factory, with a bit more effort she'd confess to the one at LeClerc's house too. 'We know you were at Mr LeClerc's house. We've got your footprints and the tracks of your car to prove it.'

If Alison had hoped to bring this woman tearfully to her knees uttering abject confessions, she was to be very disappointed.

'Who are you trying to bloody kid?' the woman snarled defiantly back at Alison. 'I ain't got no car, and I couldn't drive one if I had.'

'All right. All right,' Reg said hurriedly, to damp down the tension. It needed it, because this Shirley had looked ready to fly at Alison with teeth and claws flailing. 'Let's forget the fire at the house for the moment. You tell us, nice and slowly, so that we can write it down for you to sign, just how you set fire to the factory. In the meantime, I'll get a fellow over to check your footprints. If he says they're not yours, we'll believe you. Right?'

Brenda Phipps was feeling rather peeved. Even though she was doing what she had wanted and planned to do, it was boring just talking to all those at the shoe company who might conceivably have had a motive for killing Brian Labinski. The trouble was -and that was another thing that was annoying – the idea that the widespread fear of redundancy was a potential murder motive for all of the staff, had taken a bit of a blow. She'd found out that there were quite a few who were actually looking forward to the prospect of receiving a windfall in the form of a large redundancy sum in cash, and were confident of their ability to quickly find work elsewhere. Others were of the opinion that whatever might happen to the production workers, their tasks of invoicing, packing or dispatch just couldn't be done away with, and so they felt their futures were quite safe anyway. It was only those very senior managers with big mortgages and a specialised knowledge of an industry in rapid decline, who really feared the loss of status and the financial uncertainties of life on the dole. Of those, none appeared to know where Labinski even lived, let alone the necessary fact that he had two dogs that needed walking. Added to that, they didn't even seem to know, or said they didn't, where the Grimstons lived, or the fact that on the Monday, Mrs Grimston had had a heart attack and had been taken into hospital. It was annoying and frustrating to be here, merely flogging a dead, or dying, metaphorical horse, while the others were out and about finding new and exciting leads. Reg, she had learned, because Reg had been kind enough to phone and tell her so, had been to the burned LeClerc house, and also had been fortunate enough to come across the name of someone named Shirley who had actually had the Land-rover keys in her hands during the crucial period. That was sheer luck, but it was annoying to think that even at this moment he might be taking Labinski's killer into custody, all by himself. The Chief, too, had come up with a superb suspect in the lawyer O'Shea. They could not both be right, but the most exciting thing Brenda had done that morning was to find out where Labinski's secretary lived, and that in most people's opinion she was either quiet, shy, reserved, nice, stuck up, a bit of all right, divorced, not bad looking, well-educated, or, a toffee-nosed creeper.

Doggedly Brenda carried on. She might be an impatient person, but she knew that if a job was to be done, it had to be done properly. She had set out to question all those who had taken abusive phone calls from Gordon Grimston, or had sub-sequently been told or heard gossip about them, so that is what she would do. In the planning office, stores and dispatch depart-ment such people had been thicker on the ground, but now she was down to the very last, the van driver – and his story was more interesting than most.

'I got there just as poor old Tina Grimston was being carted off in the ambulance,' he explained frankly. 'It weren't right, the company just chopping her off like that. They'd had their pound of flesh from her many times over, and they ought to have given her a break. She'd always time for a laugh and a joke when I got there. So had the other girls. It were a happy place, and you don't find them often these days, and it made me right angry, seeing all them women in such a state. A wailing and a weeping, they was, like you see them Eastern women do on the telly at a funeral. If that bloody Labinski sod had been there then, I don't know that I wouldn't have taken a swing at the beggar meself.' Since he was an inoffensive-looking, short and fat character of at least sixty years, it seemed, to Brenda's eyes, that any swing he took would only have a chance of landing where it was meant to land, if the intended recipient had the mobility and agility of a garden snail. 'That Receiver fellow, he couldn't stick it. He just handed out some bits of paper and beggared off smartish. I did me best to help and calm them down, and most of them went off then, 'cos there weren't nothing else for them to do no more. I had to move Tina's old man's Land-rover, so they could get their cars out. By the time I'd loaded up, there were only that tall lanky Shirley woman left.'

'You actually drove the Land-rover?'

Brenda exclaimed. 'Your fingerprints are on it then. We don't want you on our suspect list, do we? Here, touch your fingers on this stamp pad, and roll them on this piece of paper. That'll save me having to haul you down to the police station.'

'Here, it's making me hands dirty.'

'Well, they're not exactly lily-white as it is, are they?'

'You still here?' George, the production director asked, when they met up in the corridor leading to the front reception.

'Just about finished,' Brenda said with a polite smile. George still looked harassed, but it was a more relaxed harassment than it had been yesterday. An explanation of that was not difficult to find.

'A shocking thing, that fire at Mr LeClerc's house, but I suppose it's taken the heat off you for a bit, even if you have been left holding the baby for a while,' she observed pleasantly.

George nodded, and wiped his forehead with his right hand. The motion exposed a bandaged wrist.

'Oh dear, it looks as though you've been in the wars,' Brenda went on, giving the usual smugly sympathetic smile of those who haven't been in wars.

'It was the bloody cat. It never did like me.'

'So there you are,' the Chief Constable announced aggressively, and unnecessarily, as Walsh came into his office. He stared at his visitor's frowning face and glinting eyes, and saw signs of tiredness and stress, and so he moderated his tone into one that was a shade milder. 'Sit yourself down.'

However, Walsh's first concern was not with chairs, but with the coffee pot that usually occupied a space on the big red-faced man's desk.

'This ain't a bloody cafe, you know,' the CC grumbled, watching patiently as Walsh poured the liquid into a cup and liberally spooned in sugar, then he frowned as some plastic containers were dug from a briefcase and set out on the embossed green leather of his desk. 'What the hell's all that for?'

Walsh swallowed the first pills with a grimace. 'Two iron tablets, because it seems I'm a bit anaemic. One antibiotic to keep the abscess healthy, and then two of these to kill the pain. I'll be almost human in a few minutes.'

'That'll make a change. I don't hold with

all this namby-pamby pill-taking business. The body's immune systems should be left to sort themselves out. If the troops in the Falklands had all run off to their doctors every time they'd had an ache or a pain, they'd still be bloody fighting.' The CC was an ex-military man, and saw, or claimed to see, most civilian situations in that rigid light. However, Walsh had a previously proven ploy to parry that attitude.

'The troops in the *Sir Galahad* should have disembarked as soon as they got there, in the safety of darkness,' was probably all he needed to say to bring an end to that irrelevant diversionary conversation, and he was right.

'I want to know what's going on with this Labinski case.'

'Me too.'

'Don't bugger me about, Sidney. I've had old LeClerc on, saying that we should have realised, after Labinski's murder and the fire at his factory, that he would be next on the killer's hit list, and we ought to have put a guard on his place. I don't know that he's not right either – and you took the minder away from Labinski's wife too soon; she wouldn't have been attacked if you hadn't. You've let things get out of control, Sidney, so what are you doing to put things right?'

Walsh's jaw gritted angrily. 'I haven't had the pathologist's report yet, so I don't know officially that Labinski was actually murdered, or when he died. Packstone's so tied up I'm not getting a lot of help from him,' he paused to take a gulp from the coffee cup. He'd instinctively uttered the kind of blanket excuses that under normal circumstances he would have scorned to mention, but he'd better get some more constructive thoughts sorted out, or else he would be in for a load of military flak, and deservedly so.

'Mrs Labinski said she was all right, and was going to book into a hotel, so I don't see how her attack can be blamed on me. Under the circumstances, I think we're making good progress. We know who set fire to the factory, and even if we can't at this moment prove it was the same person who fire-bombed LeClere's house or murdered Labinski, we're working on it. She had Grimston's Land-rover keys, so it's looking promising. In addition to that, later on we'll be confronting the person we think may have assaulted Mrs Labinski, and we're working on some other interesting characters, too.' Walsh was quite pleased with what he'd just said – because it sounded as though the investigation was being conducted positively and efficiently, which it wasn't really, but further questioning from the CC might show up the flaws, so it was time to divert his mind. 'LeClerc phoned you, did he? Well, if you know him, you might be able to help us.'

'I've met them socially. The LeClercs are a pretty well-established and influential family in the area. What do you want to know?'

'I want to know whether the younger LeClerc has really done a bunk from Manila in the Philippines because he'd been showing too much interest in young boys, and the authorities there have got wise.'

The CC's face became a picture of conflicting emotions, as surprise broke through the impassive expression that he was desperately trying to maintain.

'What the hell has that got to do with anything?' he countered testily.

'Simple. Labinski had done most of the hard work, planning the LeClerc shoe company's restructuring. Any reasonably competent manager could put most of the rest of those plans into effect. So, how is this for a murder motive? The LeClercs killed Labinski, so that the younger one could take on Labinski's job. Then, not only would they save themselves a fortune by not having to pay Labinski's huge bonuses, they'd also have a first-class face-saving reason to give to all their friends, explaining why the younger one should suddenly resign from the Navy, or the foreign office, or whichever he worked for.'

The CC said nothing, seemingly content to stare down at his fingers which were drumming lightly on his desk.

'Oh, come on,' Walsh said in exasperation. 'If the Philippine authorities are investigating something like that about one of our Embassy staff, the first thing they'd do is ask for background information from the UK, and since the LeClercs live in our patch, it's bound to end up on your desk. For heaven's sake, this is a murder inquiry. I haven't got to subpoena you to get the information I need to do my job, have I?'

'I'd like to see you try,' the CC glowered. 'What concerns me is how you ever got to hear of it. Things like that are highly confidential, or supposed to be, damn it. So, come on, give. How did you find that out?'

Having had the rumour confirmed by non-denial, Walsh simply wasn't interested in its source. 'It's on the grapevine,' was his rather curt reply.

'What? Gossip, you mean? Here in my own headquarters? By God, Sidney, you'd better spill the beans. I'm not just surprised at you, I'm appalled. If you know there's someone in this place prattling secrets, why haven't you done something about it?'

Walsh shrugged his shoulders scornfully. 'What do you take me for? Your dirty little secrets are safe, as far as I know. I learned about LeClerc through the lawyers' grapevine. Do you know a fellow named O'Shea? He was Labinski's solicitor, and just to complicate matters, he advised the Grimstons too. It was he who told me.'

Walsh's revelations hardly seemed to have reassured the red-faced man, because that red face went even redder and darker, to more of a maroon, in fact.

'Donovan Patrick O'Shea? Is he involved in all this? This could be serious.'

'You're too right it could be – for O'Shea. He's been sniffing round Labinski's wife, and it looks as though they've been having an affair, but what's equally important, he went to see the Grimstons on the Saturday morning, and while he was there he could easily have taken the spare keys to Grimston's Land-rover. So he's also a top contender in the Labinski murder stakes,' Walsh explained seriously. His head was becoming clearer now, but he was quite unprepared for the CC's next words.

'You'll have to lay off O'Shea, Sidney,' he said grimly.

'Like hell I will. Is he a friend of yours too? Tough on you. If I can pin this on O'Shea, he'll get what's coming to him.'

The CC's face turned to an even darker shade of livid, and he almost spluttered when he said, 'Your brain's getting addled with all those bloody pills, Sidney. O'Shea's a fish in a much bigger pond than the one you swim in. We'll have to step carefully.'

Walsh frowned. 'Why do you always beat around the bush? Why the devil can't you ever come out straight with what you mean? I've got security clearance, if he's suspected of laundering drug money or something.'

'Drugs? Rubbish. Use your brains if you've got any left. Do you think that someone like O'Shea can suddenly uproot himself from Dublin and come to park himself in our fair city, without someone saying, 'Hello, what the devil's he up to? We'd better keep an eye on him.'

'That's nonsense. If he was running an IRA cell he wouldn't be taking a high social profile. It'd be covert, back-street stuff. Besides, with all this so-called peace initiative in Ireland you'd think MI5 would be running down that sort of surveillance operation, if that's what you're suggesting they're doing.'

'He's acting differently to the norm, that's why he could be so dangerous. Anyway, you reckon all those diehard Republicans will just give up, without having got us British out completely, do you? I wish I could agree with you. What worries me is that if O'Shea knows about LeClerc's son, he obviously has access to a highly efficient intelligence organisation, one that's broken into our confidential communication systems.'

Walsh laughed scornfully at the idea. 'As a secret agent then he's just about useless. I went to see him as a police officer. He knew who I was. Do you really think he'd let slip the existence of an efficient intelligence net-work, by dropping out such a bit of highly secret information? I can't see it myself. I reckon he was just letting out a juicy bit of scandal he'd heard gossiped somewhere. You've got "Reds under the beds" syndrome.'

'Maybe, but you back off, until I've had consultations.'

'I can't do that. I've got to get his fingerprints somehow. I couldn't get them surreptitiously while I was there, so I'll have to go back with a warrant of some sort. I gave him a hard time too, so he won't co-operate willingly.'

'You lay off him. That's an order, see? Why are his prints so important?'

'There's some unidentified ones on the Land-rover, of course. Pinning them down could be crucial to the whole of this investigation,' Walsh explained irritably.

The CC stared at him, obviously thinking hard. 'His prints must be on file somewhere in London. If you're that desperate, I'll see if I can get them faxed up here, but if the Land-rover is so crucial to this case, how come the LeClercs are on your suspect list? How could they have had access to its keys?'

'That was puzzling me too, but O'Shea let that out as well. The LeClercs own a garage in the Fens somewhere, and it's a Rover dealership. All they'd need is the registration number, and they'd be able to get the engine number, chassis number, and the key number as well. Easy for a dealer to get a spare, even for an old model like that, and no questions asked.'

'If it's that old, any fool could start it. Had

them in the Army. The wires are just push-on terminals behind the switch. Just touch them together and the ignition's on. All you know about the LeClercs seems to have come from O'Shea, so watch it, he could be leading you up the garden path with a whole load of red herrings, just to put you off his scent.'

'In which case he's failed abysmally.'

With all five CID officers in occupation, Sidney Walsh's office seemed rather smaller than usual. Brenda Phipps lounged in her accustomed place, in an easy chair by the window, and Reg Finch occupied his favourite spot, on the opposite side of the desk where he could slouch out his long legs in some comfort. Alison Knott and Arthur Bryant, as befitted their lesser status, had to make do with more upright Spartan seating. Walsh leaned his elbow on the desk and glanced round. His head was clear again at last, and he felt well in command of himself, and this meeting.

'How did you get on today, Brenda?' He asked bluntly.

Brenda scowled. 'All right, I suppose. I've got a lot of background information on all the shoe company employees who knew about Grimston's threatening phone calls, which might come in useful, but to be honest, I've found no new leads. The only constructive thing I've done all day is set up our raid on Labinski's secretary's flat, and for that I demand the right to be in on it. I'll die of boredom if I don't get some action soon.'

Walsh grinned broadly at the expression on Brenda's pretty face. 'I think that might be arranged. I don't want your death on my conscience. How about you and Alison, Reg?'

'I think we've got on all right,' Reg said quietly, forbearing to look at Brenda's face while he spoke, in case he might be accused of gloating over having chosen the more productive line of investigation. He did not want to be involved in any bad-tempered arguments tonight. 'We went out and had a mosey round LeClerc's place. Forensic had several footprints and tyre tracks to cast and photo, but what was interesting to me was that the fire-bomb that caused the most damage was thrown through an upstairs casement window, which was only open a couple of inches or so. Whoever did that must have had a strong arm and a good eye – that makes me think it was a man. No offence, ladies, but women aren't best known for their throwing abilities. The other thing which might be important is that when the bottle exploded, the burning cloth that packed the neck was flung back out of the window, and might, in the expert's opinion, have even landed on the arsonist. So the arsonist might have singed hair, a scorched jacket or even blistered flesh on his hands,' Reg announced. 'After that we wasted some time waiting at Grimston's place, but then went to question his daughter. You need a bit of luck sometimes, and I had some today. Old Professor Hughes had actually thought about doing some sleuthing himself, and had persuaded the girl to find out and list all Grimston's phone calls, visitors and the whereabouts of Landrover keys. That shows a touch of genius. He'd thought he'd find the killer if a name cropped up more than once, but none did. That stumped him – he didn't quite know what to do with the lists, so he gave them to me. It's certainly saved us a hell of a lot of time, and put us straight onto the woman named Shirley. I wasn't thinking about the arson attacks when we went to see her, I was more concerned about the fact that she'd had Mrs Grimston's keys to the

Land-rover, but fortunately Alison spotted the brown cord carpet, and the bit of plaster on the woman's leg.' Reg paused briefly to turn a page in his notebook.

Alison turned her head to look at him. It was decent of him to have mentioned her name and give her the credit, but Reg was like that. That was why she liked him so much, in a professional way, of course.

'Well done you, Alison,' Brenda and Arthur both said in unison, and even Walsh nodded his appreciation.

'So, we tackled her on that,' Reg went on, 'and got a confession for the blaze at the factory. We then tried to hassle her on the LeClerc fire, but she wasn't having any of that. Denied it very forcefully, claiming she hadn't got a car, and didn't drive. Forensic were no help. Her feet were big enough, but none of her shoes matched the prints. So, as things stand, we can't pin that on her yet, and anyway, I doubt if she could have heaved a bottle through that window. Still, setting fire to the factory was an admitted act of revenge, so if we discount her story that she can't drive, she remains a good candidate for Labinski's murder in my mind.'

'I don't think she can drive, Reg,' Brenda

announced to everyone's surprise. 'The shoe company's van driver had to use those keys to move the Land-rover from outside Mrs Grimston's factory after the ambulance had gone to the hospital, but it shouldn't be difficult to find out if she's ever had driving lessons. As to the LeClerc fire, I think I might have a suitable candidate for you there. Would a cricketer – one who bowls the balls – fit the bill, do you think?'

Reg blinked and smiled grimly. 'Down to a tee.'

'You have a tee in golf, Reg – for driving off,' Arthur Bryant pointed out helpfully. 'In cricket, it would have to be *down to the crease*, or something like that.'

'Thank you for those words of wisdom, Arthur,' Brenda said cheerfully, perhaps her day hadn't been wasted after all. 'My cricketing man's name is George. He hates the LeClercs, the younger one particularly, with good reason, and, now I come to think of it, he may have a burn mark on his wrist. There was a bandage on it today that wasn't there yesterday. I must admit I've had a lot of sympathy for him and the way he's been treated, but if he fire-bombed the LeClerc house, he's gone too far. That's attempted murder, and is no different, in my book, to

294

aiming a handgun at someone and pulling the trigger.'

'That's not much to go on. It sounds more of a hunch than a conviction,' Walsh commented cheerfully, well-pleased at the way the meeting was progressing so far, and delighted that some relaxed, constructive and friendly attitudes had returned to his senior staff. It might, of course, be because he'd brought in the two younger members of the team. Brenda and Reg wouldn't dream of arguing, not with the juniors present.

Brenda thought about it carefully for a moment. 'I'm convinced enough to feel that we must tackle him, Chief. Besides, I've met him. He's a character who's been under great stress for a long time, and probably ready to erupt like a volcano, and do something stupid. Perhaps more than once, because he has a motive for killing Labinski which is as good as anyone else's. I've got his prints on his statement for forensic to compare with those they've found on the Land-rover.'

'Do you want to do any more work on him before he's pulled in, though? It's too serious a matter to leave in abeyance overnight.' Walsh would have liked something more positive than the mere fact that the man hated the LeClercs and was a cricketer. Still, there were times when one had to back someone else's judgement to the full, and even a stickler for detail like Reg seemed to approve.

Brenda shook her head.

'Right then, Brenda. You have a choice. Do you want to come and confront Labinski's secretary with me, or deal with this George fellow instead?' Walsh asked, giving her an amused grin.

'I'll take George, if you don't mind,' was Brenda's not unexpected reply.

'Can I go with you, please, Brenda?' Arthur asked her plaintively. 'I've been bored out of my skin today too, and you might need a man with you, if George turns nasty.'

Brenda gave an unladylike hoot of laughter. 'Do you think I couldn't handle him, Arthur? Well, why not, indeed. Come if you like.'

'You can take the forensic chap with you, the one with the shoe and tyre patterns. Wave a search warrant first, and if the shoe treads match, you can bring him in for questioning. He can be charged later. Right?'

'How did you get on today then, boss?'

Reg asked politely.

Walsh told of his meeting with O'Shea, and explained about the possibility that the LeClercs might have obtained a spare Land-rover key through the garage they owned. He omitted the story of young boys in Manila, or that O'Shea was under anti-terrorist observation, they were both things that those here did not need to know, but he did describe O'Shea's anger at the suggestion that his supposed affair with Labinski's wife, and her gaining possession of her husband's wealth so conveniently, might be *bone fide* motives for murder. That all met with their obvious approval.

'You got O'Shea's fingerprints did you, Chief? If he pinched the spare Land-rover keys, he's a first-rate murder candidate too,' Brenda declared cheerfully. 'If forensic can match even one print out of all those we've given them, we should soon have this case tidied up one way or another.'

'Weren't you also going to check out Grimston's alibi by timing the journey from Labinski's place to the cottage yourself, and from there to the hospital, boss?' Reg asked.

'Yes, I drove the route myself in my car, but I couldn't fault the calculations Pack-stone's chap had made. So Grimston's alibi still stands,' Walsh explained regretfully.

'Car? I'm sorry to interrupt, Sir, but, but–' Arthur stuttered hesitantly.

'But what, Arthur?' Brenda demanded.

'But, you said you drove it in your car, Sir.' Arthur went on.

'That's what the Chief said,' Brenda uttered impatiently.

'What's the point you're trying to make, Arthur?' Walsh said kindly.

'Well, Sir. It's not far, as the crow flies, but it's a long way by road.'

'I know that, Arthur.'

'But don't you see, Sir? You went by car, on proper roads, but Land-rovers are meant to go off road – over rough fields and up mountains. That's what they're made for. I know there aren't any mountains round here, and I don't know if its actually possible, but it's private estate land, and Grimston, or his daughter even, might know a way. If he went across country, it would also explain why no one saw him on the roads. He'd certainly do it a lot quicker that way, than you could in a car, by road, Sir,' Arthur said, blushing bright red, because everyone was staring at him.

'By George,' Reg said in a hushed voice. 'He could be right. Where's the map? The six inch to the mile one.'

They all crowded round as the large-scale map was spread over the desk. Fingers seemed to be pointing in all directions. 'That field might lead to that lane. He could have turned off here, into the woods.'

Someone said, 'No. This looks better. There's a track down here.'

'Hold it,' Walsh said loudly. 'Calm down. Let's think this out. Even if Grimston did the route ten minutes quicker than I did by road, he still couldn't have got to the hospital when he did, not if we start the whole journey time to the hospital from the moment when Labinski's watch stopped.'

'Perhaps the watch was fast, Sir,' Arthur suggested, looking rather dejected, as the enthusiasm for his suggestion seemed to wane.

'Not that make of watch, Arthur. Grimston's defence lawyers would have a field day if we tried that one. We'd need some corroborative evidence if we try to dispute it,' Walsh explained. 'Now let's look at this from another point of view. If Arthur's right, then Grimston might have come down this field by the wood, into Labinski's lane. He'd have had to have the vehicle lights on, surely, so someone in these houses on the other side of the field might just have seen him. We didn't do a house-to-house questioning down there, did we? So there is just the whisker of a possibility that someone might have seen Grimston that night, and if they could put their hands on their heart and swear to the time, that might stand up in court against Labinski's watch. It's worth a try. It's too late tonight. We've other things to do, but first thing in the morning I think we should take Packstone's Land-rover out to Grimston's cottage, and see what we can do with cross-country times.' Walsh looked round. That suggestion met with everyone's approval. 'Right, you thought of it, so this can be your baby, Arthur. I'll ask the duty officer to find you some uniformed staff for a house-to-house inquiry tomorrow morning. You'll be in charge. Question all those living in those houses that look out towards the woods. Maybe it was Grimston all along, but even if it wasn't him, one of them might actually have seen just who the driver really was.'

Ten

George lived in a boxy-looking, modern house, which was typical of many built on estates for the middle income, semi-executive types. Within there would no doubt be an impressively large lounge, with a dining area, or even perhaps a separate dining room, but upstairs, even with cunning space-saving devices like fitted wardrobes and cupboards, all would be cramped, and if there was that most desirable of extras, the fourth bedroom, then it would hardly be big enough to swing round the poor proverbial cat.

Brenda Phipps rang the front-door bell.

The door was opened so promptly that Brenda found herself staring in surprise at the distraught face of the lean, pale woman whose mousy crimped brown hair was so long that it hung down from its central parting almost to her waist.

'Thank God you've come so quickly. I just didn't know what to do.' Her hands twisted and twined in her long tresses.

301

'What's the matter? What's happened?' Brenda demanded sharply. She sensed an urgency, but the woman before her showed all the outward signs of someone ready to lapse into hysteria rather than effective action.

'It's George.'

'Why? What's he done? Quickly now.'

'When he got home he rang the hospital, to see how young LeClerc was getting on, and they said he'd died of his burns. Well, George took it really badly. I've never seen anything like it. He went so pale and weak, I thought he was going to fall down. I tried to help him, but he just pushed me off. His eyes were all staring, like he was in a trance or had seen a ghost. Then he just wandered about, looking at photos of his cricket matches, and pictures of us and the boys. His face looked so – so hopeless. I know he's been under a lot of stress lately, but I think he's having a mental breakdown. He needs help,' she stuttered and started to sob.

'But where is he now?' Brenda almost shouted.

The woman shook her head. 'He just walked out to the car in his slippers. He hadn't even got his coat on. I'm so worried. And what would he want with a garden hose? I don't understand.'

'I do. Which way did he go? How long ago?' Brenda cried, grabbing the woman by the shoulders and actually shaking her.

'Up towards the woods,' she blurted out eventually. 'About fifteen minutes ago.'

'You stay here. Alert HQ, and get an ambulance quick,' Brenda snapped sharply to the forensic chap who had been keeping in the background. She turned and ran back to her car, with Arthur hot on her heels.

Arthur barely had time to get in the passenger seat before the car accelerated away. He knew they were heading in the wrong direction, but he was quite unprepared for the sudden handbrake turn, and the screeching of tyres and burning rubber. He was flung violently from side to side.

'Hang on,' Brenda yelled, and her accelerator foot went flat to the floor and stayed there as she snicked up through the gears, speeding like an insane rally driver through the estate – more often than not cornering bends on two wheels rather than four – out to the unlit country road that led through the woods.

'Go for it, girl,' Arthur said, encouragingly. That was nearly as bad as telling a blatant lie, because he was in fact scared out of his wits, but he was damned if he was going to let her know that.

'Put your window down,' Brenda said in what was obviously meant to sound like a calm voice. 'Keep a sharp lookout your side for his car. We might be in time. Sometimes suicides sit for ages in a sort of coma, before they actually start the engine.'

There was a wire fence to bar entry on Arthur's side that gleamed long thin silver lines in the glare of the headlamps, but that came suddenly to an end. He peered intently into the seemingly tangled under-growth. 'Cut the speed, or we'll miss him,' he yelled.

Brenda braked hard, and Arthur cracked his head on the windscreen, but for some reason he felt no pain, because at that moment he had seen something – a flash of light on metal or glass, deep in the wood, and there was a rutted track too. 'Over there. There's something over there,' he cried. He was out and running almost before the car had skidded to a halt. His feet slithered in mud, and he nearly went flying. Yes. Brenda had been right. A car with a hose jammed round with cloth, coming from an exhaust pipe. He wrenched it free, and saw puffs of smoke escape, but the car's offside back door was locked, and so too was the driver's. He dashed round to the other side, but that wouldn't open either. Brenda raced up and saw the problem. She started swinging high kicks with her foot at the rear side window but, for some reason, glass, even the toughened variety, only breaks easily when you don't want it to, and she had no success. Arthur's method was more effective. He leapt on the bonnet and stamped on the curved windscreen. At first even that only crazed; it needed two more kicks to make a hole big enough to be able to reach in and lift the door latch, and get it open. A cloud of acrid fumes flooded out, but Brenda had to lean right in to release the man's seat belt. Seemingly he had had no desire to die of a road accident while he was in the process of killing himself. Her eyes were streaming as she hauled George out of his seat, leaving him on his back, sprawled out on the muddy track.

'You do the mouth-to-mouth bit, Arthur,' she croaked hoarsely. Then she used her radio to summon thither the assistance she expected to be already on its way.

They had been extremely fortunate to find him so quickly, so there was a fairly good chance that George would survive, but whether that individual would thank them or not, was quite another matter. However, the forensic chap could check the tyre tracks and shoe prints at his leisure now, and if they all matched up, the LeClerc fire-bombing incident, at least, could be considered neatly closed, from the investigators' point of view.

Arthur was down there on his knees, manfully blowing air into the sprawled man's lungs. He had been alert and quick-thinking tonight, and it did no harm to acknowledge the fact. 'Well done, Bryant old boy,' she said huskily, and got a brief wave of a left hand in appreciative response. Most of the day may have been boring for both of them, but it had certainly ended with a bit of excitement.

Emily, the late Labinski's private secretary, lived on the first floor of one of four virtually identical blocks of flats, which were just off the road from Cambridge to Ditton and, fortunately for those living in Ditton, much nearer the former than the latter. Ditton is an attractive, nearly unspoilt little village which Clifton-Taylor might have described as having 'rural charm', if that Oxford man had ever got there. Certainly, without its cars, it might slumber yet by its sweeping river bend until the next influx on a 'bumps' race night, but surely the young females of Rupert Brooke's day never deserved being immortalised as *mean and dirty.* Something perhaps to rhyme with *thirty* – or had its ladies hurt his ego, for him to write in scribbled verse, that all its sweets were cheap and nasty?

The brown-painted first-floor landing of the block of flats was so cold and bland that the description of 'tasteless' might even be considered flattery.

Sidney Walsh rang the door bell for the second time. It could clearly be heard ringing within, but just in case the occupant had any doubt what its message was, he gave a couple of hefty knocks on the door, with the back of his hand. That indeed brought an immediate response, but not from where it was expected. The door opposite opened abruptly, revealing a bald-headed, stocky, ear-ringed man in a sweaty tee shirt and tracksuit bottoms, who had the physique and bulging muscles of an over-the-hill Olympic weightlifter.

'What the hell's going on?' he demanded, staring suspiciously at Walsh and his two companions.

'Nothing for you to be concerned about, thank you,' Walsh replied politely.

'Oh, it ain't, ain't it? Well if it were you lot that pushed your way into old Mrs Harris's flat downstairs and nicked her pension money, you ain't doing it up here, see?'

'Do we look like muggers and vandals?' Walsh asked in surprise, waving his hand at his companions, Reg Finch and Alison Knott.

'Yer. Wanna try mugging me, huh?"

An interesting conversation might have developed, but at that moment there came a rattle of a chain, and the door Walsh had actually knocked on, opened a fraction.

Walsh held his identification card to the gap so that the person inside could see it. 'Mrs Emily–' he started to say.

'She ain't a common or garden Mrs, she ain't. She's got a proper title. Lady Emily's what you call her, see. I seen it on her letters, and she's a Lady by name and a Lady by nature, she is too. So you mind your bloody P's and Q's,' the lone vigilante guardian instructed.

The chain rattled again, and the door swung right open, revealing a flushed and obviously highly embarrassed dark-haired woman of medium height. She was in her middle thirties, dressed casually in fawn slacks and a light green mohair jumper.

'Thank you, Mr Gregory. I shall be quite all right, I'm sure. These are police officers,' she said in a clear, well-modulated voice.

'Okay, but you sing out if they cause trouble, and I'll come right in and sort the beggars out.'

'I know it's unkind to say so, because he obviously means well, but I'm afraid he utterly terrifies me really,' she explained with a forced smile as she ushered her visitors into her sitting room.

She sat down on a hard, carved-oak chair, which was one of a few nice pieces of furniture about the place, leaving the more cushioned variety for her uninvited guests.

Walsh stared at her plain but not unattractive face. There was a slight twitch under her left eye, and the suspicion of a tremor in the fingers of the hands that rested demurely on her knees. He had guessed that this woman might be of a nervous disposition, and he was sure that he was right. She might, even at this moment, be absolutely terrified. That would have rendered most people speechless, but this woman had, perhaps, been well-schooled in the art of hiding her fears under a facade of apparently relaxed normality, and was still able to engage in small talk and polite conversation.

'May I introduce Detective Sergeant Finch, and Detective Constable Knott? I am Detective Chief Inspector Walsh,' he explained in a relaxed and friendly voice.

Lady Emily nodded politely at each in turn.

'Do you really have a title?' he asked cautiously. He couldn't remember off hand whether it was the daughters of Dukes or Earls, or both, who were courteously 'Ladies' by right.

She hesitated momentarily, but then nodded reluctantly. 'It would not be difficult for you to find out all you want about me. So I might just as well save you the trouble. You must be wondering, perhaps, why, with a titled family, I live here in this small flat. Well, my brother farms all that remains of the family estates, and he's nearly bankrupt now, because of the beef crisis.' She looked down at her hands. It seemed to Walsh that this woman almost wanted to tell them of her private life, as though the doing of it might bring her the benefits of the confessional, with an expiation of sins, and a better life then to come. So he did not interrupt her. Specific questions could wait.

'My marriage, which started so well, ought to have ensured me a life of reasonable affluence,' she continued quietly, 'but I was quite unaware, at the time, that all the apparent assets were securities for my husband's fraudulent loans. When the house of cards finally collapsed, I found that I was fortunate to escape with a mere nothing, while my husband, my ex-husband that is, still has several years of his sentence yet to serve. Such a thing might normally pass through the law courts unnoticed by the general public, but when the press found out who my father had been, photographs and articles positively gloating over the downfall of a so-called rich man's daughter, appeared in nearly all the papers. Since then I have tried to fade into the background, and live like everyone else. Fortunately I can speak several languages, and use a word processor. Those are the only assets I now have, and with them I must earn my living. I have become a personal secretary, no less, and to the society in which I now live, that is a position of high status. The title and family connections, are, I'm afraid, more of an embarrassment to me than an advantage, and they have brought me nothing but bad luck anyway. Unfortunately my solicitors seem unable to forget them when writing to me. So now my secret is even known in this place, and again I'm a figure to be pointed at, and whispered about.'

'I see. Thank you for being so open with us,' Walsh uttered politely, and pulled his mind back to the purpose of his presence there. 'We have come, I'm afraid,' he went on rather sadly, 'with a search warrant, to recover the briefcase that belonged to Mr Brian Labinski, and which was taken from his house yesterday by someone who forced an entry, and unlawfully restrained his wife. Do you have that briefcase? Or do we need to search for it?'

Lady Emily's self-control very nearly faltered. Her bottom lip fluttered momentarily, and her eyes glazed as tears started to form, but they were hurriedly blinked away. It was her shoulders that drooped despondently, and stayed drooped. 'That won't be necessary. The black witch who haunted my christening still plagues me with bad luck, it seems. Yes. I have Brian's case. It's in the bedroom. What will happen to me now?' she asked resignedly, while bravely bringing those shoulders back square again, and obviously preparing to face with whatever fortitude she could muster, the new trials and tribulations that beset her.

Walsh felt intensely sorry for her. It must have been a cold, hard and unhappy childhood for her – being brought up to never show her emotions. Now she was a woman who was unable to relieve her feelings naturally, with floods of tears. She must be suffering terrible miseries and stresses in her mind.

'What is there in the briefcase that you didn't want us to find?' he asked her quietly.

'Receipts and things. Brian was so meticulous at keeping records, but these couldn't go with his company expense account claims, you understand.' She gave a brief but unhappy smile. 'Of course you don't understand. I shall have to explain. Let me tell you the whole sad story.'

'That is a very good idea,' Walsh acknowledged.

'I've been Brian's secretary for over six months now, and he was already trusting me with his confidences, not just business ones, but those of his private life as well. One of which was that he was not happy with his marriage. It's awfully unkind to say so, but the truth is that his poor wife was not living up to the standards that Brian had planned and expected from her. He told me of the foolish things she sometimes said on subjects she didn't properly understand, and how she blurted things out in company that should have been kept personal and private. Her dinner parties had embarrassed him so much, in fact, that he had just stopped entertaining at home, and he gave up taking her to any important business events as well. He was a very clever man, you see, and although he hated to admit it, he had realised that he had made a mistake. In spite of her undoubted good looks, she couldn't cope with the kind of society he wanted to be part of, so she obviously wasn't the person he wanted to spend the rest of his life with. It's awful, isn't it? I'm sure his wife was doing her best, but when a man like Brian decides he has a problem, he starts doing something about it. It was quite clear, even quite some time ago, that Brian was intending to get rid of her when it was convenient to him, and had already started to look around for someone more suitable to replace her. He even listed to me the qualities that person would need to have. Someone who could entertain, converse in different languages, and generally hold her own in society, and not be too unattractive as well. He knew my history – I could hardly keep it from him, could I? Anyway, he became convinced that I was an ideal candidate for the job – when it became vacant.' She held her hands out in a brief gesture of helpless resignation. 'I tried to put him off at first, but that is very difficult when you work so closely with someone, and you're desperate not to risk losing your job. What else could I do? It was not I who was breaking up his marriage and driving his wife away. Besides, life with Brian would certainly be much more comfortable for me than it is now. So, I did not stop his boyish familiarities with me. Well, to cut short a story that I'm quite sure you already think is far too long, last weekend was to be the final test of my suitability. To put it crudely, I was to be tried out properly – in bed.'

'But last weekend Mr Labinski was still in India,' Alison Knott contradicted suspiciously.

Lady Emily slowly shook her head. 'He flew into Paris on the Friday night, and I met him there, in the hotel. It wasn't a bad weekend, really. It was nice to dine out expensively again, take taxis everywhere and to sit in comfort at the opera. Even the in-bed bit was quite bearable, and I understand that I performed my part – satisfactorily. We came back together on the earliest Eurostar train to London on the Monday morning. I then came straight up to Cambridge – to arrive in the office at the normal time – while Brian went down to Heathrow to pick up his car. The Bombay flight came in at ten that morning. So everything was timed to perfection. That's it really.'

'I'm still not quite sure I understand,' Reg Finch said quietly. 'I can see why you wouldn't want to be involved if this case draws the media attention in court that it might, but what precisely was in the briefcase that you took such risks to get?'

'The hotel receipts, of course. You would have known from them that Brian came back from India early, and that I was involved. I'm not a very clever crook, am I?' She sighed ruefully. 'I should have just taken the receipts and left the briefcase where it was in his house – then I might have got away with it. I'm afraid I panicked. I was so frightened of someone coming and seeing me.'

'You were a bit hard on Mrs Labinski, weren't you? Tying her up like you did,' Walsh observed.

Lady Emily shrugged her shoulders phlegmatically. 'I had hoped the spray would blind her long enough for me to get in and out quickly, but she turned away so quickly that I couldn't be sure that it had worked. So I had to pull her jumper over her head, and tie her hands, to stop her taking it off. I'm not proud of what I did, and no doubt I will be punished severely for it.'

'If Labinski had told you that you were – er – satisfactory in bed, then, as you say, you had obviously met all the criteria of his ideal consort. Did he then tell you when and how he would get rid of his wife?' Walsh asked quietly.

Lady Emily nodded ruefully. 'Oh yes. He'd become rather eager by then to get it all over and done with as quickly as possible. He rang his solicitor on the Monday afternoon, and told him precisely what he planned to do. They had arranged to meet the next morning to go through the draft of an offer which he was prepared to make to his wife. A legally binding divorce settlement, that would be quite generous, provided she accepted it immediately, and vacated his house promptly. It was a fair proposal, I thought, and she'd have been a great deal better off than I ever was. I was to move into his house as soon as she had moved out. He would get another secretary, and I was to polish up my title, and start entertaining the rich and powerful, so that he could set about getting himself a *Sir* to go with it.'

'His solicitor knew all this on the Monday?' Walsh asked with his eyebrows raised inquiringly.

'Oh yes. The only thing his lawyer didn't know, was my name. Brian refused to tell him. He said that for the time being, it was none of his business.'

'Where were you between eight and ten on the Monday evening?' Reg Finch asked, since the boss seemed loath to pose that direct question.

'Most of the time I was downstairs, trying to calm poor Mrs Harris, after the tearaways had messed up her flat. Mr Gregory, across the landing will vouch for me, I'm sure. Besides, Sergeant, I'm hardly likely to have bitten the hand that was to have fed me, am I?' she replied.

So, another loose end was tied up, Walsh thought dryly, but a loose end was all that it appeared to be. He had really learned nothing much from the Lady Emily interview that he had not already surmised anyway. That was depressing, but then so was his abscess, and the weather.

Denise Labinski's evening attire was extremely suitable for a widow. It was a black dress, of course, with long sleeves and a neckline that this time was proof against any peering eyes. A pony tail had made her look too young, so she had rolled her fair hair up into a rather matronly-looking bun, that was quite fetching really.

In the hotel she felt perfectly safe – safe enough to dine with, and even enjoy the witty conversation of the man who was to sort out for her all the intricacies of probates and such things. Obviously that could not happen if she refused to talk to him. Even if she did think he was a deceiving rotter, he was still very good company.

'Shall we finish off with Irish coffees?' Donovan O'Shea suggested as the hotel waiter came to clear away the used plates and glasses.

'Why not? It would be sort of appropriate,' Denise Labinsky agreed a little sleepily. She was tired, but she did not yet want to return to her chilly hotel room, and be alone with her depressing thoughts. 'I've really had too much to drink already, but I ought to be able to manage another one. I'll probably fall over if I stand up, then you might have to help me up to my bedroom,' she added ingenuously, when the waiter had gone out of hearing, then she realised that wasn't the sort of thing to say – he might think it a hint. 'But you're not going to force your attentions on me tonight, understand? I'm a woman in mourning, and it's not right,' she explained hurriedly.

'I've never forced my attentions on any woman in my life, as far as I know,' he replied hotly.

'Well, we shouldn't have done what we did the other night, not with Brian lying out there dead somewhere. That was very wrong. It was wicked.'

'Oh absolutely. Terribly wicked it was, and we should be utterly ashamed of ourselves,' Donovan O'Shea agreed so humbly and readily that she looked up at him suspiciously. 'Where I come from we say it's only wicked – if you enjoy it. So it must have been very very wicked, because I enjoyed it a hell of a lot,' he went on, looking at her very seriously indeed. Then he waved a bony finger admonishingly. 'Come on now, be honest. Admit it, Denise. It was very good, wasn't it? I rather felt you enjoyed yourself too, with all the noises you were making.'

'Shh. Not so loud. Someone might hear you,' she whispered, frowning disapprovingly.

'Well! You did, didn't you?'

Denise put her lips together stubbornly, determined not to make a reply, but for her, the truth could not be denied outright. 'Well – yes – I did. Of course I did. It was nice to let my feelings come out naturally, and be a real woman again,' she admitted with reluctant embarrassment, 'but I've got to stop that sort of thing now, and sort myself out.'

'What's wrong with being a real woman – when you are a real woman?'

'You don't understand,' she retorted. 'I've been doing a lot of thinking, and I've realised that I'm just a failure when it comes to marriage and relationships. I tried ever so hard with Brian, but my parties were a disaster, and when we went out I always seemed to be saying the wrong thing and making myself look stupid. It wasn't really fair, because all the people Brian wanted to mix with were those clever types with hard eyes, who look straight through you half the time, as though you aren't there, and all they wanted to talk about were shares and markets and dividends and deals and things.

321

It was always money, and I didn't know half what they were on about, and they knew it too, so they'd say things to make me look even more silly than I was. Poor Brian. I know in my bones that he was going to get rid of me soon. Now the poor man's dead, and even though I failed him, he's going to make me a wealthy woman. It's quite depressing, if you think about it.'

'Well don't think about it then. You and Brian just weren't cut out for each other, but somewhere there's your Mr Right, if you can recognise him when you see him. What are the kind of things you love doing?'

'That's easy,' Denise said seriously. 'I love dressing up in pretty clothes and trying to make myself look glamorous, and I love it if I can tell from people's expressions that I do look good. It's awfully vain and selfish I know, but that's me. I love talking too. It used to annoy Brian ever so much, but I can really talk to all sorts of people about absolutely anything that comes into my head, as long as it isn't money, or too clever things. It's good for people to talk, you know. It does them good. It's like taking a tonic. Do you know that old Mrs Grayson comes into my salon at least twice a week? Not to buy anything, but just to have a chat. I don't mind. It's because she's lonely. It brightens her day up – and mine too, when I see her come in looking miserable, and go out looking happy. And there's the old lady near the village post office, sitting by her window because she can't get about. I always wave, and if the window's open, go and say something. You should see her eyes light up. Old Mr Hamilton next door is just the same. I think he watches out for me, because he's lonely too, so I always make time to have a little gossip about the weather or what's been going on – it brightens his day up too.'

'You've a kind heart,' Donovan said with a twinkle in his grey eyes. 'What else do you like? Music? Travel?'

'I like ballet, and Gilbert and Sullivan, and old ruins, and old churches and junk shops too, and I love walking on the beach looking for sea shells and driftwood, and tucking my skirts in my knickers and paddling in the sea. I used to love making sand-castles too, when I was really young – and still would, if I could,' she admitted earnestly. Her eyes had a faraway, dreamy look.

'I used to know a girl like you, years ago,' Donovan said, so softly that it seemed he was afraid to hear what his own voice was saying.

323

'Did you?' Denise asked, staring at his sombre lean face with some interest.

'I'd already got my degree in London, and I was doing Irish law, in Dublin. She was – well – not quite as beautiful as you are, but she was lovely all the same, with long flaming hair, and she was as wild as the wildest kitten you ever saw, and I loved her. I loved her so much that it hurt. The sun really did shine when her sapphire blue eyes smiled. Two years we were together, always on the go, never stopping, and whatever we did, even if it were just a walk in the park, it was like a big adventure. It was wonderful – and it was tragic too.'

Denise's mouth unaccountably fell open in horror and sympathy. 'Oh dear, how awful. What happened? Was it an accident? Did she die?'

'Oh no. Nothing like that. One day she just ran off with the drummer of a rock band. It's funny, you know – it was as though all the colours in life had suddenly gone dull grey, yet everywhere I went in Dublin I could see her face in my mind, smiling, all bright and full of life, but she was gone from me for ever, and I was all alone. I stuck it for a few years, and then decided that if I stayed in Ireland I'd go mad, so I packed my bags, closed my eyes and stabbed a pin in the map, and went to live where it had made a hole. Well that's not quite true,' he admitted with a rueful grin, 'because the first pin landed somewhere in the North Sea, and since I didn't feel like living in a diving suit all the time, I tried again, and low and behold, the pin landed in Cambridge. So that's why I'm here.'

'It must have been awful about the girl, if you loved her that much. I'm so sorry for you.'

'I was sorry for me too, but I'm not sorry now. I wouldn't have met you otherwise.'

'Am I really beautiful?' Denise asked, frowning with annoyance at having asked such a brazen question, but nevertheless still looking earnestly into his eyes.

'I think you're the most wonderful creature God ever made. Don't all the roses smile when you go by, and the birds start their trilling all over again?' He took one of her hands and stared down at it for a moment. When he spoke again his voice was even softer, and a little hesitant. 'You know, Denise, what I'd like us to do, when things have settled down a bit and the weather's warmer, is to toss some things in the back of the car, and just drive off together to somewhere where the sun always shines and the birds always sing. We can climb mountains, make sand-castles, have sandwiches in a country pub, and cheer up any poor soul we think looks lonely. Then at the end of the day we can watch the golden sun sink down over the horizon, and dine in a little oak-beamed hotel by candlelight, and I'll tell you over and over again, just how lovely you are.'

For some reason Denise's bottom lip fluttered. She shook her head slowly, and then started to cry.

'You're tired. It's time you were in bed. I'll come to pick you up in the morning, after breakfast, and we'll go and get Brian's papers and bills sorted out. Then maybe we can find a little pub somewhere with a roaring log fire, and have some lunch,' Donovan suggested.

Denise dried her eyes and nodded reluctantly. She swayed a little on first standing, but found she could walk unaided up the broad stairs to her hotel room, while Donovan O'Shea could go into the bar for a last drink, and stare thoughtfully down at the dark white-topped liquid in the glass, as sip by sip its level sank lower.

Sidney Walsh woke up suddenly. It wasn't the kind of waking that makes one jerk upright all tense and alert, instead he stayed relaxed and comfortable. It was just that his eyes had opened, and his brain was wide awake. He'd probably just come out of a refreshing period of rapid eye movement, or what the scientists called REM, the time of dreams. Not that scientists really knew much about what the brain got up to during sleep. They'd only just got to the point of knowing that the lack of the right kind of it could bring about some strange mental behaviour. Walsh had rarely ever remembered any of his dreams, and so had difficulty believing that his brain must be doing the same sort of thing as everyone else's. This time though, even as his eyes identified the vague shape of the dressing table in the dark gloom, he was seeking to recall the dream, if that was what it had been, because somehow it was important. Lady Emily was in it, for heaven's sake. He was sitting beside her on the plane coming home from Paris one moment, and then the next minute they were standing together, with the chill salty wind blowing through their hair, on the deck of the Dover ferry. That was all utter nonsense. Lady Emily had travelled on the Eurostar train. Was this so-called dream merely to make him admit that he'd never used the Eurostar train, because he was scared of that long passage deep under the English Channel? Well, he'd admit it to anyone, if he had to, but he still wouldn't travel on it. He grinned to himself – even the Dartford Tunnel was bad enough. He always drove the downward slope of that as fast as he could, all tensed up, with white knuckles showing on the steering wheel, then as soon as he'd passed the lowest point, he could relax, because if the water did break in at that moment, it would blow him safely out of the tunnel, like a pea from a peashooter. He peered up at the faintly luminous hands of the bedside clock. It was two-thirty in the morning. Dawn came earlier in Paris, because it was nearer the east and the rising sun, although it wouldn't come this early, of course. Over there it would only be three-thirty in the morning. Now he did jerk upright. Of course. What he and Lady Emily would be doing on that plane, and on the ferry too, was resetting the hands of their watches to good old Greenwich Mean Time. Yes, it was still GMT, the hour didn't go on, or was it off, for British Summer Time, until next weekend. But Labinski had been on the Eurostar train to London, not the flight from Bombay, which was several time-zone hours different. Every single train to London, except that one, was always on, and never left, England's soil, where no traveller ever thought about such things as time zones. Was it possible then, that Labinski's expensive watch had still been showing Paris time – an hour out from GMT? If that were true, then Grimston's alibi had a really big hole in it, because Labinski must then have been run down at seven o'clock that evening – not eight. It was a good argument, and a brilliant one too, if it could somehow be proved. Even if it couldn't, a clever lawyer might use it to throw doubt on the precise time of Labinski's death into the minds of a jury.

'Are you all right?' Gwen asked sleepily.

'Yes. Sorry love. I didn't mean to wake you.' He laid his head on the pillow and was soon asleep again.

Eleven

It was just before eight-thirty in the morning when the dark-blue police Landrover came out of the woods, and stopped in front of the cottage. A rare sun, much weakened by the effort of piercing the thinnest of grey clouds above, had just enough power left to lighten the surface colour of the red brick, so that against the darker background of woods it almost seemed that the building was floating on a calm sea of green.

Even without the use of his telescopic sight, Jamie Hamilton could see the word *Police* painted on the side door of the vehicle. He wasn't interested in them, but their arrival might make someone come to the front door, and so he steadied the crossed lines of the sight on that door, took a deep breath, and waited. This might be his opportunity, he thought dimly, because his mind needed more effort to make it think at all now, so numbed was it by this extended period of active service. That phenomenon did not worry him too much, for he knew what it was by its symptoms – combat fatigue. At least an hour had passed since he had crawled up onto the ridge near the old oak, a position which gave him an excellent view down the long field to the old ruin and that little red-brick cottage, yet he was no longer really conscious of the passage of time. He had changed his position from the one he'd been in all yesterday. It was wise for a sniper to do that, in case some Jerry watchers had seen signs of his movements and were preparing to do to him what he wanted to do to them. Yesterday had been a fruitless day, as they were sometimes. He'd seen some harmless civilians come and go. They were probably collaborators, but he was not interested in them. His orders were quite clear, it was the man in that cottage who was his target, he was the evil one who tortured and violated helpless women and made them unhappy. Yesterday the cunning bastard must have sneaked out the back way, and kept to the woods. He'd been worried about the dogs, but wherever they had been, he must have been downwind from them. They were a worry though, they might give his position away. His other problem was the cough on his chest that had grown worse as the damp and cold had permeated into his body during that long yesterday. The combat fatigue was worse than he'd ever known it before, and it had taken all his strength and willpower, when darkness had come, to make his way back to his base and his billet, where he could dry out the wet and clinging Ghillie suit and fall asleep on the floor before the gas fire from sheer exhaustion. When this operation was over maybe they'd give him some leave – and he had dreamed in sporadic flashes of smoke and bombs and blood and bodies, of Winston and Monty, and of his home-coming to that little bungalow of which he was so proud, and of his wife and that nice girl next door, who would both be so pleased to see him. Next day, preparing to carry on the fight to free the world from the bloody tyrant, had been a slow and fumbling business, but he hadn't let the side down.

Was that door opening? He coughed and spat, and had to resettle. There was the man. He was just moving down the path. He was unmistakable. That open green anorak over a baggy red sweater, and brown trousers. The crossed lines wavered on the red sweater, steadied, then Hamilton's finger lightly touched the trigger. The strength of the recoil into his shoulder took him by surprise and he saw grey sky through the lenses. He jerked up his head, even as he worked the bolt and reloaded. The figure of his victim seemed to have been flung backwards to the ground by the bullet's impact. Which was as it should be. He was a marksman still. One of the civilians was getting in the line of fire, going to his victim's aid perhaps, but that would be a waste of time, for he should be beyond any medical help now. Yet to be on the safe side he steadied the rifle and fired again at the sprawled body. Then his tired brain bethought him of what would happen next. The Jerries would go mad with rage at what he'd done. They always did. They might not know where he actually was, but very soon they would be wildly spraying the most likely spots with every weapon they could lay their hands on. Machine-guns, mortars and even shells from their supporting artillery would shortly be ranging down on this low ridge. Which was good in one way, because that would be betraying their positions for other spotters to pinpoint, but his task here was done, and he could leave that to them. It would be wise to start moving back at once, to the relative safety of the trees. Besides, he needed to report the success of his mission to base HQ as soon as possible, and then he could tell his wife and the girl that they were no longer in danger. They would be so pleased. Now that he'd flushed the Jerries out and crippled their command structure, the advance could continue. The blessed peace of Victory could not come again soon enough for the nearly exhausted old man.

There was an air of excited expectancy among the four police officers in the field-support Land-rover, when it drew up outside Grimston's cottage. Walsh had felt better than he had done for ages. The swelling in his jaw had noticeably gone down, and the pain had virtually disappeared. There had been an added pleasure too, when he'd explained his Paris time zone theory to the others. 'What I thought we'd do is to tell Grimston that this exercise will finally disprove his alibi, and get him to show us all the possible crosscountry tracks to Labinski's place on the map. Then we can firm up on precise distances and times, then I'll set up a meeting with the CC and the Crown

Prosecution Service, and they can decide whether we have enough circumstantial evidence to arrest Grimston for Labinski's murder,' he had said.

'And if Arthur comes up with someone living on the far side of the fields near the green, who actually saw Grimston in his Land-rover that night, that would button it all up nicely,' Brenda had added eagerly.

'And if Lady Emily said that she couldn't remember him altering his watch when she did hers, that might help too,' Alison had suggested helpfully.

'True! Reg, you and Alison had better stay with Grimston while Brenda and I are out in the Land-rover. We don't want him doing a bunk now,' Walsh had said firmly.

As they walked over to meet the tall bulky man who was emerging from the cottage front door, the prospect of possibly tying up the case of the murder of Brian Labinski had resulted in a light-hearted, jovial, almost holiday mood.

That mood was instantly dispersed by the crack of the rifle, and the tinkling of glass as the lower pane in the front door shattered. That sharp sound was familiar enough to officers who had regular firearms training on special police ranges, and triggered some instant responses. Brenda, who was in front and nearest Grimston, sped forward and launched herself in a flying dive at the man who's face was stunned into frozen stupidity, and who was clutching at his left arm as though he had been stung by an out-of-season wasp. Her weight hit him knee high and sent him crashing backwards onto the cottage path. A second shot screamed over her head and thudded into wood or soft brick, and set her scrambling forward on her knees to grab the big man's arm, and start dragging him into the doorway. Grimston's senses returned quickly though. He twisted off his back, and as soon as his knees were on the ground, in spite of his injured arm, he was crawling faster through the door and down the narrow hall, than Brenda could heave him.

The other officers had dived flat to the ground, but save for the Land-rover, which anyway could hardly be expected to turn or stop a high-powered bullet, that ground was far too open for comfort, and the front door of the cottage was too obviously in the sniper's sights.

'This way,' Reg shouted, demonstrating the obvious course of action by scampering like some weird long-legged crab round the side of the cottage to safety. The other two quickly followed. They burst in through the back door just as a cursing and blaspheming Grimston was pulling his shirt and red sweater over his head and staring at a profusely bleeding weal across the fleshy muscle at the top of his left arm.

'Shut up, blast you,' Walsh snapped at him. 'Are there any binoculars anywhere? There're some on that gun cabinet over there. Reg, Alison, your eyes are better than mine, get upstairs and see if you can spot the beggar. Keep well back from the windows.' He turned to the big man who slouched on the kitchen chair, and whose normally weatherbeaten face was now made pale and anxious by shock.

'Who the hell wants to kill you, damn it, Grimston?' Walsh growled angrily, as he reached in his pocket and drew out his radio.

'How the bloody hell do I know? But my Tracey's out there with the dogs, somewhere. She'll have heard them shots. She knows a rifle from a shotgun, so I hope's she's got the sense to keep her head down and not come running back here to see if I'm all right. By God, if he hurts her, I'll kill the bastard. You see if I don't,' was his spluttering reply.

'Shut up and keep still,' Brenda said irritably. She had torn a tea-towel into strips, and was using them to bind the injured arm. 'That's not brilliant, but it'll stop the bleeding for now. He must be on that ridge near the skyline, Chief. Near those lone trees.'

'Where do you mean? Show me.'

Brenda ran into the sitting room, knelt and lifted the corner of the net curtain carefully. 'Up there, on the ridge at the end of that field, near those trees. Ideal spot for a sniper, but he won't be hanging about there.'

'Don't I know it?' Walsh snapped as he held his radio phone to his mouth. 'Headquarters! Sidney Walsh here. I'm at the Grimstons' cottage, off the Barton Road. This is an emergency. We've come under fire from a high-powered rifle. Position not seen, but possibly six hundred yards south. One civilian casualty, but not serious. Don't, repeat, don't, send an ambulance into the danger area, but keep it handy.' That was the easy bit, that message was as neat, precise and concise as it could be, but what the hell was he to say next? Most likely situations involving firearms had been anticipated as training exercises, and flexible schemes designed to deal with them, but they had nearly all been urban-based – armed robbers holed up in a bank with hostages, or a distraught mental case under siege in a council house – and none had set a lone sniper into wide open country. He must make up new rules as he went along. A bird's-eye view of the area would be useful. 'Get a helicopter over the danger area, which is an arc south, one-mile radius from here, and growing. There are thick woods as well as fields, so get a thermal-imaging device on it. Now, I want flak jackets for us here pronto, and the Armed Response Force handy nearby, for when the sniper is located; and you can get all the road patrols you've got circling the danger area. Observing only though, on no account are they to approach any suspect. All right? Any questions?' No doubt there would be soon, but at this precise moment HQ would be buzzing like a disturbed hornets' nest.

'Chief, we've got Arthur and a team down in the village near Labinski's place. If they spread out and get safe into cover, we could have the whole of that end of the woods under observation,' Brenda suggested,

340

pointing to the area on the map with a finger.

Walsh nodded, and used the radio again to give Arthur the instructions to put that idea into effect.

'Right Sir,' Arthur replied promptly enough, but then he went on to mumble, 'Sir, I've found out that–'

Walsh heard the words, but just then Reg shouted urgently from upstairs, 'For crying out loud, boss. What the devil are you playing at? Grimston's just gone running off into the woods, to the left of the track we came in on, and he's got a rifle too. A light one. It looks like a .22. It's definitely not a shotgun.'

'Bloody Hell. Do whatever you think best, Arthur,' Walsh snapped hastily into the radio as a load of new problems rushed into his brain to compound the existing complications. He stuffed the radio back in his pocket as he ran back into the small kitchen. Sure enough it was empty, and the gun-cabinet door was open. Some .22 cartridges lay scattered on the floor. If Brenda had not been with him Walsh might have jumped up and down in blind fury. His prime suspect was now armed and loose in thick woods, where some other maniac with a high-powered rifle was already on the warpath, and an innocent girl (or was she innocent?) was walking two dogs. He'd got to do something. He couldn't just do nothing.

'I'm going after him. At least I'll be handy if anything happens,' he announced, turning towards the door.

'Good for you, Chief,' Brenda cried out. 'You lead on. I'll follow with this,' she snatched up a double-barrelled shotgun from the open gun cabinet and fumbled in a cardboard box for cartridges. 'At least if we get shot at, we can shoot back with something,' she explained excitedly.

'You lot take care,' Reg warned anxiously. 'We'll use the Land-rover as cover, and see if we can get up to that ridge. We might be able to see what's going on from there.'

Walsh yelled, 'Right,' as he disappeared at full speed round the corner.

Reg Finch, and Alison Knott followed them cautiously, then made a dash for the safe side of the Land-rover.

'Keep your head down, Alison,' he warned as he wriggled in, wound the driver's seat as far back as it would go, and started the engine. He was lying almost prone, to reduce the size of the target he might be presenting to the rifleman, but he had just enough vision out of the bottom of the windscreen to see where he was going, and long enough arms to still shift the gears. They started off very slowly along the edge of the green field, towards the ridge, but no shots were fired at them, and soon, feeling bolder and less at risk, Reg eased himself and the seat more upright. There were signs of trampled wheat stems coming from where an old oak still grew, and they led into the wood. He could presume those to have been made by the sniper, so he used his radio to inform Walsh of the fact, and drove slowly and cautiously on, peering into the trees for signs of movement.

Walsh and Brenda ran fast into the wood. It would seem that Grimston was intending to follow the edge of the field up to that important ridge whilst keeping in amongst the sheltering trees. There were no natural paths, so that meant forcing a way through brambles and thickets. Initially, trailing Grimston was no problem, for he had left a trail of trampled vegetation a child could have followed, but further on, where the trees opened out, Walsh needed to be alert to spot his tracks, and to do that he had to slow down. Senses other than sight soon came into use, for as he had neared the danger zone, Grimston too had obviously slowed down, which allowed his pursuers to come within hearing distance, and he was making a surprising amount of noise. Too much, for an experienced woodsman, so probably he was deliberately trying to draw the attention of the unknown sniper towards himself, and away from his daughter, if she was out there somewhere. To that extent, Grimston may have succeeded, because there came the heavy crack of the high-powered rifle again, followed almost immediately by the snappy pop of the smaller calibre .22.

Both Walsh and Brenda dived to the ground, and then looked at each other in embarrassment, because the bullets had been long gone to wherever they were going, before even the two police officers had heard the sounds. Then began a wild period for the two of them, of scratches, tumbles in mud and the ever-present danger of twigs intent on gouging out an unprotected eye, which afterwards Brenda would recount with an amused look on her face that had not been apparent at the time. Even Walsh's panting conversation with the

CC was later hilarious to recall.

'What's all this about bloody helicopters, Walsh?' that worthy had snapped out over the ether, 'and how many armed men am I supposed to send you? Surely you can surround a lone rifleman and pin him down until the marksmen get there?'

'And pigs might fly,' the Chief had snapped breathlessly. 'This is thick woodland, and there's not one but two riflemen popping off at each other now. You'd love it here. Anyway, we're heading south-east, in hot pursuit.'

'Back off, Walsh. Wait for armed assistance. I don't want people getting killed.'

'Neither do I, but there's civilians about, so I've got to keep in contact. Besides we are armed, we've got a shotgun. Get off the air. I'm too busy. I'll report in when the situation clarifies itself.'

'Hell–!' but then there came the sound of a woman's scream, and Walsh ignored the crackling words from the radio, and with anxiously set face, ran doggedly on. For him this race through the woods was becoming a nightmarish blur, because his brain was racing other thoughts through his mind as well. What Arthur had said was linking up with other stored data to form new patterns, which needed deep consideration, but there was no time to do that, because there could be real danger ahead. When the sniper was cornered, he might turn and fight like a cornered rat – to the bitter end. Walsh was on a roller-coaster ride of action from which he could not yet escape, but when the ride stopped – he would need all his wits about him.

'Do what you think best,' the Chief Inspector had clearly said.

Arthur Bryant pulled back his shoulders and held his head up proudly. This was definitely being given responsibility, for there was no doubt that whatever he now did, lives in his charge might be at risk. Nevertheless, what had to be done, had to be done, and he set out to deserve Walsh's trust by minimising the risks as much as he could. He hurriedly gathered his small team together, and gave them instructions in as confident and authoritative a voice as he could muster, which was completely at variance with the strange sick feeling of anxiety that had come to swirl round in the pit of his stomach. He positioned most of them at intervals across the village green, well back from the woods at the western side, and told them to lie down, stay there, and merely watch carefully, but he, himself, with the petite, black-eyed Mary Innes as support, would take the most dangerous spot, as a good leader should. So he drove round the green and up the lane, and parked his car, seemingly very untidily, because it was almost blocking access to the row of older bungalows, just before the entrance to Labinski's house, and almost, but not quite, opposite that same track leading to the green down which a man had been so cruelly deprived of his life.

His forces thus deployed, there was nothing left for Arthur Bryant and Mary Innes to do, but crouch down behind the shielding car, and watch and wait; but waiting, when the adrenaline is already flowing and the body is primed to explode into instant action, can be nerve-wracking and seemingly interminable. It gave time too for doubts to eat away at confidence, but patience, even when there is no other alternative to it, can bring its reward, and suddenly, out of the woods and into the lane came the weirdest and most grotesque figure that either watcher had ever seen in their young lives. Long lengths of seemingly grey hair, matted with snagged dead leaves and grasses, streamed out behind it, as the gruesome creature loped erratically along, with one of its arms incongruously waving a rifle wildly to help keep its balance, because its head was turned to look behind.

Mary Innes voiced a low cry of shock and alarm, which was abruptly cut short as Arthur pulled sharply on her arm, to bring her head down below the level of the car's bonnet. Then, keeping low himself, he waddled towards the boot end, and the gap between the car and the hedge. He heard the steps of the running figure falter, no doubt at the sight of the obstructing car, but then the creature came on again, accompanied now by wheezing coughs and gasps for breath. He must time his move to perfection, and at what seemed to be the right moment, he suddenly straightened up and leapt at the figure, with both hands reaching out for that all-so-dangerous rifle. He was a fraction of a second too soon though. The figure gave a hoarse, strangled yell as it tried to stop its forward motion and draw back, but that very combination of movements aided an instinctive defence action, and the butt end of the rifle thudded hard into the pit of Arthur's stomach, causing him to double-up helplessly into the hedge, gasping for air.

Mary Innes sprang up to defend her fallen comrade, but he was in no danger, since that unearthly creature had turned and was running, with loud agonising gasps, into the gravel drive of the late Brian Labinski's elegant house. He must not be allowed to get away, and Mary had, at that moment, no thoughts for her own safety. She jumped lightly over Arthur and dashed in pursuit. She saw a blue police Land-rover come out of a field, and head towards her, which brought her a great feeling of relief, but then, out of the corner of her eye, confusingly, more figures appeared from the lane. A tall heavily built man with another rifle clutched in one hand, but also clinging to that rifle, and trying to drag it away from him, was a red-anoraked girl with wild flying hair, and two black dogs which leaped excitedly about the struggling pair. However, Mary Innes was not to be diverted from a purpose once it was set in her mind, and she ignored the lot of them, and went hurtling after the wheezing figure. The yielding gravel slowed it more than it did her own light weight, and when she dived forward she managed to grasp an ankle and bring the creature crashing down

349

on its face. The rifle broke free from its grasp and slithered away across the shingle. She ignored it, and scrambled forward onto the figure's back, trying to grasp its still flailing arms. Then she was callously barged to one side, as the big man, now without his rifle, started kicking wildly at the fallen figure. He was not content with doing that for long, for he suddenly reached down to grab the netting folds, and heaved the figure bodily upright, then set about pummelling it with his spare hand. Mary pressed her hands to the ground and dug in her toes ready to spring up and re-enter the fray, but suddenly there was no need. Ample reinforcements had arrived. A staggering Arthur, a Chief Inspector half covered in mud, Reg and Alison, and the girl, while a cool Brenda was calmly bringing up the rear with the shotgun over her arm, looking more like an aristocratic lady out on a pheasant shoot, than a policewoman in hot pursuit of armed men.

The big man had torn away most of the ragged Ghillie suit, and when he himself was under restraint by the newcomers, he let the still struggling old man with the bloodied face drop with a thud back onto the gravel. Jamie Hamilton's fighting spirit was now restricted to gasping for breath between rasping coughs.

Alison Knott hurriedly knelt down beside him, and putting an arm behind his back, raised him into a sitting up position, which helped him a little with his breathing. She looked up at Walsh, and shook her head slowly. 'I don't like the look of him. He needs help. It might even be pneumonia,' she said anxiously.

'Call the ambulance in, Reg,' Walsh instructed, looking round quickly while trying to get his mind into some sort of order.

Then the CC's gruff voice came on his radio.

'Your helicopter will be in the air in twenty minutes, Walsh. What's going on? Why haven't you reported in?' he demanded aggressively.

'Because I've been too damned busy, but you can cancel it now,' Walsh retorted bluntly, 'and you can stand down the armed squad too. We won't need either of them. It's all over. We've called in the ambulance, but that's just for an exhausted old man. I'll be coming in shortly,' he announced.

The CC acknowledged that with merely a grunt, but there was a recognisable sound of relief in that grunt. Walsh felt that relief too.

Things had happened so quickly. From the fear and dread of the slaughter that those two rifles might have caused, to a sudden safe state of confusion, must be like the mood swings a madman might experience. All he needed to do now was give the orders which would wind things up in a proper professional manner, but then came a diversion.

Attracted no doubt by the noise outside, the frowning lean-faced Donovan O'Shea had emerged from the front door of Labinski's house. His glance scanned the strange assortment of people gathered before him, and his eyes seemed to twitch nervously. Then one particular object caught his attention, and he stared down as though mesmerised by the sniper's rifle, lying incongruously on the shingle.

Slowly O'Shea reached down to pick it up.

'Leave it!' Walsh said sharply, and at the same moment Brenda Phipps stepped forward. The breech of the shotgun in her hands snapped closed with an ominous metallic click, and the barrels swung menacingly round to point at the Irishman's feet.

O'Shea's trance-like state was broken by

the threatening gesture, and he straightened up and stepped hastily back. Perhaps, like Reg Finch, he too was uneasy when there were guns about, for it seemed as if he looked round for a way to escape from those weapons and the suspicious eyes staring at him, but finding none, was forced to stand his ground. He stared coldly at the muddy dishevelled figure of Walsh, clearly recognising in him the neatly dressed individual who had visited his office only the day before. His jawline hardened and he spoke out aggressively.

'Why is my client Mr Grimston being physically restrained in such an unnecessarily brutal manner?' he demanded arrogantly, pointing to that individual, who was being firmly held in the grip of Arthur Bryant and the red-anoraked girl, and in the process of being handcuffed by Mary Innes.

'Mr Grimston and his daughter are very kindly helping us with our inquiries, thank you very mu–' Walsh started to say.

'Grimston? Is that *the* Grimston?' Denise Labinski cried out in a voice full of anguish and fear. 'What's he doing here? He killed Brian, Donovan, and he tied me up hoping I'd die too,' she went on, clasping for support or protection onto O'Shea's arm.

353

'I never bloody did,' Grimston shouted back, his face a confusion of bewilderment and anger.

'Oh yes you did. That's what you said you would do on the phone, and you did it. You did. You did,' Denise insisted petulantly, as tears began to flow from her big round frightened eyes.

'That's what you seem to have said to almost everyone you've met recently, Mrs Labinski,' Walsh said calmly but wearily. 'Did you think that if you said it often enough, it would come true? You'd got marriage problems, but if someone did kill your husband, then your problems would have gone away, wouldn't they? As indeed they have done. Were you hoping some besotted knight in shining armour would rescue the innocent maiden who was being so cruelly treated by that wicked husband of yours? You certainly seem to have made sure that as many people as possible knew of your problems, but if that was your plan, your aspiring knight in white shining armour very nearly got it all wrong.'

Denise Labinski stared at Walsh in utter amazement. 'I don't understand a word you're saying. I've never asked anyone to kill Brian for me. I wouldn't do that. I didn't ever wish him dead. It's just not true, and it's not fair.'

Walsh glared back at her. 'Well, maybe not in so many words, you didn't, but that's what your words must have sounded as if they were saying, in the mind of this poor old man,' he nodded down at the still coughing figure of Jamie Hamilton.

Denise followed his glance, and saw Hamilton lying on the ground for the first time. She gave a little shriek of horror, and rushed to kneel by the old man's side.

'Oh, you poor Mr Hamilton. What have they done to you?' she cried, reaching out to touch the swollen face that was now deathly pale. His grey eyes suddenly gleamed with the warmth of recognition.

'I got them for you. I got both of them,' he wheezed proudly between coughs, but loud enough for most of those gathered round to hear. 'You'll both be safe now, my darlings,' he croaked more softly. 'Mavis, I think I've copped it. I think me number's up.'

'Both of them?' Mary Innes asked with a puzzled frown on her face.

Walsh grimaced wanly. 'He's confused. He thought he'd killed Grimston as well this morning. Unless you mean the two darlings. That would be Mavis, his wife I would guess, and Mrs Labinski here.'

'Good God, are you suggesting that it was this old man who killed Brian Labinski?' O'Shea asked, incredulously.

'You heard what he said, and he's the one I feel sorry for. An old man, isolated by a society that seemingly had no use for him, and driven in his loneliness to a form of pathological schizophrenia, in which his past life was often more real than reality itself. Into that haze came a pretty woman who chatted to him as though he were still a human being. She must have become a ray of sunshine in his day, and her tales of a husband's unkindness, and more latterly of actual threats to her by big-mouth Grimston here, must have made him feel she was in real danger, and it was his duty to protect her. Unfortunately he seems to have had a really lethal piece of equipment to do that sort of thing with. That rifle and that camouflage outfit belong to a trained sniper, and that's what I think he must once have been. The funny thing is though, on the night Labinski died, I think Hamilton here was really out with his rifle gunning for Grimston, not Labinski.'

'How come, Sir?' Mary Innes's dark eyes stared inquiringly up at Walsh's face.

356

'Well, Grimston was the main threat to Mrs Labinski in Hamilton's sick mind, not her husband, so that night I think he took his rifle with him through the woods to Grimston's cottage, intending perhaps, to just warn Grimston off, but possibly quite prepared to use it. However, our friend Grimston wasn't there, was he? He was at the hospital. Hamilton here must have seen the old Land-rover, and had the bright idea that he might use it to kill two birds with the one stone. He could stop Labinski's unkind treatment of his wife for a good long while, and also put Grimston in jail. He knew enough about old cars to be able to by-pass the ignition switch and get it started, and all those lonely walks in the woods meant that he probably knew the paths and tracks of the estate nearly as well as Grimston himself. Anyway, I think he drove the Landrover through the woods, waited for Labinski to take his dogs for a walk, and then drove at him, and knocked him down. Possibly he thought that just the one bump wouldn't keep him hospital for long enough, so he backed up, and thus caused worse injuries than he really intended. However, Hamilton didn't know that at the time, because he was driving the Land-rover back to the cottage for us to find later, when we went after Grimston. Which we duly did, after we'd learned of the threatening phone calls. When Hamilton got back home, I think he was shocked to find that no one else had discovered Labinski while he'd been gone. So he had to pretend that he was on his way home from the pub, and find Labinski himself, but by then, of course, Labinski was already dead. Hamilton should have gone home and stayed there. Arthur here found out this morning that Hamilton hadn't been to the only pub in the village that night, or indeed any night for a week. The landlord has barred him from the premises for at least a month, because he'd been too aggressive to other customers.'

'But can you prove that Hamilton was the driver of the vehicle, Inspector? That's the vital question,' O'Shea asked. Clearly, even at a time like this, he was concerned about such legal niceties.

Walsh shrugged his shoulders phlegmatically and looked down at the old man who was now, in fact, breathing a little more easily. He might yet live a long time then, but on mental grounds it was unlikely that he would ever stand a trial. The McNaghten rules on pleas of insanity would keep the lawyers arguing for years. 'There were oil smears on the Land-rover's passenger seat which forensic will probably find came from the linseed oil that's on the wooden stock of that rifle. They'll probably find more evidence too, when they get working on the old man's clothes and fingerprints,' Walsh bent down to rub a knee that was stiffening after all the running he'd been doing, then he straightened his back, and went on unfolding the sad story. 'Hamilton's plan to incriminate Grimston didn't work though, because Grimston had an unshakeable alibi, and we couldn't arrest him. Then Mrs Labinski was attacked in her house, and left bound up, and even though she didn't see the person, she still insisted to Hamilton that it must have been Grimston who did it. We know she was wrong, but Hamilton believed her, and he clearly felt he must deal with Grimston properly this time. Being an old wartime sniper, who killed at long distances, he obviously thought that was the best way to do it. However, good marksmanship needs practice, and fortunately for Grimston, Hamilton missed both times. He came mighty close though.'

'So that's how it all was. It all makes sense now. It's a pity, it was just getting interesting,' Mary Innes murmured regretfully.

'You're a right little fire-eater, aren't you, young woman. Just like Brenda here, but what about the arsonist, the fire-bomber and the attack on Mrs Labinski? It hasn't been boring for some people, you know?'

Then the ambulance turned up to take Jamie Hamilton away, and after that a very distressed Denise Labinski came to pull on Walsh's arm.

'I know I always talk too much, but honestly, Inspector, I never ever wanted anything horrible to happen to anyone. I feel so awful about it that I'll hate myself for the rest of my life.' Genuine tears were running down her face, and no one there could have had any serious doubts of her sincerity.

Walsh sighed and scratched his head, and found himself patting her hand consolingly. 'I don't suppose you should really blame yourself, Mrs Labinski. You just got caught up in some of the weirder workings of fate. That happens to all of us sometimes, to some degree or other. Perhaps I was a bit hard on you. I'm sorry,' he said reluctantly.

Thinking about it more deeply, it was clear that she had unknowingly primed a lethal pump, but that was only because she wanted to be kind to a lonely old man. He was right to apologise, and he was glad he had done so, but his words had surprised her, and stopped her tears, but not another question.

'If it wasn't Mr Grimston who tied me up, then who was it?' she asked with a puzzled frown.

'Ah!' Walsh said, and pulled on his chin thoughtfully. 'Well, I suppose you'll have to know sometime. Let me put it this way. Your husband wasn't very happy with the way your marriage was going, and he had, sort of, made alternative plans.'

'You don't mean to say he'd got another woman already lined up, ready to walk into his house just as soon as he'd kicked me out of it? Why, the rotten pig. Of course I knew our marriage couldn't last much longer, but – oh I don't know, I don't know anything any more,' she said despondently, 'but was it this other woman who did that to me? But why should she?'

'Your marriage break-up wasn't her fault. Your husband sought her out, and she, like you, was someone caught up in the wild workings of fate. If the press had found out that she was involved, her life would have been made more miserable for her than it was already. There were papers in your husband's briefcase identifying her, and naturally, she didn't want us to find them. That's why she came here. She didn't intend you to suffer as you did. She panicked,' Walsh explained and shrugged his shoulders.

Denise Labinski pouted and frowned at him. 'You're sorry for her, aren't you? You don't really want to charge her, do you?' she exclaimed accusingly.

'It's not up to me. If you want charges pressed, then I'm sure they will be. She did wrong, and she knows it, and she'll probably take her punishment with her head held high. I just think she's had enough knocks from life already, but that's a personal opinion, not an official one,' he admitted, frowning to himself, because he was getting into Lady Emily's affairs a little more deeply than was wise.

'Everyone wants to blame me for what happened, and it doesn't seem fair,' Denise said sulkily.

Support for that view came from a surprising quarter. 'Well, I don't think it's fair either. If your husband hadn't broken his word to Mrs Grimston over the shoe business, none of this would probably ever have happened,' Brenda Phipps pointed out soberly.

Denise looked at her gratefully. 'You know, you're absolutely right. Well, I think there's been enough suffering in this business already, and I don't want her to suffer as well, not on my account. You've got a kind heart too, Inspector, so please don't charge her.' Her face seemed happy now that that was settled, but then her forehead creased into a deep frown, and her jawline hardened. She suddenly swung round, setting her long fair hair swirling wildly, and waved a finger at O'Shea accusingly. 'He said Brian's plans to kick me out were already made. You must have known all about it, Donovan O'Shea. You were Brian's solicitor – you would draw up all the papers to make it legal. If you knew I was to be dumped without a penny, there was no need for you to set me up, so why did you come to the reception that night? You knew I'd be there. Why? We'd met before, but you never showed any interest in me then. You couldn't have been after my money either, because Brian wasn't dead then, and I didn't have any. So why?'

O'Shea reddened and shuffled his feet like a nervous child. 'How could I take an interest in you, while you were still married to Brian – but as soon as I knew he was going to kick you out, I thought I'd better leap in quick, and try to catch you on the hop, before anyone else did.' He was gazing down at her face, and looked worried and anxious. Clearly both of them were now totally oblivious of their surroundings, but the watchers still watched, with absorbed interest. O'Shea reached out to put his hands lightly on her shoulders. 'I've loved you from the moment I first saw you,' he said hoarsely.

'Oh Donovan,' Denise cried as she flung both her arms round his neck. 'Do you love me so much that it hurts?'

'It's worse than that. I can't live without you.'

Out of the corner of his eye Walsh saw Brenda Phipps playing a serenade on an imaginary violin, using a shotgun as an unlikely bow, and Arthur was sneakily, but unsuccessfully, trying to get hold of young Mary Innes's left hand, while Reg was just standing there grinning broadly. He shook his head in bewilderment when he heard Denise Labinski ask if they could now go and start building sandcastles.

He turned away and started walking back

to the Landrover.

'Move your car, Arthur, and you, Mary Innes, take those handcuffs off Grimston. He's calmed down now. Do go home Grimston, and take that miserable look off your face, or take your daughter to see your wife. Somebody must need you. I know I don't. I can't put you in jail for being shot at, or worrying about your daughter, but don't go threatening anyone else again. Next time you mightn't be so lucky.' He climbed wearily into the passenger seat, and felt in his pocket for his pipe and tobacco. There was no pain in his jaw any more, so perhaps life might get back to normality again. It was about time.

Reg carefully thumbed on the safety catches of the two rifles, and tossed them onto the rear seat, then climbed in as well, but he had hardly sat down than he was starting with alarm as the shotgun barrels were thrust at him from over the driver's seat. Brenda's smirking face appeared. 'We are jumpy today, aren't we, Reg?' and she grinned cheekily as she tossed the vital two red cartridges into his lap.

'You know, boss, I'm glad we've got this business sorted out at last. There's been too many diversions for my liking, and too many times when things were not exactly under our control,' Reg Finch admitted ruefully.

'But we did all the right things, though, Reg,' Brenda pointed out, seating herself behind the wheel and fastening her safety belt. Then she beamed a big broad grin at her two companions, 'but not necessarily in the right order.'

Walsh nodded his head wisely, in agreement with both of them, but these two had probably never known the pain of a tooth abscess and the mental disorientation that it brought. Perhaps they would suffer one day, then they might understand a little of what he'd been through. No, they wouldn't. Memories of pain soon passed. He'd have forgotten it himself, in a few days.

The publishers hope that this book has given you enjoyable reading. Large Print Books are especially designed to be as easy to see and hold as possible. If you wish a complete list of our books please ask at your local library or write directly to:

Magna Large Print Books
Magna House, Long Preston,
Skipton, North Yorkshire.
BD23 4ND

This Large Print Book for the partially sighted, who cannot read normal print, is published under the auspices of

THE ULVERSCROFT FOUNDATION